ISBN – 978-0-9947769-0-7

Jacket Art by Author

2015

noun \pis-'tōl\ Middle French

First Known Use: 1592. An old gold 2-escudo piece of Spain; *also*: any of several old gold coins of Europe of approximately the same value.

Figure 1: Thomas Jefferys's *Carte d'une Partie de l'Amérique Septentrionale*, 1755. This is the British version of Bellin's map. The line hachures represent different administrative boundaries in the 17th century while the dotted lines illustrate British (larger) and French (smaller) definitions of Acadia/Nova Scotia. See F/200 (1756), Library and Archives Canada (LAC).

Forward

I must first of all advise the reader that this novel is a work of *fiction with actual historical reference to period events*. The dates at the beginning of each chapter hold the timeline of actual events rewritten with the author's imagination.

I had read Author Peter Landry's historical book *The Lily and the Lion* and immediately my overactive imagination was stimulated enough to set in motion a "what if" scenario. Research into the subject of the "Battling Barons" as Landry called them, pressed me to read historical period accounts by Nicholas Denys and American author Harriet Vaughan Cheney. They both gave rich accounts of the period 1641-45 reporting hostility between the two Governors, perhaps as there would be expected between two strong personalities with reputation and wealth at stake.

Author Beamish Murdoch wrote *The History of Nova Scotia or Acadie* in 1865 and reported, as accurately as his research allowed, to the events surrounding Port Royale and Charles de Menou d'Aulnay. His general character description of d'Aulnay and LaTour guided my impressions of how these two men may have interacted in that era.

Author M. A. MacDonald in her work, *Fortune & LaTour* provided a wealth of details and allowed me to keep a timeline of actual historical events to fuel my imagination. I simply loved reading her detailed summations based upon her incredibly complete research spanning two continents.

The hardest part for me to understand from historical accounts is mutual intolerance and the bitter religious persecution between Catholic and Protestant in the 17th Century. There were many references showing the Catholic influenced Crown struggling to coalesce the nation by providing tolerance to protestant endeavors. Matters of state were overseen by Catholic Cardinal Richelieu, who was a relative of the d'Aulnay family.

Charles LaTour's father, Claude LaTour, was apparently comfortable in both churches. Claude

LaTour had also become very comfortable in England in the decade before this book. Claude had been captured at sea by the English and returned to England where he married an English woman. He obtained the name Baronet of Nova Scotia and accepted a Baronetcy for Charles as well. When Claude approached Charles in 1630 at Cape Sable with his English wife, two man-of-war military ships and colonists, he assumed incorrectly that Charles would capitulate. Claude was thrown from Fort Lomeron and a two day battle ensued of epic proportion. The English captains were under order to accept surrender of the fort or take it by force. After the two day siege however, Claude LaTour and the English expedition backed down and went on to Port Royale. These events clearly show Charles LaTour was loyal to France, and primarily why he was granted governance to a portion of Acadia by the crown.

Bitterness and fierce competition existed between the two governors of Acadia – a predictable clash with the personalities required to explore new frontiers... A collision of titanic wills.

One fact has been clearly recorded about the siege and ultimate fall of Fort LaTour in Saint John, Easter Day 1645, in which the principal antagonist, Charles de Menou d'Aulnay de Charnisay, "hung" the occupants of the fort one by one. He spared LaTour's wife, child and maidens along with the hangman and guard who had simply opened the gate while everyone was attending impromptu Easter prayers in the main Lodge. What struck me as unforgettable was the horrific manner of their death as he had hoisted each person up and let them slowly strangle.

Further, he had forced Madame LaTour watch each execution with a noose around her own neck.

Nicholas Deny had written 'the act as most barbaric by any standard' in his book from that period; *The Description and Natural History of The Coast of North America (Acadia)*.

With all this swirling about in my mind, d'Aulnay made a perfect villain only by his indisputable act of evil. I still cannot imagine the depth of contempt he must have felt to perform his heinous actions.

There was actually a naval skirmish in the Bay of Fundy in the summer of 1644. Charles d'Aulnay did have his ship dismasted and one man killed. d'Aulnay's sawmill in Port Royale was also burned during the incident. My ideas for the book come from the basic sentiment that as humans the root of crime is established in love and/or money.

Money laundering, or re-stamping a less valuable to a more valuable coin seems reasonably plausible, but it is fabricated in this book. It is pure fiction and perfect for my plot.

It has been reported that Madame Françoise Jacqueline (while in detention) died shortly after the fall of Fort Saint John from a broken spirit having witnessed so many deaths. Her burial location was never divulged, thus her remains have never been discovered to this day. Her mysterious untimely disappearance left an interesting opportunity for yet another fictional plot twist in my overactive imagination.

New Brunswick is rich in historical significance as the first stop for many European explorers and settlers since the early seventeenth century. My retelling of New Brunswick history is built on the timelines of original events with no attempt to defame descendants of families named, or relate to present day characters. There have been times in my research that I imagined, awestruck, the type of courageous people it must have taken to brave the Atlantic Ocean and colonize strange new lands.

Europeans meeting indigenous peoples had to have been an incredible experience. The indigenous were the original colonists of North America after crossing the land bridge in the North several millennia before. It has been duly recorded by many historians that the first Europeans were surprised that Native people were expecting their arrival as a result of spiritual leaders sharing their visions.

There may be some who feel that Mi'kmaq and Maliseet people were under written in this novel, but as I studied what little material was available to me, I understood the relationship established as a symbiotic, but separate existence. There was an established culture and almost nomadic lifestyle that had worked for centuries before Europeans attempted change. The most memorable research was on Henri Membertou, the grand Mi'kmaq Chief. My novel as it relates to him is as accurate as I could make him. If he seems to have been exemplified it is because historically I know of no greater leader of any nation.

Treasure gold, has always been rumored on Catons Island and for that matter several other locations around southern New Brunswick. Pistole re-minted in San Sebastian to produce more coins with a higher value is fictitious, but plausible. My reasoning comes from research unable to ascertain why the silver écu was commissioned by the King of France and minted to replace their gold coin during the period this novel covers. The French coin of that period was made of pure fine gold, greater quality than any other nation at that era.

This book has retained the original place names to remain authentic. A full list of place names used and characters is at the end of this book.

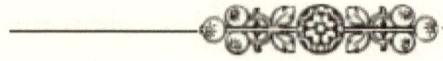

"Earth provides enough to satisfy every man's needs, but not every man's greed."

— Mahatma Gandhi

Of Things to Come...

Port of Saint John,

Acadia 1641

"So, just what do you feel are your rightful lands?" demanded the irate Governor LaTour "I have the King's assent to administration of all lands on this sovereign ground and as such... *MONSIEUR*"... he continued with a menacing growl, "you are unwelcome here."

Before the red faced Governor d'Aulnay could utter a retort, a large muscular fist flew from beneath LaTour's cloak while yelling "LEAVE AT ONCE!" Sergeants from both sides of the spectacle jumped in pulling both noblemen apart. "Get away from me!" growled LaTour shaking the pain from his hand. "Leave us be!" said the other, blood already running down over his lips from his bleeding nose. As LaTour pulled free and straightened, he roared —"alright , *you* d'Aulnay, and *you alone*, will come with me and see for yourself what the king has sanctioned on paper by his hand as charter showing me as the rightful Governor of this land!"

The pair strode free of the grim faced crowd gathering and passed through the gate towards LaTour's trim cabin within the palisade walls. Neither spoke until the door was closed and in the dim room d'Aulnay immediately noticed the table set with wine and fresh bread, a knife was lying beside the round of goat cheese.

"Are you two done making fools of yourself?" demanded LaTour's wife. "Madame LaTour! You startled me" said d'Aulnay crossing the room—"and might I add, you are as beautiful as ever" kissing her hand.

"Charles, I hope your journey across from Port Royale was uneventful. Did you make the tides correctly?" She added quietly.

 "Twenty feet of tide is indeed a nuisance when making the approach to this harbour with a Nor-Wester on the nose"... while tide is falling slack they all said in unison. "We made good time" sighed d'Aulnay. "Why in God's name did you feel the desire to inhabit this treacherous harbour?" LaTour chuckled and said "no problem for an old salt such as you" d'Aulnay smiled thinly and while gingerly feeling his nose replied "SO... did you have to hit me that hard?"

LaTour sobered saying "you and I must be the only ones to ever know the real purpose of our *apparent* animosity. Our future and prosperity must endure scrutiny... if the truth were ever to escape of our plans we would suffer greatly at our king's hands... come let us talk while we can. Francie, please give him linen that he may clean up from my overzealous acting."

Françoise Marie Jacqueline, Lady of LaTour enjoyed her pet name; it gave her a feeling of intimacy towards her business partner husband. She passed a handkerchief to d'Aulnay as they all sat at the table.

"Our first concern is how much we invest in this venture" said d'Aulnay firmly. LaTour eyed him carefully and replied in a halting voice "next, would be *who* retains the converted pistole, and I must confess I am not a trusting man, nor are you for that matter I am sure."

The two men sat impassively staring at each other with a large impasse forming between them. Françoise intervened from her side of the table and firmly said "as I am the only one here that must trust you both, I suggest I cache all the pistole upriver. Here in Saint John and away from you two."

d'Aulnay licked his lips furtively and said "If I take the pistole to Spain for re-minting, and you buy as many gold French écu as you can find... we may indeed have a plan." He cast his thumb towards Françoise and said "her honour is impeccable and although she is your partner, I agree... she is the obvious person to cache our new double escudo. We must both trust her."

The three figures were huddled around the table talking intently, when a loud banging began in earnest at the door. d'Aulnay's burly lieutenant had grown concerned with d'Aulnay's time spent away from his protection and with uncertainty of his commander's safety, began roaring "monsieur's, open the door at once." As he reared back to hit the door once again, it opened brusquely and d'Aulnay appeared --eyeing his protector with a grave look. "Remy, please give me a moment longer to give attention to the details of LaTour's document. Everything appears to be in order"—then smiling weakly—"merci, you are a comfort. I will be fine, but you must get the men ready to depart, and Remy" he said emphatically… "No trouble today, I hold you responsible to remain orderly," he further added while closing the door again. Neither d'Aulnay nor LaTour had seen Remy's look of recognition when he spied Françoise-Marie Jacqueline, 'Lady of LaTour' sitting at the table.

Once settled again the talk began quietly—"So it is settled" began Lady LaTour. "I will take two Mi'kmaq canoes upriver to scout a suitable location on the premier branch, to the right of the main Wolostoq River. If I find a suitable location, I will employ our Mi'kmaq friends to aid in construction of a cache to hold all the pistole. It would be wise to not involve any of our people and secrecy will be our greatest asset... I am worried how long the King will endure this apparent rivalry" whispered Lady LaTour ominously.

d'Aulnay offered enthusiastically, "The King is giving great latitude to the governance of Acadia as it is all so far from the palace in France, and unimaginable to the hardships and relations with savages. He does enjoy a profit from our efforts without fail and this, coupled with favorable reports from the Company of One Hundred Associates are forming his conscience... of course not withstanding colonizing a new world for France! Trading will allow diversion to the main task of meeting our Spanish connection and of course resupply."

 LaTour added "I propose a trip to Boston is also in order to determine their quantities of pistole, although I am less thrilled with allegiances so close."

As the conversation began to wither with details forming, it became apparent that another meeting would be required before summers end. "We will stay our courses and meet in the fall" said LaTour.

"New England would be most pleasant this July" a smiling d'Aulnay murmured. Both men nodded and shook hands while giving a light kiss to each cheek.

Françoise turned to the hearth and stared intently into the fire, seemingly oblivious to all else. "God's will, be safe" said LaTour. He received only a faint smile in return as d'Aulnay straightening himself at the door murmured "God be with us all."

"We are leaving!" declared d'Aulnay loudly as he cleared the door to the outside. Remy was relieved that this dreadful encounter was at a close, and true to his word, the men were in the longboat with oars held high. They stared straight ahead and refused to allow LaTour's men to taunt them to action. They were all men of valor, including Remy; proving themselves on the battlefields of the Siege of Montauban, the naval battle of Saint-Martin-de-Ré, and during the Siege of La Rochelle. They were indeed disciplined and loyal, ready for action at the first order… countrymen or not. Remy tried in vain to read d'Aulnay, there was only a detached evasiveness. d'Aulnay never looked back at the fort as they left, not even when his pinnace cleared the harbour and made way south to Port Royale. For all his time with d'Aulnay, he had never seen such contemplation and depth of thought. Remy thought *what actually just happened here? Where did Françoise-Marie Jacqueline fit in?*

1 Pistole

Port Royale, 1610

Henri Membertou was growing older. It was not something that was seen as a hindrance to the old man who was now over one hundred years old, rather he enjoyed ongoing learning of new skills and studying people, all leading to greater wisdom. The muscle stiffness in the morning and his knees were more of regret than debility.

He towered a head taller than many and still retained a full head of black hair. He was unanimously voted Grand Chief of the six nations because he had earned their respect as being both a visionary and honourable. Membertou was the head autmoin, the spiritual leader – leading many to believe he had powers of healing and prophecy. He knew his ancient customs coupled with *belief* of the healing powers in traditional methodology were his tools... age and experiences his guide, thus lay his real power. The ageless leader had met explorer Jacques Cartier, and after being given a tour of his large ship instinctively knew change was coming. Common theory for human instinct would have been to fight that which was feared, but Membertou could see collusion as a benefit to his people. He did not back down from a righteous fight however; having proven his leadership by leading over five hundred warriors across the Bay of Fundy to battle the Passamaquoddy in retribution for an attack that had killed one sakmow, or chief from his council. At over one hundred years of age he commanded the attack with ruthless precision, culminating in the death of two chiefs and destroying their settlement. He had exacted a severe consequence for their ruthless and violent raid.

He had met the first of the settlers in Port Royale with respect and open arms, leading to cohabitation as he had stated would occur from his visions. It was during this era that Membertou had first met Claude de Saint-Étienne de la Tour and his son Charles. Through the LaTours, and accompanying Recollect Friars he had learned French fluently and had studied Christianity leading to his baptism. He was given his Christian name of Henri in honour of King Henri IV when Baptized. Over time he had insisted that he became Baptized and learned French, then Jesuits that had replaced the friars at Port Royale must learn Mi'kmaq to ensure equality and proper instruction of

Christianity to his people. Many Mi'kmaq were thus Baptized with Membertou... first to prove his faith.

It was during a vision that Membertou was shown the LaTours long before they arrived in Acadia. He was saddened by what he saw in this vision and firmly decided to stoically keep it all to himself. He genuinely enjoyed their company and enthusiasm for all things Mi'kmaq. When young LaTour, or Tia'm as he had been named, became enamored with one of the local young maidens, he had joined the two as partners despite knowing the outcome from his earlier visions. Visions he had decided, were God's way of punishment for mistakes he made throughout his long life. The visions had also shown him events for his son Mooin—he could understand young LaTour joining forces with him, but could not understand the remainder of the future vision. It was all so senseless and devious in a quest for the maligned wealth. He foresaw Mooin as the catalyst

for change, but would he fall to the charms of gold

coins? It was unbelievable that he would forsake his

heritage to become as a white man would live. The

visions were centered on the evil of a man he had

not met yet, but the gold coins were the source of all

that was pitting man against man. He could only

show Mooin the proper path as a young man and

advise him of the visions. He begged the great

creator to give Mooin both strength and wisdom to

follow the righteous path in life.

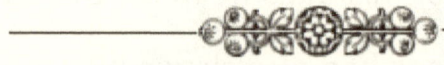

2 Pistole

Port of Saint John,

Acadia 1641

Françoise-Marie was still staring into the hearth when she realized the fire was almost out. She usually had her maidens attend to such matters of the home, but had learned the value of hard work and did her share of domestic duty as well. They had been sent out gathering wild blueberries allowing privacy within the house.

With a shiver she stood and attended to the kindling and soon had the fire dancing around the large pot. It hadn't been easy these last few years and she knew it was only by God's grace and the local native people that they had even survived this long. She thought how true that Mi'kmaq translated to "friend " in Algonquin, and her respect towards their closest allies had grown.

The beginning at Port Royale had seemed as exciting an adventure as the mind would let believe. She had reservations of leaving a comfortable life in La Rochelle for the certain hardships in Acadia... but the adventure called to her spirit.

It was a reasonable distance even then for a young lady to travel from her hometown Nogent-le-Rotrou, in the North, seeking a life of her own in Paris. Her Father, a Doctor, had demanded so much from her in as much as could be expected of a young woman. No, she was definitely not going to lay down her lot in life in such modern times! Paris had seemed such a grandiose plan, but she felt she could perhaps create her new life away from her Father and the thought of a mere two days away still seemed so close to home. The better choice was travel to La Rochelle on the West coast, a longer four day journey, to attain her independence. Getting there safely would be the problem and thus kept her tethered to her home town.

The Nogent-le-Rotrou town square contained a large abundant water well that travelers frequently used, and over time the town became a stopover with roadside Inns and stables. The largest inn was overshadowed by the newly constructed Saint Jean Castle and had provided accommodations for the engineers.

It was during such a respite by soldiers riding through to La Rochelle that the young free spirited girl asked if she could ride along. The equally young Lieutenant agreed... providing she could keep up, as he winked to the others with a laugh. Early next morning as the soldiers prepared to leave town, Françoise-Marie Jacqueline resplendent in riding attire and astride one of her Father's dapple grey Percherons inquired "why the delay?" "I was here earlier and not a soul had arisen."

The Lieutenant was agape at the vision before him of a magnificent horse reined in with head held high and ears forward, tacked in fine black leather and saddle. By the time the group had arrived in record time at La Rochelle, all agreed she was as courageous as qualified a rider... leading at times. The sergeant appraised her skills as good as any cavalry soldier, but easier to the eye. All agreed with sergeant Remy Martin's assessment.

While she had an air about her, a subtle humility that spoke of civility left many curious to her meager funds and mysterious lack of details to her past. The priest of the church arranged accommodations for Mademoiselle Jacqueline with the Morin family and they agreed to her staying for a short period of time as they were making anxious plans for New France in the spring. It had hurt to see her new found family embark in April aboard the *St. Jehan* and there was not enough room for her, try as they may to get her aboard. She began to dream of ways to make the journey and decided that she would save her wages and pay passage at the first opportunity. It came unexpected, as good things usually do, a year later.

She had strolled to the pier while on errands to watch the ships and passengers bustle about and waved to the Company of One Hundred Associates agent. Monsieur Tourneau noticed her while talking to a middle aged man whose crestfallen face suddenly looked a little happier as he turned and eye contact was made. He had just disembarked from a weathered pinnace that had arrived from Acadia.

"Mademoiselle Jacqueline" called the smiling Trading Company agent waving her over. "Still dreaming of Acadia I see. I would like to introduce you to Monsieur Guilliame Desjardins." Tourneau continued quickly "She comes here daily you know since her friends left last year." After proper introductions, Desjardins informed her that he was on personal business for Governor LaTour asked if she would be interested in dinner that evening. Details arranged, Françoise-Marie anxiously wondered what the

Secretary to Governor LaTour in Acadia could possibly want.

The Inn was comfortable and suitably resplendent in furnishings suitable for travelers accustomed to finery. It had been a great struggle for her to dress for the occasion. All that she had with her when she left home was now gone along with her horse and working as a maid had allowed her to save carefully. The duress in her heart deciding to spend all of her savings on one complete outfit had seemed so careless, yet the decision just felt right to her intuition and she sat at the table looking as fine as any socialite in town.

Desjardins began with answers to her rapid questions about Acadia. Her interest had her sitting forward and hanging on his every word. With the meal complete and questions answered, he looked at her and said quietly "you are a wonderful Lady and adventurous at heart," he drew a breath and continued "I have asked you to dinner, not so much in interest personally, rather my employer Charles de Saint-Étienne de la Tour." "You can only imagine the incredible difficulties in colonizing a new country with the minute details and expense." He leaned forward and continued slowly, "you do understand that just met you I have only the highest regard for you." She nodded; caution filled her heart from his obvious mounting discomfort. "I mentioned my mission to the Trading Company agent and he spoke highly of you and your desire for the new colonies and our meeting seemed heaven sent." He bravely looked at her and exhaled "Yes, well to the point, you see I have been tasked with finding *you*, as a suitable candidate, as wife to Governor LaTour."

He waited, eyes downcast awaiting a response. As the silence grew and with the absence of a slap he had fully expected, he finally looked up to see her looking at him with a silent penetrating stare. He felt small in her gaze and regretted his mission, yet it was her manner that had unnerved him, she seemed unfazed and when she finally spoke it was measured and firm.

"That is it? You meet me upon landing in La Rochelle and would have me wed your Governor? You say you respect me, yet you do not know my depths and capabilities" she said speaking quicker. "Do you think of me as a whore?" she hissed at him disgustedly so as not to attract attention. Even though she had not raised her voice, or for that manner threaten him, he felt much like a trapped animal. It was extremely hot in the Inn suddenly and he felt the sweat coursing down his back in rivulets.

"No Mademoiselle Jacqueline, I do not think of you in any such negative fashion" he answered quickly, too quickly. She had him on the defensive.

This mission was not something that was supposed to be difficult; women were never this bold in France, excepting of course the tenure in any long term marriage allowing it. Women usually would jump at the opportunity to become an aristocrat and enjoy the comforts of privilege. She suddenly had him feeling unsure and indeed at her mercy, much like LaTour would have him feel. She could communicate as effectively as LaTour just by her eyes alone!

The thought was delicious at once. He smiled and looking at her with reappraising eyes said "Mademoiselle, you misunderstand. I see you as the only choice of "Lady" for our Governor LaTour. He has already left for Paris seeking aid for Port Saint

John and expects me there to begin my mission of finding you. He remembers meeting you in Paris when you attended the King's ball with your father several years ago. He has remembered you since that meeting and is infatuated" he divulged to her quickly before sampling his wine. "He was very distressed at not having found you in Nogent-le-Rotrou and learned you may be here in La Rochelle. Thankfully Tourneau knew of you, and my mission is over before it begins and all by a chance meeting... will you accompany me to Paris?" implored Desjardins.

They left next morning after Desjardins had made suitable arrangements for passage aboard a large stagecoach called a *diligence.* The clumsy carriage was a two story carriage that allowed tent covered seating on the roof. Desjardins paid a premium to leave promptly although they were the only passengers.

It had been mentally unbearable for her sitting in the carriage with leather curtains drawn as the horses were watered in Nogent-le-Rotrou. *I am here* she thought. In all dreams she would never have guessed her fortune just two years before. She had no desire to talk to anyone at this point, not yet-- especially her father, but the road to Paris passed through and she would endure quietly. The time for her return would come soon.

They continued on, mostly from her urging, even though the Norman Horses and carriage men were exhausted. The countryside had flashed past and they arrived in Paris with dark looks from the carriage men towards the regal young "Lady" that pushed them incessantly. They had never travelled so hard and saved a day doing so. Desjardins smiled continuously.

Their first meeting had left them both reeling. LaTour was intrigued to learn Desjardin`s opinion. He had faith in his confidant to know his needs, and felt him a better judge than himself. He wished he had been advised with his first marriage to a native woman. As usual, Desjardins was correct when LaTour had tired of her lack of sophistication and easy going attitude. It had been so easy for him to learn the native language and desire the complete native experience that included a wife. It had also been an easy matter for him when she had simply left the Fort one morning and did not return. The other people of the settlement had said she felt alone and not part of anything important as LaTour traveled the seas. The partnership *expected* of native couples simply did not exist. He now desired a proper Lady for his burgeoning empire.

Mademoiselle Jacqueline indeed had the necessary sophistication and looks and she also possessed the mind of a natural leader. He also had remembered her father being a wealthy Doctor of high society. Françoise felt it was love that attracted her... and not just convenience. It was obvious that Charles was a natural leader, both clever and capable. Some of colonists felt he was arrogant or aloof, she felt that he was more occupied looking for opportunity, than concerned with drivel. He was definitely not the type of man who let others make his decisions. She had found him more interesting than any suitor her parents had approved from her home town. He was considerably older and his confidence coupled with experience was his allure.

She was taken aback at first mention, when he reluctantly told her of a first marriage in Acadia to a baptized native girl, the daughter of a great chief who was the first to be baptized for all natives. It was all so heady that such a great adventurer and yet nobleman could be actually interested in her.

The brisk daring ride through the forest on two of her fathers' famous dapple grey Percherons proved both the new horse breeds worth and that he had found his true partner. They drew their horses in to walk side by side and he reached his hand to hers. He suddenly held her hand up soberly looking her in the eye and asked pensively for her hand in marriage fearing she might actually say no. He was so elated when she had said yes that he instantly also agreed to her demands as an equal partner in his new colony. It truly was a proper courtship and when it was all agreed; yes she would indeed marry and be Lady LaTour... *a Governess.*

Her heart soared as the pinnace under full sail left La Rochelle two months later. Her father had brokered a contract as a business partnership for his daughter and after many changes to the agreement allowing fairness and protection for all parties; Dr. Jacqueline had agreed to the union. The Trading Company agent had waved hardest from the dock.

After a turbulent crossing the ship entered the calm safety of Port Royale and her first glimpse of Acadia landfall was partially covered in snow as was usual in late spring. She didn`t think she would ever be warm again after the late winter passage from La Rochelle. She had learned quickly the nautical terms and purpose of the rigging on the ship and would even gain the approving nod from the Captain while at the helm. The crew had practiced regular drills with canon and weapons during the voyage and after pleading, she herself had learned a small amount of sword use. For Françoise the terror from each terrifying crash of the cannons had been reduced with an understanding of their operation and resulting by-product of noise and smoke. Eventually, she barely blinked as canon boomed, and cheers had roared out as she hit flotsam tossed overboard for target practice with a Musket on calmer days. She felt full of promise and ached to see her fiancé again.

Once docked, she emerged from the aft cabin once again dressed regally, looking very proper and relaxed. Her maidens followed carrying her belongings as they were duty bound to do in a parade of finery trailing the elegant bride to be. Those milling about the small wharf hoping for a first look at the future Lady LaTour were astounded when all ship's crew stood to attention and with looks of admiration, their respect evident.

The wedding was a dignified exchange of vows uniquely expressing their union as partners with the colonists all on hand including the elder Claude LaTour and wife in attendance. LaTour's wedding was the most lavish the colonies ever held in Acadia by the Capuchin Fathers from Fort St. Louis. Festivities included a marvelous feast and excellent wine from France. It was all so promising for the new partnership of Lady and Lord LaTour. Yet now only four years later she was contemplating her incredibly dangerous and stealthy mission. She decided the companionship of their friend, Mooin, christened 'Louie' in honor of the King, would make the adventure possible if not bearable.

3 Pistole

Port of Saint John,

Acadia 1641

Charles LaTour was a man in motion seeing to every detail in the new forts defenses and as well as his new home within the stockade. His wife was a born task master and soon had everyone working at a fever pitch preparing for winter from her many itemized lists. He had been incredibly fortunate in Port Royale to have befriended *Mooin* (Bear) who was able to communicate in both languages fluently. What had first caught his attention was his low humming that was actually old songs Charles had heard as a boy in France. The Native merely shrugged when asked where he had learned the songs. Languages proved immaterial as they seemed to have an instant working relation with little need for words to communicate.

Before they had left for Port Saint John, Charles had asked the Mi'kmaq if he would consider being helping colonize the new fort LaTour in Port Saint John. Louie had agreed to the request, but when LaTour left Port Royale Louie had not boarded for the trip and was nowhere to be found. Two days later, when LaTour opened the stockade gate early in the morning, there was Louie sitting on a rock at water's edge. "Louie!" cried out Charles. "How did you get here?" The Mi'kmaq smiled and said "The great waters were calm and I left when you asked" pointing to his canoe. "I watched you arrive from the hills behind us while hunting" added Louie.

"Game is plentiful on the ridge in the hardwoods, if you have time to enjoy a hunt and become one with the Great Spirit" said Louie rising from the rock. "I brought the venison to help feed everyone" he said quietly. Approaching the shoreline LaTour could see the large deer by the canoe. As they embraced in friendship, LaTour said "thank you for coming to Port Saint John. Seeing your deer makes me think a hunt is in order to clear my head, you must come and share in our food and rest."

Striding into the trim stockade house he recovered his hunting bow and arrows from the pegs over the fireplace mantle. Swinging his leg between the string and bow, he deftly hooked the loop in the top end groove. Picking up the bow he slowly cycled full draw and back to test his craftsmanship from a past life in Port Royale. With mounting anxiety he changed to his skins and moccasins, and told his sentry he would return by nightfall.

He began scouting the best game trails leading towards the high ridgeline behind the fort only pausing for breath when the view had allowed a breathtaking scene of the harbour. As the sounds of the forest filled his senses, he realized how badly he needed to be grounded once again, alive and part of the surroundings. By the time he stood on the ridgeline his strung bow and arrows on his back with belt and knife, he would have appeared to anyone in the distance a native of the land. When he returned to the fort in late afternoon he too had returned with venison and most importantly—serenity.

While many nobles of the era were well versed in the art of sophistication, they were also ingrained with a sense of elitism that prevented them from hands-on tasks. Charles had grown to a teen with privilege within France, but soon learned that elitism could be lethal in the new frontier. Those who waited on others to provide usually did not survive their first winter. When his father had befriended the native Algonquin Mi'kmaq upon arrival, they were well received and learned the skills needed for winter as well as camaraderie. The cold winters were a time of preparation for the Mi'kmaq people by carving new arrows, bows, and spears for fishing or hunting in the coming summer. The simple times and laughter made the campfires feel even warmer. Hunting was a way to survival as vital as the fires to keep them warm. Charles remembered his pride as he had returned to the encampment late one afternoon with a pair of rabbits and a small deer to be shared. The fact that he had made the bow and arrows himself and built his snowshoes made him feel he was doing his part within the hunting parties. It did not seem possible how much time passed. Decades ago he had learned all these skills along with the language. But, the most valuable lesson he had learned was patience and acceptance of circumstance.

"You cannot change the weather, you must change for weather" the old chief had once stated simply. The LaTour men had learned to adapt and overcome hardship while gaining respect for the Mi'kmaq people. The Mi'kmaq had benefitted and learned as well, they suddenly had iron arrow and spear tips, fishing line, nets, and cooking utensils. The local iron ore had been forged by blacksmiths to the absolute amazement of locals. At first they jumped back, alarmed when the large air bellows pumped the orange glowing charcoal to hot blue and pink tipped flame with a whoosh.

The fishing methods with the large long boats and nets provided a greater abundance of winter fish which was shared equally with French and Mi'kmaq alike. The respect that grew between cultures was born of understanding the Native people as spiritual equals and not the savages reported a century earlier by the English settling New England.

Port Saint John would indeed become a bustling trade center if LaTour inherently gave Algonquin Wolastoqiyik people respect and honest treatment as he would have wanted. Marrying Mi'kmaq and French traditions together was logical for LaTour and he demanded as much from the colonists within the palisade walls. Although he had forged a warm bond with the Port Royale Mi'kmaq Natives, he felt certain that success with the local Native Wolastoqiyik known as Maliseet here on the Saint John River was equally possible. The nasty lack of civility shown by d'Aulnay towards the Mi'kmaq of Port Royale became as common place as his haughty mannerisms.

When LaTour had attempted to reason with d'Aulnay's obvious racism, it had been rebuffed and made clear that he thought them less intellectual and a nuisance to the colony. He simply snorted shaking his head and walked away when LaTour had ruefully advised "there would never have been a colony if not for the Mi'kmaq skills and charity." LaTour would leave it alone for now, but fortunes or not, an escalation in animosity to the Native people would draw LaTour into the fray.

Time was running out. d'Aulnay had related that he learned a great deal of gossip in his recent trip to France, stating the King was making a serious change in currency. By edict, the King was lowering the value of the gold coin and finally dropping the gold coin that was in circulation in favor of silver. He

had to get to Boston, Charles had plans in place; he

just needed a little more time to be certain of

success.

4 Pistole

Paris,

France 1641

Charles d'Aulnay was trying to feel something he was not used to feeling... trust. Françoise was given the task of hiding the wealth of coins as neither LaTour nor d'Aulnay were comfortable trusting each other. Françoise made a good compromise with her heritage and honesty.

d'Aulnay had not overtly grieved when his uncle Isaac Razilly had passed away from health complications; it was not an emotion he allowed himself. His position as lieutenant of the resident military had kept him busy training and building fortifications, yet knowledgeable in the affairs of governance in the colony.

Charles had been a child of diminutive size and the brunt of bullies until he fought back with an aggression that earned him his own reputation. Those who had overlooked the small stature of d'Aulnay and dismissed him as a threat never forgot the encounter. His almost bored appearance with flat affect was his greatest weapon, unnerving even the battle hardened warriors. Military training was an outlet for his abundance of frustration and he excelled with officers observing his unique blend of viciousness and pompous manner as vital to a commission.

He had disagreed with his Uncle`s fraternizing with native people, but most of all the sense of partnership he had brokered with the LaTour family.

It had been a bitter moment when his uncle`s last will and testament specified his administrator to inherit his governance of Acadia. He had wanted all of Acadia to govern. It had only taken a trip to France to weave his deceptive version of how France was better with his governance in Acadia. He visualized himself an altruistic pioneer for the advancement of France, and this narcissism, coupled with a gift of speech writing, bid well with the Royal Council.

The King, without having the firsthand knowledge of the frontier, relied on his court officials opinions to place d'Aulnay into the dual governance role that had existed with his uncle, and LaTour.

d'Aulnay, feeling he had pushed hard enough for one visit, would deal with LaTour later. His cohorts in France would have to negatively sway the King's opinion of LaTour as co-Governor of Acadia.

Thinking of LaTour always left him wondering how a nobleman of means could cavort with savages and still think he was worthy to lead a colony. He was confused how the man could live like a savage and still request audience with the King and court. He was a grand orator with credible time in Acadia for colorful reports, and being a strong handsome man of valor seemed to bolster the king`s confidence in him. Deeper than personalities and vanities however, d'Aulnay knew it was the steady shipments of furs, salt and other natural resources that bought favor with the king.

As the carriage jostled him on the long ride to La Rochelle from Paris, he thought of all the requirements to take over governance of Acadia. LaTour, he mused might become an issue if his share of an incredible fortune kept him in Acadia. Greater than any fortune was the allure of becoming sole governor, and d'Aulnay was far more interested in power than fortune. LaTour would have to go, and perhaps if possible without his share of pistole.

His greatest trepidation in dealings with LaTour was the fact that there were two of them. It seemed preposterous to deal with a woman, but they had proven themselves both capable and cunning in the required leadership skills. By using their partnership to an advantage in management of the fort, LaTour could focus on myriad details with his wife managing matters in his full trust whether he was present or not. It made him realize that perhaps he should have been more careful in choosing his bride for skills instead of a bride chosen by beauty alone. Lady d'Aulnay could manage the domestic staff and matters of the home, but never questioned him or offered opinion. It was not proper for a Lady of the period to infringe on a Lord's affairs. Seeing Lady

LaTour manage the fort as good as any man made him envious to a much darker level.

 He knew loyalties ran deep with new colonists and left little chance of an implanted emissary within the fort to keep him apprised. No! He decided. It was all too convenient for LaTour to deceive him. He would have to rely on his intuition that all men were somewhat deceptive and craved dominance. The only fact that had remained true was the fate they both shared if caught in this scheme to wealth. *Ironic that the king trusts me*, thought d'Aulnay.

He would continue to work with LaTour and when the wealth had been created, take over governance of Acadia and find a way to capture the pistole. He knew Denys' lands to the north-east were of little consequence at this time and would be taken when needed. He knew that Deny had settled within the

Native lands as LaTour had, with a difference that he was not in Royal favor...he would fall easily. It all seemed so possible now and he was anxious to get back to sea with a first stop in Spain.

He realized the journey from Paris to La Rochelle was seemingly long and questionable to the Royal Council, when Honfleur was a closer port to Paris. It had been a simple matter of logistics he had explained once when asked. La Rochelle is closer for the ship to Acadia. When asked this trip why he travelled overland, he advised the Council that the New France Trading Company was in La Rochelle. He of course had other reasons; it was closer to Spain, and it was a chance for clandestine meetings. As he walked towards his pinnace tied to the wharf he wondered if the ship had been replenished as requested. He needed to make good time for Spain before the Atlantic crossing and one of his contacts had discreetly supplied the latest sea charts for San Sebastian at his last overnight lodgings.

Tourneau was present, as was his custom on the wharf overseeing the affairs of the Company. As d'Aulnay climbed out of the coach and gathered his trunks, Tourneau announced his pinnace was indeed loaded and replenished as requested. Tourneau then added quickly, "Monsieur Emmanuel Le Borgne was here a short while ago seeking you. He asked me to tell you not to leave port without seeing him." Tourneau glanced at the baggage and as he stared at the extra trunk asked if he wanted a worker to load his extra trunk. When he caught the silence, Tourneau swiveled his head to look at d'Aulnay, as their eyes met Tourneau was the first to uncomfortably look away pretending to shade his eyes from the summer sun.

d'Aulnay never answered Tourneau, but seeing Remy on the aft deck had circled his finger at the trunks when Remy finally saw him on the wharf. "You are certainly observant, Tourneau. I hope you were as observant to replenishing stores on my ship as you are to matters that do not concern you" added d'Aulnay as he walked away, walking stick thumping on the planks.

Tourneau exhaled slowly and realized his heart was beating staccato. *Pompous Ass*, he thought as d'Aulnay entered the doorway to Emmanuel Le Borgne's building. Those eyes were like large, unblinking deep black pools. d'Aulnay was one to be more careful with in the future, reflected Tourneau.

5 Pistole

San Sebastian,

Spain 1641

Hernado Galeana was looking towards the ocean with a steady sweep of his long telescope. His view from the island prominence of Santa Clara lighthouse was nothing short of spectacular. He had felt giddy when appointed as master of the station and given a new telescope to use. He took his role seriously and had once relayed a warning by flag to the station on land in San Sebastian of a dangerous looking corsair ship approaching the bay.

When an armed garrison had been waiting at the pier for the corsair, it was by all accounts determined there was little doubt of the pirate's intentions. With the corsair turned away from port, Hernando had been acknowledged as the man saving the port city from danger with his scope. It was a miracle to see distant details with this new device and thus a novelty for people to beg a look. King Phillip had ordered them placed in every lighthouse since the new invention from Netherland had been discovered aboard visiting ships calling in Spain. It had been decreed a matter of safety, and while it did serve to spot sailors in distress, their greater purpose was early detection of possible danger. Hernando also was charged with reporting all traffic that approached or departed San Sebastian. Of the list of duties he performed, the latter proved the most profitable to him.

His first meeting in San Sebastian with the small Frenchman named d'Aulnay was profitable enough, though always made him uncomfortable. The Spaniard was not easily intimidated and could hold his own, but felt uneasy with the haughty Frenchman. d'Aulnay was always very precise with planning and timetables for their meetings such as today. It was an easy matter for him to accept the bribe allowing passage to and from San Sebastian unreported.

Hernando never received an answer when he had inquired how d'Aulnay knew he was responsible for such duties, and suspected that the "chance" meeting in the cantina was staged, d'Aulnay merely shrugged and with a mechanical smile set gold coins in front of the man. Standing and adjusting his tunic, d'Aulnay with an almost whisper had said "take the gold and live well, betray me and the gold along with your life will disappear."

True to form and on time, distant billowing canvas sails were bearing down on the island heading for San Sebastian when expected. Hernando sighed; his rendezvous with d'Aulnay was approaching. He had arranged for his alternate keeper to arrive that morning allowing him to be at the cantina to receive his gold. It was never a large amount, but allowed a little better life style than his wages permitted. The arrangement kept d'Aulnay's pinnace out of records and gold in his pocket. Hernando rationalized that bribes were a part of life and the Frenchman was obviously not about to attack San Sebastian, so he could care less the purpose of his clandestine operations.

As he thought about it, he had noted that the pinnace always arrived late in the day and had left at first light with tides always in d'Aulnay's favor. Perhaps it was a questionable affair he wondered.

Hernando would take the telescope with him this time.

He made good time with his rowboat from the island to San Sebastian so as he waited in the cantina savoring each mouthful of lamb and sausage stew, d'Aulnay could be seen on the wharf with a wine cask at his feet. A burly sergeant at his side had commandeered a hand cart which they set the cask into with obvious effort. After a brief dialog, the suddenly unhappy sergeant wheeled around and boarded the pinnace's long boat floating at the wharf. The longboat was quickly rowed towards the waiting ship at anchor and d'Aulnay melded out of sight with the crowds.

Interesting thought Hernando as he sat back from his meal. "Rosa! Do you still want to see through my glass? I will show you how to use it!" said Hernando proudly. Rosa thought he was just boisterously anxious to show her the telescope when he hurriedly flipped open the box and began focusing down the street.

The ruse had allowed him to see d'Aulnay enter a small shop at the end of the street carrying the cask with aid from the shopkeeper. A metal working shop owned by Giovanni Cellini, son of the famous Italian goldsmith. He wasn't really listening to Rosa's excited observations as next she looked through his miraculous new invention. He had cleverly used the cantina waitress's previous requests to see through the scope for a look down the street and watch d'Aulnay. *What could be in that wine keg other than gold* he thought.

Later, as d'Aulnay sat down at Hernando's table, he noticed the cantina was filling as he carefully surveyed the room. He regretted having taken so long with Cellini as he inconspicuously stood out from the Spanish regulars.

Removing his gloves and flattening them onto the table, he then fixed his gaze on Hernando. "So, how was the view from your lighthouse today? Did you see a ship worth reporting?" he asked.

"I do not *think* so Senor d'Aulnay" replied Hernando carefully. "You do not *think*, eh?" quizzed d'Aulnay sharply.

"Yes, well you see" said Hernado clearing his throat "I think such a service to *not see you* must certainly be worth a little more gold to the success of your dealings" stated Hernando firmly.

Before d'Aulnay could react, Rosa arrived at the table with a flourish and blurted "have you ever seen the amazing seeing glass that Hernado has there?

The details from a distance are truly a miracle!" as she continued her prattle of all the people she could see far down the street earlier while pointing excitedly out the window. d'Aulnay first looked at the narrow long box holding the telescope hanging from the back of Hernando's chair with an improvised leather strap and then to the window she was pointing at. He was looking down the street that he had just walked from Cellini's shop.

As he turned back to Hernando, his eyes were as black coals that burned into Hernando's sole. "I see" was all that came from d'Aulnay's mechanical smile.

Rosa! "Leave us be!" cried Hernando quickly. Rosa sulked while stomping away, mumbling obscenities to him.

"It must have been difficult asking for more" said d'Aulnay evenly. "I came to pay you the fee we had agreed, if you must have more, you can come to the Inn after our meal to receive it all" continued d'Aulnay. They sat quietly with d'Aulnay eating his warm meal and enjoying the wine while Rosa glared at a nervous Hernando.

"Drink up" said d'Aulnay ordering more wine from Rosa, watching the evening grow darker outside.

Hernando had already consumed numerous goblets of wine waiting for d'Aulnay and after a couple of bottles had become inebriated. d'Aulnay quietly announced it was time for him to retire. He whispered to Hernando "here is enough coin to pay the cantina... meet me outside when you are done."

It only took a few moments later for Hernando to arrive outside the cantina squinting in the darkness looking for d'Aulnay. "Here" came a quiet voice from the darkness near the wharf. Hernando swayed over to the wharf and was about to speak when heard the rhythmic thump of d'Aulnay's walking stick on plank coming his way. Had Hernando not been inebriated he would have realized the thump had disappeared as d'Aulnay came into view in the dim light of late evening. The world suddenly exploded in light and he had just begun to feel the intense pain in his head as the world swirled and turned dark.

d'Aulnay looked down at the fallen man and with a sneer, mocking him with a disgusted "fool!" A large cask of water sat on the wharf edge next to a post and he pulled Hernando over to it. Picking the limp figure up, d'Aulnay shoved Hernando's head under the water. With his elbow on Hernando's back, d'Aulnay leaned over and rested his chin on his fist while thinking of; the LaTour couple, pistole, how delicious the stew had been, and what he would do for the winter provisions at Port Royale. The flight of thought allowed him enough time to realize that bubbles had stopped burbling and Hernando was very dead.

Slipping the telescope from Hernando's shoulder and onto his own, d'Aulnay scooped the dead man to his shoulder and proceeded to the wharf's edge where he guided him into the darkness beneath the wharf.

With his clothes straightened and broad hat with long feather plume in place, d'Aulnay slowly thumped into the darkness towards his inn for the evening.

6 Pistole

Boston,

New England 1641

Richard Bellingham sat in his study overlooking the bay. The *L'Amitye de la Rochelle* sat at anchor below in the harbour and her master lounged back in the overstuffed wing back chair sharing the view with Bellingham.

 "So Charles, what brings my good friend to Boston?" boomed a smiling Bellingham. LaTour smiled back and said "in honor of your new Governorship of course!"They both cheered and with a clink of their glasses drank to their health and good fortunes.

LaTour sat up in his chair, setting his glass down after a moment and looked soberly at his friend. After a further moments silence he spoke slowly. "I did indeed come for more than your congratulations; I need your support old friend." Bellingham following LaTour's example set his glass down and had arisen. "What do you need, I will do all I can... what is it?" came the instant reply. "I am speaking in confidence old friend" began LaTour. "You are familiar about my acrimony with d'Aulnay in Acadia I presume?" queried LaTour. Turning his chair to face LaTour, Bellingham sat again. "Yes, it is known, even here." said Bellingham tersely.

"There have been rumors from Port Royale suggesting that I fortify my position in Port Saint

John. I cannot believe it may be so, but it seems that d'Aulnay is planning an attack once the King has officially given him Governance of Port Royale... *And*," he said for emphasis, ``I know he is in France as we speak, seeking support for his sole governance of Acadia."

"Lord Almighty!" exclaimed Bellingham. "He is your fellow patriot, is he not?" added Bellingham angrily. "That little ass is most certainly not to be trusted, and I never cared for his pious attitude" grumbled Bellingham.

LaTour began pacing the room while forming his thoughts. *There were details he had to work around when speaking of d'Aulnay, but no question remained that Bellingham had spoken the truth... d'Aulnay was not to be trusted.*

Feeling that a small amount of actual information could help his plans while providing viable reasons for any rendezvous with d'Aulnay, he added "d'Aulnay is treacherous I believe, but I must work with him and at least try to be honorable. I think it would be wise however, to prepare for all possible contingencies. The issue of his being Catholic and me being Protestant is most likely at the root, and I know his support in France is solely non-protestant. It seems the persecution I sought to leave, is still haunting me" finished LaTour quietly.

"My only issue to lie on the table, at this point, is *who* you are asking for help" pressed Bellingham. "Me or Governor of Boston, there can be no confusion of the difference in my roles."

"For today old friend, I need to make plans by being introduced to your friends and contacts that I may make a plea for aid in short notice and be well received." replied LaTour firmly. "But I may need your help on a personal level at some point. Can I count on your support?" asked LaTour quietly.

"You can be certain that I am going to do all I can in your aid!" Standing quickly, a jovial Bellingham said "We will begin at once to meet the worthy people of Boston." By night fall the pair had made the rounds throughout Bellingham's extensive network of colleagues and mercenaries. Some were loyal, others not quite so, but LaTour had learned in record time; names, places, and who could be trusted for his dealings.

Bellingham spoke as the carriage rolled towards his mansion, "these are dangerous times my friend, as yet I do not fully know who are, or are not, against my Governance. I was careful to arrange meetings of mutual advantage to us, and these alliances will hold over time for you. They are all good men. Our adventures today however, have proven to me that there are politics at play by the discomfort of some you met... It is the old lawyer in me that always reads people" chuckled Bellingham.

LaTour politely chuckled, but was aware of the supposed impropriety Bostonians had charged when Bellingham had wed his young wife Penelope. The objections persisted with charges of misconduct because he had officiated his own wedding, of course it was led and perpetuated by the rival to his governance John Winthrop. LaTour had more pressing issues and Bellingham's guilt was of little consequence, though he had to admit the old magistrate certainly was happy with young Penelope.

"And so Charles," continued Bellingham, "you are able now to trade here in Boston on your own accord as you have before, but with confidence. I read you as a solid man to engage business and I am in your service... further, I will talk to an associate on the south shore with impeccable character. You will be able to find Robert Compton easily. Sail south of Boston until you find the only stairs reaching to the cliff top. His ship called the *Norma* is moored below-- and Charles," he said pointing his finger, "you will be able to trust him."

After a reflective pause in silence, he continued as he surveyed the bay below, "I do not know if I will be Governor for long, but this day has given you the required assistance for the foreseeable future. If Winthrop is successful in returning as governor at my expense, you will need Compton's assistance. Your greatest problem with Winthrop is his previous alliance with d'Aulnay." They then agreed that if Winthrop was indeed successful and had replaced Bellingham on LaTour`s return to Boston, he would immediately pull anchor and head south along the coast to seek Compton.

The parlor doors glided open framing the young, beautiful Penelope who was soon cajoling and chasing the two friends to the dining room. After a jovial dinner with stories of success and failures shared from both colonies, Bellingham and LaTour returned to the parlor for a nightcap of sherry and conclude their discussion.

"d'Aulnay is most likely going to betray you Charles" began Bellingham. "I expect I will soon see his pinnace in the Bay and without your knowledge of his whereabouts. Other than basic trading, he will not receive my assistance in matters of military support.

You however, should take the four seasoned soldiers I introduced you to this morning as well as two twelve pounder cannons I liberated from a recent Norse troublemaker."

As Bellingham drained his sherry they stood and setting his glass down walked to LaTour to put his hand out. Bellingham spoke barely audible "If you are in need of assistance henceforth, but cannot attend in person, you will pass on this special handshake to them as proof of friend or foe. Be careful who you show this handshake, for presently only three in the know are you, me and Compton."

LaTour agreed and advised Bellingham he would depart in the morning after settling his accounts in full. They talked for a short time until their tired eyes were blinking and agreed it was time to retire. LaTour felt elation on a successful voyage and was anxious to be with his new wife, sleep came much later.

Sunrise had found LaTour already dressed and heading to the main wharf. When he finally had a return signal from his pinnace, a long boat was boarded and oars were soon flashing in unison through the early fall morning. He could see Desjardins sitting in the middle of the long boat on the wine cask.

The sailors of the *L'Amitye de la Rochelle* were his most capable, trusted and loyal men. They had spent their day at anchor; swabbing, re-lashing, mending sails and preparing for their return to Saint John, so this would be their chance to see Boston. It was LaTour`s chance to see the goldsmith.

7 Pistole

San Sebastian,

Spain 1641

As Charles d'Aulnay strolled in the early morning sun, he was pleased with his progress. All of his obstacles aside, and finding partial favor with King had been rewarding, many of the Royal Council were now in his favor as well, and within a short time he would realize his plan to be sole governor of Acadia. He strolled along the narrow street thinking how he should attempt to gain holdings in San Sebastian. *Spain was so lovely* he sighed.

As he neared the waterfront there was a large gathering of people on the wharf. He eased through the throng of people until he could see a body being pulled from the water. Someone said loudly "that is Hernado! Someone has killed Hernando." d'Aulnay looked nervously about the crowd and began to back away from the agitated mob of people. The man that had pulled Hernando from the water began looking through his pockets and speaking loudly announced "he still has coins, he was not robbed. Rosa began pushing through the crowd upon hearing that Hernando was the body found at daylight. She looked down at him and was nauseated at once by his open eyes and blue color. His head was already showing the large contusion and wound. Shaking her head, she said "the fool left the cantina full of wine last night. He probably fell to the rocks beneath the wharf."

d'Aulnay stopped and listened as the crowd began loudly repeating Rosa's presumption. Some began walking away from the wharf while others were breaking into little groups forming the day's gossip. As the human tempo increased like a large wheel starting, San Sebastian was returning to a bustling sea port. Exhaling his breath through his loose lips making a brief flapping sound, he could see Remy making rapid preparations to board the long boat. His crew lined the railings of his pinnace and up the ratlines, as were other ships at anchor in the bay. He would have to move quickly now.

Hurrying up the street in fast strides, he soon had returned to Giovanni Cellini's shop. As Giovanni Cellini closed the door, his bloodshot and puffy eyes hinted a long night for the metalworker. "I trust we are finished here" said d'Aulnay airily. It was more a statement than a question not lost on Cellini who tired and hungry turned quickly placing his hammer on d'Aulnay's chest. Measured and precise he spoke in French for emphasis "if you ever come here again speaking with disrespect to me, I will be forced to teach you proper manners." He glowered while slowly lowering his double ended hammer and said "I must work through the night after my regular shop hours to perform my artistry. Show me respect." d'Aulnay stared impassively. "You do not scare me d'Aulnay. If *we* are caught in this treachery, *we* will face the wheel." Using *we* with emphasis. Cellini swore as he walked to the back of the shop and tossed the hammer on his bench. He turned as d'Aulnay approached the bench and was suddenly forced to lean back over the bench as d'Aulnay's long dagger came from beneath his cloak. He held it close to Cellini's right eyeball and began to bring it slowly closer until Cellini cried out in terror. d'Aulnay lowered his dagger tip to Giovanni's cheek and holding it firmly brought his knee to the man's groin. The resulting pain caused Cellini to flinch forward enough for the dagger tip to dig in. d'Aulnay stood back and returned the dagger to its sheath, then threw his handkerchief at Cellini. The goldsmith pressed the handkerchief against his cheek and sank into a chair.

"*Get up!* And finish our business, and Giovanni, if you ever threaten me again, I will kill you...slowly" d'Aulnay said with a cool detachment. Cellini groaned as he stood and walked to d'Aulnay's small wine cask on the floor. He opened the bung and said "You brought me a total of one thousand one hundred and thirty gold French francs. I have replaced them with; one thousand one hundred and seventy five gold Spanish doubloon. I am sure you already knew the count." Reaching into the bung hole with his fingers, Cellini brought out what appeared to be a used double escudo. He passed it to d'Aulnay for inspection. Turning it over in his hand he exclaimed "do *all* these coins look so well used?"

Cellini allowed a smile and said "yes, they are magnificent are they not? I used a few handfuls of smooth stones with lime, charred sticks, and cloth rags in a cask. I then had my children roll it around the floor as a game and voila." d'Aulnay returned the coin to the cask and Cellini used a wooden mallet to drive the bung firmly.

"I will begin the cask you brought yesterday after I get some rest. When are you returning?" asked Cellini. d'Aulnay remained silent for a moment staring at the goldsmith. When he finally answered he was obviously evasive and stated "if you begin soon you will be ready in time." The silence continued until Cellini already tired and drained from d'Aulnay's encounter merely shrugged and said "very well, the matter of my compensation and you are on your way." d'Aulnay removed a leather pouch from his cloak and held it dangling by the cord.

Cellini took the pouch and opening it, looked inside nodding his head. He walked over to his bench and poured the contents to his bench. The gold coins were spread with a sweep of his hand, allowing Cellini to count them. Leaning forward quickly and snatching a silver coin from the bench Cellini exclaimed "what is this?" He turned it slowly to catch light on the surfaces until looking up at d'Aulnay in astonishment. "Yes, it is what you think... a new écu minted in France to replace the Louis d'or. It is meant to equalize the monetary systems within France, but my information from the palace yesterday points to clipping and counterfeiting the gold coins as the biggest reason." d'Aulnay continued, "Time is now against us, so my partner and I will attempt to trade as many gold coin as we can. It is obvious that France will not be paying gold in the near future as the new silver coin replaces it" d'Aulnay continued carefully. "Consider it a tip for your services. You are a true master of your trade Cellini, and I appreciate your talent. Let us try to forget our unfortunate encounter shall we?" urged d'Aulnay.

As Cellini dabbed his cheek he nodded slowly, and seeing that the nick on his cheek was no longer bleeding, threw the bloodied handkerchief under the bench. "Agreed, but I believe *your* threat was as real as *mine*, and so we will continue, but with *respect* would you not agree?" replied Cellini firmly. The two men shook hands over the completed cask of coins.

As d'Aulnay rolled his cart down the street he was so engrossed in the task of navigating the street crowd with his gold, he did not see the figure on the roof of the church. In fact, nobody noticed the cloaked observer in the shadows of the bell tower.

Had d'Aulnay noticed, he would have realized the bell tower had an excellent view from the waterfront to the Cellini shop on Agosto Street and the corner Inn on San Jeronimo.

8 Pistole

Boston, New England 1641

LaTour was able to quickly sequester a carriage with horse, and after loading the cask aboard, was on his way to North Boston. He arrived at the small goldsmiths shop and was soon inside with help from the proprietor John Reverie. After friendly and familiar greetings, the bung was removed from the cask and Reverie reached into the hole and pinched out a gold coin. He turned it over in his hand and nodded. "So, how many coins have you here?"

LaTour walked over to the cask and pointed to the inked wine stamp with a smile. "*Sixteen Hundred and forty* was a good year for good Spanish Tempranillo!" They enjoyed a good chuckle and hoisted the small cask to the goldsmith's bench. Reverie was soon able to free the coins and after counting out the stacks of coins agreed to the total of coins.

"I must admit, Charles," said Reverie as he wrote in his logs and made calculations. "I really don't understand why you want French coins. They are a nuisance here because they are basically clones of the Doubloon, why not trade and maintain the doubloon; they are worth twice as much!"

LaTour sighed and spoke ruefully, masking his deceit, "I trust in your honesty and integrity to keep our affairs private. I must trade with France and return there with our native coin, and an abundance of doubloon would be questioned. I am supposed to trade in France solely, but as you can ascertain, I am more -- shall we say *vigorous* in my trade practice."

"All is well with me Charles" said Reverie. "I guess I understand your intentions, it seems like you are getting the bad end of the deal, but if you are pleased, than I am pleased to be rid of the Louis d'or."

Reverie placed LaTour's gold in a chest and secured the lid and locked it. "Give me a moment Charles, and I will retrieve your coins, I have kept them in my secure area. Please, relax a moment" said Reverie pointing to a comfortable chair." I won't be long."

LaTour soon heard a voice calling outside and realized that Reverie had obviously exited the rear and was now at the front of the building. As he exited the shop front, he noticed Reverie had loaded a small chest on the carriage floor. When he arrived at the side of the carriage, Reverie passed him a key and said "Godspeed Charles. Please take a moment and check your fee from wine trade" laughed Reverie.

LaTour nodded and inserted the key in the lock and found forty two stacks of twenty Louis d'or. He turned to Reverie and said "there appears to be a shortage John. There should be forty two and a half stacks if it is valued at half of a doubloon."

"You will have to excuse my levity Charles; you have taken all my remaining francs! That is why I asked you to count them" beamed Reverie. "Give me a moment to get your coins" and trotted into the shop. He returned before LaTour could climb to the carriage and passed him *fifteen* gold doubloons. "It is always good to deal with you John. I won't forget your honesty and generosity" he added while shaking his hand.

The longboat was made ready when he returned to the wharf. The crew was waiting casually on the boardwalk and everyone anxious to get home. LaTour was amazed at the speed in which the longboat glided through the water, powered by enthusiastic men. The tide was headed out and the light breeze had LaTour clearing the last point of land two hours later.

The mate had just responded to heading change and called out "turning to zero three zero. Aye, aye captain." He ordered the yardarms set and the crew sent aloft to unfurl topsails. They were soon making ten knots toward Port Saint John. LaTour was standing on the poop deck watching the crew as Lieutenant Nicholas Gargot walked over and stood beside him. "You seem quiet. Good trading Sir?" he queried to break the silence.

"Yes, very successful trading. We will have winter coming soon and my worries of supplies for the fort are lessened for now. I am hoping Françoise is getting local forage for store as well" replied LaTour thoughtfully. "Gargot, I wish to talk to you about something deeper at hand. When I spoke with Governor Bellingham about the affairs between d'Aulnay and myself, he felt compelled to warn me about d'Aulnay's possible betrayal. I think the reality of a full scale war with d'Aulnay is upon us" said LaTour regretfully. "We have had our moments to be certain, but I have not been to France so long I fear he may have gained favor with the King at my expense. Bellingham seemed certain of betrayal" he trailed off.

Gargot was a formidable soldier and had been with LaTour for many years. He respected and trusted the decisions LaTour made and was able to read him well enough to know there was a tangible threat. He relished the thought of battling with the pompous d'Aulnay personally. As the *L'Amitye de la Rochelle* surged though the Atlantic under full sail, the silence on the aft deck was palpable. Any other time the art of trimming out a ship and settling for the trip was thrilling with the ship almost seemingly alive. He knew LaTour was forming his thoughts carefully and therefore remained silent to avoid distraction. He was starting to feel the rhythm of the surges and hear whispers of the broken bow waves along the sides of the creaking ship when LaTour finally spoke again.

"When we return to the fort and unload, I want you to return to Boston and trade. You will take the shallop at anchor at the fort and a few trusted men with a smaller load of pelts. I am going to meet d'Aulnay in Port Royale as quickly as possible and determine his veracity. I know I can trust you implicitly" LaTour paused a moment and said "With my trust, your discretion, and respectful audacity you will also seek military aid from Governor Bellingham." Lieutenant Gargot was humbled at LaTour's trust in him and was only able to muster a nod in silence while holding LaTour's gaze.

LaTour turned and looked about the ship; walking first to the port rail and scanning the distant land, and then the starboard to observe the Atlantic. Raising his voice he ordered the mate to ease offshore in the growing darkness to avoid any of the possible hazards.

He turned once more to Gargot and said "Thank you Lieutenant, we will talk tomorrow of our plans. Take time to plan further defenses in Saint John at the fort with the extra canon we have below ships... We may soon be at war!"

9 Pistole

Port Saint John, 1641

The winds were favorable and steady to result in record passage time from Boston for LaTour. As the *L'Amitye de la Rochelle* entered the Saint John harbour sails were reduced. The incoming tide heading for the mighty Saint John River pulled her quickly towards the fort and the awaiting crowds. The colonists had gathered around the outside of the fort and were all cheering and waving. LaTour looked proudly to the fort and waved back as he saw the LaTour flag with his shield raised up the flag pole for a proper homecoming. Francie's work no doubt he chuckled to himself. The sails were furled and secured around yard arms, halyards secured or coiled to dry and the longboat unlashed. As the anchor splashed, heading for the muddy bottom, all the men cheered loudly. LaTour scrambled down the side of the ship to the longboat that was already in the water alongside the pinnace. He ordered his travel chest and the small locked chest lowered first and then his lieutenant and oarsmen. They were soon ashore and heading for the fort while many hands made light work unloading the pinnace.

The Lord and Lady walked arm in arm to their lodge in the fort. After a long embrace followed by an equally long kiss, LaTour stood back and looked at Françoise while holding her hands. He searched her face looking for clues and then asked "What has happened? You are holding back from me... what has happened Francie?" he asked sternly. Françoise gently pulled her hands back and while pointing to a chair offered "You had better sit down Charles; this is going to be hard to take. Before I begin, understand that I have told no one else here at the fort." Charles nearly jumped into the chair and looked expectantly at her. "Go on, please Francie, you are killing me... what has happened?" Françoise took a large breath and said "You had hardly left for Boston when sails were spotted coming from Port Royale. I thought it might be d'Aulnay at first, but it was a shallop with a small crew with some Jesuits aboard. They were polite and never caused any issue. They simply talked pleasantries while looking the fort over and left the Jesuits here! The Jesuits say they prayed in God's service and felt that God has commanded them here. They have set up an altar and expect us to conform to God's word." Charles began to rise his eye's blazing, but was cut short by Françoise's raised hand. "Stop! That is the least of it all. The Jesuits have informed me that the King has ordered your arrest and seizure of all assets by none other than *Governor Charles de Menou d'Aulnay de Charnisay*!" She said his name with slow, deliberate, pronunciation in disgust. Her eyes welled up and she put her hand over her mouth to stifle a cry and sobbed out "Oh Charles! I am so sorry, we are lost here... We have been betrayed... The King wants you to answer for treason! We... I have given everything for this trade post." LaTour was crestfallen and despaired for Françoise as she quietly choked her sobs back with her head down. He slowly got up from his chair and effortlessly picked her up as if she were weightless. As he hugged her close, her feet dangled six inches from the floor with her face buried in his shoulder and gently cried. They remained that way until she finally stopped and LaTour slowly lowered her to the floor. He turned as she looked at him, but she saw the wetness on his cheeks. All LaTour could manage was "I am so sorry Francie... I will make this right. *I will not fail us.*" Charles de Saint-Étienne de la Tour was ready for bloodshed. He trembled and even his eyesight seemed twisted with his rage. He stripped immediately and donned his buckskins and moccasins. He strode to the fireplace and snatched his bow, arrows, and knife belt. "I will return soon" he mumbled. The colonists all smiled and waved at him as he trotted through the gate for the high ridges around the fort. He never stopped until he made the summit of the ridgeline, and as he breathlessly panted, turned to view the fort, harbour, and distant Port Royale. He was overcome with emotion. His arms outstretched, he roared for all he was worth D'AULLLLLNAAAAY! YOU! BASSSTARRRDDDD! He dropped to his knees and with his head down and palms upraised he made his vow to God. *Forgive me Lord, I will kill the devil incarnate d'Aulnay.*

He then prayed; for strength and the courage to fight d'Aulnay, for Françoise to have comfort, for all the settlers that believed in him and for guidance and finally with his King to see truth. He then begged forgiveness of his sins against others before going silent. When his breathing returned to normal with rage subsiding, he raised his head to see Louie sitting on the ground with legs crossed a short distance away watching him. Neither spoke, but Louie could see his friend's pain. He finally spoke in Mi'kmaq to LaTour using his Mi'kmaq name Tia'M (moose, for his strength and comfort in the water) given to him in Port Royale -- "Tia'M, Gisu'lgw will hear you for your heart is right to receive him. It is what separates you from d'Aulnay. You are a great man of honor and strength. Only Gisu'lgw can avenge d'Aulnay's evil spirit. Tia'M! You must remember your teachings as I too learned them." LaTour felt drained and could only manage a faint smile at his friend. He finally slowly replied while nodding "gegnua'tegeieg," *We do what is proper or correct.* LaTour stood as did Louie. LaTour put his hand on Mooin's shoulder and said "A', maja'tinej *"O.K., let's leave.* "Mi'watm ta'n teliapoqonmuioq." *I am thankful for your help.*

 They walked back down to the fort with LaTour feeling renewed with hope. He would best d'Aulnay, and he knew how he would do it... by deceit as he had been deceived. He would not surrender his fort to anyone, but he would hurt d'Aulnay where it would hurt him most-- Pride and pistole.

When LaTour entered the lodge, Françoise was by the fire place with a hot bowl of stew in her hands.

She looked at him balefully, asking "What are we to do Charles?" He returned the bow, arrows and belt to their place on the fireplace and placed his hand on her shoulder. "I had to remove my rage Francie, to think clearly and make the right choices. The answer is very simple in theory, but it will take a great deal of fortitude on our parts to implement." He continued, "The Jesuits are here as d'Aulnay's spies... so we will use them for *our* purposes. They also removed any element of surprise that would have occurred had we not known of this deceit... *we can prepare*. Most importantly though Francie, d'Aulnay does not know that *we* are aware of his deception... we can deceive him and we will manipulate the pistole to our advantage! He will wait to attack until he is at strength and can take the pistole as well. If it were not for the pistole..." he paused and said ominously "we will defend our fort from all attackers including King and countrymen alike. We will overcome this."

"You know you will have to go to France and plead your case Charles" said Françoise. "It will require the King to be swayed on your actions alone. You must make him believe in you as I do, and realize you are a true patriot" she declared standing. "Now let's get you out of those dirty skins and into a hot bath" she said with an arched eyebrow, pointing to the large copper tub. The buckskins became a neat mound on the floor instantly... as were her clothing. They were unusually late to arise in the morning.

Late morning found the pair at the table once again making their plans. LaTour was able to formulate a comprehensive plan that would include efforts by Nicholas Gargot, Françoise and Louie. As LaTour reiterated the series of events required to unfold,

Françoise interjected where she could see issues or conflicts until they sat back in silence. Françoise began, "Yes Charles, I think this is all doable with a good chance of success. Let's meet with our other two now and turn this mess around, but no worries... I am more than able to meet d'Aulnay again for *his* deception!" Charles could only beam at her enthusiasm.

Closing the door firmly, LaTour joined his Lady at the head of the table and looking at Louie and Lieutenant Nicholas Gargot began his campaign. After placing their hands on the Bible at the center of the table, they made oath to never reveal any details of their meeting. LaTour stood and delivered his plan, "It is time for all truth to be cast at this meeting, and apprise of our current situation. Lastly, make a formidable plan to correct the problems." LaTour looked at each person. "I have been ordered arrested and returned to France to face inquiry with the King. As yet, we are the only ones to know this, other than the Jesuits who are here as scouts for d'Aulnay. They are not to be trusted. I must accept that d'Aulnay has betrayed me using politics in France with members of the Royal Council. The king has been misinformed to d'Aulnay's advantage. To regain my governance of Port Saint John, I must first defend it at all cost. Gargot, you will commence immediately to increase fortifications and add the two new cannons as we have already discussed. You will drill the men on siege tactics and have them remain vigilant. We are now at war, civil war, with d'Aulnay and to a minor degree France. We will surrender to no one! As soon as you have met the obligation of preparing our Fort, you will depart for Boston and seek aid from Governor Bellingham. We have need for another warship and soldiers to help defend us." At that

LaTour stood and said "I have made good contact in Boston and our aid is in Bellingham. Also to the south there is contact named Robert Compton in Bellingham's absence. I will now show you people the secret hand-shake that will determine your credibility in New England." LaTour began with Françoise and moved around the table shaking each hand to divulge the secret. When he was finished, LaTour said "There are only we four, Compton, and Bellingham who know this hand shake. Use it wisely and divulge it only with discretion."

"My next step is to sail at once for Port Royale and meet d'Aulnay. He must be deceived into believing that I am unaware of circumstances" continued LaTour. "I know he is not ready for a confrontation yet. He will wait until he has grown in strength at both Port Royale and at sea, as we are presently much more powerful." Nicholas Gargot spoke lowly for effect and said "the little dwarf does have some growing left does he not?" LaTour joined in the laughter that provided comic relief" before continuing, "This will not last though, as he most likely is returning from France with preparations to take siege." LaTour grew somber again and eyeing Françoise said "I will be alright this trip, though I doubt it possible in the future. Françoise will be in command of our fort in my absence Lieutenant; please ensure the men all realize their respect is required in your absence for both Louie and Françoise."

With the meeting over, Charles and Françoise were once again able to speak privately.

"Francie, tell me of your adventures up river while I was gone. Are we ready to hide our pistole?" asked LaTour. Françoise revealed her trip upriver and how

Louie had been instrumental in securing an old cave for the cache. Louie had been scouting and learned from a local band the existence of the "Maiden" as a landmark and offered to scout it as the potential area. He was gone for a week and just appeared one morning at the fort, Françoise confided.

"He told me he was at my service and was ready to take me whenever I wanted to leave" she said with obvious admiration. "I took all the gold there Charles, and only kept a few francs here at the fort. Trade has been good though and we will be ready for the largest trade shipment to France in history."

"I will need it to support my position with the King" said LaTour with relief as he stood. "Forgive me my dear, but I must prepare for Port Royale. I will most likely have another installment of Doubloons for exchange with my francs from Boston. If all this deceit is true Francie, it will most likely be our last transaction with d'Aulnay I hope our reserves are enough." LaTour finished his conversation at the door and was soon heading for a review of their defenses against possible attack.

10Pistole

Port Royale, Acadia

Summer, 1641

The *L'Amitye de la Rochelle* sailed into Port Royale Harbour with the fleur-de-lis marked foresail full and LaTour's coat of arms banner fluttering from the fore-mast. Her cannons were loaded and prepared to run out the gun ports in anticipation of possible trouble. LaTour ordered the sails stowed and anchors aweigh. As the Pinnace turned her nose to the wind the longboat was readied and in the water when LaTour reemerged from his cabin. He was resplendent in all finery for the occasion along with his chest of Francs, and was soon met at the wharf by d'Aulnay's Lieutenant Remy Martin. Remy had been ordered to offer a cordial reception, but he would not let his guard down after seeing LaTour lash out at the last encounter. He led LaTour up the hill to the fort where d'Aulnay was waiting in his main Lodge. d'Aulnay pointed to the small chest at LaTour's feet and said "trade is still prospering I see. How was your trip old friend?"

LaTour smiled as he was expected and remaining amicable saying "It was a most excellent crossing, and yes we have all the francs from Boston, our contact there has traded everything he had!"

d'Aulnay turned and walked to the window and looking outside said "We have a problem Charles." LaTour fought panic as he realized d'Aulnay's possible trap. He waited silently for d'Aulnay to continue. After a long pause, he sighed and said "Charles when I met with the King he revealed a new currency to replace the Louis d'Or. It seems we are going to be challenged with finding Louis d'Or to trade."

LaTour caught the silver coin as d'Aulnay turned and flicked the silver coin with his thumb with a ting. He examined the coin and walking to the window for better light exclaimed "The stamping is so precise and clean! It must have been created in a machine. Where are the coins to be made?" "The king has hired an engraver and sculptor named Jean Varin to create a large screw press machine to make the coins in Paris" replied d'Aulnay.

They both stared out windows of the lodge in silence until LaTour asked "Did you receive your official

Governorship of Port Royale from the King? Were there any issues?"

"Yes, I received the warrant, and no, there were no concessions" replied d'Aulnay. LaTour waited a moment before accepting that d'Aulnay was not divulging anything further and decided to play along as he had planned and said "So, how much pistole do we have for safe keeping?"

As he waited for a response he scanned the room and noticed a small wine cask on the table and a long narrow box with **Hernando Galeana** emblazoned on the top. d'Aulnay walked over and rested his hand on the top of the cask, then while patting it said "with the conversion in San Sebastian of melt down and re-stamping; it gave us a total of one thousand one hundred and fifty five doubloons. Not so bad my friend?" smiled d'Aulnay.

LaTour forced a smile and patted the small chest and removing a key from his cloak opened it to reveal the contents. "We have six hundred and forty, Louis d'Or" said LaTour proudly. d'Aulnay grinned and said "and I have seven hundred and seventy to a total of thirteen hundred and forty for our man in San Sebastian!"

"What is the total in San Sebastian to be converted?" queried LaTour thoughtfully.

"We have one thousand, five hundred and eighty Louis d'Or from my last delivery there" replied d'Aulnay. He added in a questioning tone, "Perhaps when this round is done with exchanges we should stop for awhile on the side of caution."

"Is there a problem in France, or San Sebastian I should know about?" said LaTour cautiously. In the long pause LaTour determined d'Aulnay was deliberating how much information to divulge, until picking his words carefully said, "You seem ahhh distracted or distant. Do we have a problem here LaTour?" diverting the question. He knew d'Aulnay was being deceptive by using a question to answer and now LaTour was certain of trouble with France.

With all his strength to not lash out at d'Aulnay and kill him where he stood, he feigned shock said "We have so much to be cautious of, please accept my apology, for I am sorry to have questioned your honesty! I am worried of being caught in these, well frankly speaking treasonous operations."

d'Aulnay became placated, and while he wished to kill the weak, savage loving conniver, he would wait a little longer and have it all! He said condescendingly "Leave the King and France to *me* and just do *your part* of this operation. It is our efforts we reward, the King is receiving a large portion and all is fair. No we have no problems in France to be concerned of my friend. I will return in the spring and complete the dealings in San Sebastian. Then we take a little break to avoid any chance of raising questions would be in order. I too have no wish for being caught and charged with treason" smiled d'Aulnay.

LaTour only wanted out of the building and get as far from d'Aulnay as possible. *What has he done to my reputation with the King* he wondered... *He knew* d'Aulnay was smiling at the paradox of treason.

LaTour stood and walking to d'Aulnay said "Well old friend, we are doing well then. Yes, we will end the exchanges after you are done in San Sebastian in the spring. When you return we will have nested a sizable fortune and perhaps we will not have need to restart."

d'Aulnay looked LaTour in the eye and said "Very good, take these coins. When I return in the late spring, we will both go to the cache your lovely wife has found as safe repository of our wealth."

 LaTour nodded amicably and passed d'Aulnay the key for his small chest. Gathering the wine cask of doubloons he paused at the door and turning said "If the Order of Good Cheer is still being held here in Port Royale during the winter, perhaps Francie and I will venture across the Bay and join in the fun with you and Jeanne." It seemed to catch d'Aulnay off guard for a slight hesitation before he offered graciously; "Yes, we still feast weekly in the winter... please come. It does alleviate the doldrums of winter."

LaTour returned to the pinnace and having timed his tides correctly, was fortunate to catch the favorable outgoing tide allowing full sail to Port Saint John. He never once looked back at his old home settlement of Port Royale and as he looked at his dirtied hands from manning the ropes with his men, he thought wryly; *at least this dirt will wash off...*

The days were getting shorter and the sun was now lower in the sky. As LaTour entered the harbour he caught occasional scents of the decaying poplar leaves reminding him yet again of the urgency to prepare for winter. From the foredeck standing on the bow sprit, he could see the many cords of winter hardwood piled under the parapets for extra protection. Realizing how well the fort was operating under Francie's direction allowed him the veracity to make travel plans to France. He would go to France when d'Aulnay would not expect during the winter, and for good measure, if he was successful with the King, he would go to San Sebastian before d'Aulnay and take possession of the gold doubloons.

Despite the ordeal in Port Royale, LaTour was whistling his favorite tune *Sur le Pont d'Avignon.* as he walked through the main gate. As he strolled along he heard his men begin to whistle along with him to the bewilderment of the recent New England recruits. Louie was stacking pelts and told them the name of the tune was a child's song from France. He said "LaTour told me it was song used by soldiers to identify friend from foe when the smoke from canon and Musket obscured the battlefield." He shrugged and said nonchalantly "I think it is a nice song, it is a happy song." He joined in whistling along with LaTour despite himself and went back to work.

11Pistole

Port Saint John,

Autumn, 1641

Louie never understood the ideals of many of the Frenchmen he met. He was born and raised with French influence at Port Royale finding them mostly honorable hard working people. It was an easy transition for his father, the Great Chief Membertou, to accept the French as equals. They enjoyed a symbiotic relationship while sharing liberally with everything from technology in construction or farming, health care and hunting. The native spirituality had a great deal in common with

Christianity allowing a simple transition from the understanding of the term God. Louie was versed in scripture and the Native spirituality wherein he found the duality of respect for fellowman, yet here was d'Aulnay and others that would betray anyone for their own gain... yet they honored their God in their churches and pronounced great faith. He knew what his forefathers for generations had known; that the end result of treacherous behaviors would end in purgatory. It was a mystery to him.

Razilly, Charles LaTour and his father Claude had arrived in Port Royale with expectations of working *with* the locals and adapted easily with Native ideals of fairness. They dealt fairly with Chief Membertou in return; the golden rule from the Bible had been quoted many times to the occasional detriment of the colonists. Those who remained after the first winter had learned survival techniques from the local Mi'kmaq and prospered.

The Mi'kmaq had prospered from increased yields in farming, fishing and better buildings. When Louie had been a boy, he saw the Order of Good Cheer begin its humble origins one night in the main lodge with plays, songs and feasting. The actors had performed the song *Sur le Pont d'Avignon* and Louie never forgot it. The colourful costumes and dancing was performed with laughter and clapping from all in attendance, Native and Frenchman alike.

Louie had fond memories of the early colonial life and as a boy had seen Charles become comfortable with the Mi'kmaq language and customs. He had grown to respect him as unique among the Frenchmen, for he could at once be comfortable in either culture while remaining a noble leader. He like many of the others had accepted LaTour as an equal when he had married a native girl (e'pite'sl in Mi'kmaq). Membertou had blessed the union and claimed to have had a vision predicting the marriage years previous of the event. As Grand Chief, his blessing had spread acceptability for interracial union throughout Acadia.

When d'Aulnay had arrived in Port Royale, young Louie was abruptly introduced to the concepts of racism. He had heard an Osprey chirping and searching the sky saw the majestic giant struggling to gain altitude with a fish in its talons. The raptor was fascinating to watch and as Louie gazed at the spectacle he had his hand shielding the sun. d'Aulnay, walking in his direction had simply slapped him a hard smack, cart wheeling the teen out of his way. "Move you stupid *SAVAGE*" he had growled as he continued on, laughing. It was a pointless attack;

Louie had been standing in an open area... and nobody to witness the senseless cruelty. Louie had refused to cry. There would be another day he had promised.

LaTour's offer to settle at his fort was attractive because he would have reason to leave Port Royale.

His time hunting or helping at the fort in Saint John had kept him occupied. Lady of LaTour had given him a mission resulting in a weeklong voyage to store kegs upriver in the cache. It was easy to work with Francie, and her laughter moved him many times. She had been as hard on the paddle as he had been, making the trip memorable. It left him with confused feelings how he would adapt to the new fort. He could fit in and stay at the fort, he knew he was welcome, but he also had LaTour's support for anything he could not manage on his own.

The recent addition of d'Aulnay's pious Jesuit "spies" made him uncomfortable as they felt the need to encroach primarily upon the Wolastoq (Maliseet) people that had made the fort their home. LaTour had severely warned them to treat Maliseet peoples with respect, yet he allowed the Jesuit to stay... much to Louie's dismay.

He made his decision, preferring the sanctity of his own wigwam set against the steep north ridgeline behind the fort. He had built his wigwam with the traditional method of Birch bark stitched with spruce root. The doorway had a view to the south as was proper for design, but had an advantage of looking over the fort and out the harbour towards Port Royale. On nice days in the winter he could sit in comfort with the pelt aside sitting in sunlight from the open doorway.

He had prepared for winter with beaver pelts over the birch bark and covered it all with old sail canvas at LaTour's urging. With a small fire in the wigwam he sat on furs barebacked on the coldest nights. Life was good for Louie and he would sit in his comfortable wigwam cooking his saltwater rinsed meats on his fire pit grill.

The meager possessions were all he required for sustenance, but the one gift from Francie was the small silver container he used for making the yellow birch tea he loved so much. Francie had exclaimed it was the most delicious drink she could imagine when they had travelled upriver that summer. He chuckled to himself when he remembered of her drinking her silver mug full and quickly asking for more while apologizing. They had erupted into laughter together... good times he thought. Maybe he would tell her sometime his recipe had a magic ingredient of sweet clover heads.

As the first snow came, Louie was ready and had a second mini wigwam built for storing firewood, tools and wood for a new bow and arrow making, along with his materials for snowshoe making. He had what he needed and nothing more; it was the way of the Mi'kmaq, because more than necessity was waste. It was good to have the cookware, iron arrowheads, and the sharp tools making him realize that ironically the gold that the Frenchmen wanted so badly was of little use to actual survival. Life was starting to feel like the early days for Louie in Port Royale.

After a return from the Order of Good Cheer one moonlit night, he began to feel the natural pang of needing a companion, someone to share his life and laugh with and continue to make memories with. He was usually able to shake it all off with the many chores required for his sole existence. He seemed to require a break from his thoughts and rely on meditation many of the long winter nights as he thought of Francie at the fort.

12 Pistole

Port Saint John,

January 1642

The day had broken clear with a warm front filling Port Saint John with above average temperatures. LaTour knew time was upon him to return to France. He had kept the ship prepared during the early winter in anticipation of such a day. He turned to Francois and said softly "it is time for me to return to France. There may be no better day than this one of warm weather."

She had earlier made the large fire for warmth and it was now perfect for cooking. She made a large breakfast which they ate in silence. They stared at each other in silence until she nodded slowly and said "it will be alright; you are a good man and the King will have no choice but reinstate your honor with your claim to holdings.

Preparations were ordered for departure by noon with crew roll called and supplies loaded after the full cargo of pelts. The fort leapt to duties and by eleven the ship was ready to make way. The long boat was alongside with the last of supplies as the anchor was ordered aboard and stowed. Men scrambled about their respective duties until the pinnace was moving to the ocean in light breeze. With the long boat aboard and lashed firm, full sail including staysail, topsail and gallants were ordered and trimmed loose for the soft air. As the *L'Amitye de la Rochelle* leaned to her sails the fully loaded creaking hull surged forward throwing a formidable bow wave. LaTour knew from experience that the north Atlantic was a dangerous place in the winter, but he had no choice. He had learned that d'Aulnay had improved his fortifications from what he had seen in the fall visit, and when d'Aulnay dicovered he had sailed out for France; LaTour knew there would be trouble from d'Aulnay.

LaTour knew that the fort colonists had all been talking of the last minute trip to France and thus the Jesuits knew. The Jesuits had anchored a small 4ton sloop at the fort in the late fall when the brothers had traded places between forts, and he was certain they would be off to Port Royale within the day if not preparing already. He felt that the fort was in capable hands to repel any advance or siege, but he knew d'Aulnay would be in a rage because he had been deceived by LaTour. With the deception, d'Aulnay would also know LaTour would make a stop in San Sebastian to take the last pistole. d'Aulnay however, did not know where the pistole was cached, and for that matter even LaTour had not seen the location. Regardless of who knew the location, the LaTour's had absconded all the pistole. Yes, d'Aulnay would come to Port Saint John and make his move while LaTour was away, and he would be seeing red.

He had people watching d'Aulnay in France and would check information when he landed in Le Havre, it was his alternate port from La Rochelle and the situation definitely required steering clear of La Rochelle until he was cleared of charges... something he could not do if locked up. His need for a clandestine spy came from the fact that he never really trusted d'Aulnay enough to entrust his future to him. d'Aulnay in retrospect, was in need of

LaTour's help and the discrete location his new fort in Saint John, but LaTour knew that the next meeting in Port Saint John between them would have ended in a violent encounter. He had no doubt that d'Aulnay would have killed them all for the pistole cache; if he ever doubted it, the new silver écu was the pivotal event to capitulate his demise... time as up.

He would prepare his defense on the month long crossing, using the aft facing cabin deck railing as a private "court room bar" to practice speech portions. His first speech however, was the crew briefing; to keep them steadfast he would have to tell them the reasons for such a harried departure and importance of returning to France in harsh risky winter conditions.

The large aft deck was his stage and the men all gathered mid-ship to hear their leader's word. There was no need to practice, for the facts were simple and the deception real. The current recourse was their only purpose. The men all cheered at LaTour's audacity to foil d'Aulnay with a risky return in winter and confront none other than the King himself.

With the detailed briefing complete and the affirmation of the men's support to the mission, the lookout in the crows-nest began singing loudly *Sur le Pont d'Avignon.*. LaTour thought of the irony of a nice song, a happy song becoming the battle song of Port Saint John. As the song ended, and LaTour turned to look back, he was surprised that they were beyond sight of land.

13 Pistole

Port Saint John,

January 1642

The three Jesuits gathered quickly to observe the men of the fort running and gathering supplies or trade pelts. They spoke quietly and asked each other if any knew of the reasons behind LaTour's obvious rapid departure in the pinnace. One of the priests said he had overheard that LaTour told the mate he was going to France and the amount of provisions gave the rumor credit.

After the departing ship had been reduced to a small white dot on the horizon, Françoise stood impassive and with her arms crossed as she stared at the Elder

Jesuit Burdett. He had just informed her that it was time for their rotation back to Port Royale. After an uncomfortably long silence he had grown fidgety and said "is there a problem Madame? You knew we are here on a rotational basis, and I have decided to leave."

"Interesting timing" Madame LaTour snapped in reply. She finally turned after staring him down and walked back to the lodge without ever saying a word.

Father Burdett stood alone in the courtyard and as he looked around, noted the colonists were turning away from him. Some were going inside buildings while others returned to their chores. He realized his time here had perhaps not been as clandestine as he had hoped and that meant he would depart as soon as possible. His work here was complete for now, and God's work would have to wait.

The young priest remaining at the Fort was advised to maintain the Lord's work and remain devoted to his rosary until the rotation returned. As he watched from the beach, the sloop headed south out the harbour for Port Royale. It had all started in the morning with LaTour's rapid deployment for France and now even his fellow Jesuits were abruptly gone. It was unsettling for the innocent man of God, but not nearly as much when he turned away from harbour seeing everyone in the fort had gathered to watch the departure. They were talking among themselves and it was clear that something was very wrong. There were unfriendly, unsmiling contemptuous people between him and his small altar building within the fort. Only a blue jay was heard screeching in the silence from a rooftop. He summoned strength and willed his foot to move forward and then another until he was walking to the gate. In a show of their dislike and solidarity, they would not move aside and the young priest was forced to slide himself through the silent, unyielding, human forest. He could not understand their obvious hatred; he was here and could deliver communion and prayers. The young Priest was hurt at their display towards him, and he rationalized possibilities, but finally accepted he could not understand why they seemed angry.

Port Royale,

February 1642

The old Jesuit priest named Burdett was slowly

stepping backwards in horror as Charles de Menou

d'Aulnay de Charnisay, Governor of Acadia,

screamed a long agonized roar and kicked the table

over. He kicked the box that had resided on the table

moments before with such force that it flew past the

cowering priest just missing Remy who stood quietly

at the door appearing almost bored. The box

exploded sending letters and official documents

flying. He was in full blown tantrum and the rage was

only starting, the table was destroyed next and the chair followed. When he was done his destruction there was nothing left whole or untouched in the room. He was reaching for his sword when Remy stood to attention, raised his eyebrow and placed his hand on the hilt of his sword and firmly asked "Are you finished? If not, what are your intentions?" They were the first calm, sensible words spoken in the room since d'Aulnay launched into his uncontrolled tantrum, screaming nonstop obscenities or fractured curses and mostly "LaTour".

Burdett was whimpering and cowered at Remy`s feet willing the door to open, unable to watch the violent spectacle. Remy`s question had pierced his commander's rage. d'Aulnay blinked a few times, relaxed his stance and breathlessly wiped his mouth from both sides with the back of his hand. Remy resumed his bored pose nodding almost imperceptibly. Remy looked down at the pathetic priest begging for Remy to open the door with furtive glances at the latch. Remy stared at d'Aulnay and put his hand on the latch. d'Aulnay waved disgustedly at the door saying "Burdett, you will not speak of this incident" whereby Remy obliged the priest by pulling the door open allowing the priest to flee. Remy looked at the floor and said ``the *man* of God wet himself I see. I think he may have been scared of your wrath." d'Aulnay kicked the shattered table leg again and said "Remy, I am beyond rage. The scoundrel LaTour has absconded a great deal of wealth from me and to make matters worse, I was to seize the Fort of Saint John and return with LaTour to France that he answer to charges of treason and rebellion. I left him alone until spring and now I find he has fled. I know he will work against me as I am now in a position to seize his fort."

Remy stared impassively and as was his custom, never offering comment. Not that d'Aulnay wanted a comment; Remy knew he had become a sounding board to bounce d'Aulnay's ideas and speeches off. If anything was certain to Remy, it was the fact that d'Aulnay would never divulge all details. He couldn't understand how LaTour returning to the King was an issue, if indeed LaTour was doing as asked. *Something is a little questionable with his rage, and the wealth remark was probably a mistake with too many details in his furor* he thought.

d'Aulnay proclaimed loudly "Remy, have the *Vierge* prepared for battle. I want the stores to be filled aboard for a possible siege. Also, talk to Burdett and see if we can get some understanding of defenses in Saint John. If you need any extra labor, get the savages to help." He finished his orders with a simple gesture and "that is all for now." Remy bowed respectfully and left the destroyed lodge as d'Aulnay continued his curses at LaTour.

Remy was a firm leader in the garrison by giving orders to his subordinates and leaving the minute details for them to solve. He also expected his orders followed as efficiently as possible, but today he would manage many of the details to expedite the departure. The men were grousing about the sudden midwinter sailing; with the cold, ice, snow, and frozen gear all serving to increase the complaints, until Remy having experienced enough foul nature for one day exploded with desperation... promising a blade run through the next complainant. The outburst stunned the men to silence.

Because the *Vierge* was moored until spring, it looked un-kept with odd lines hanging and seagull guano everywhere. Remy gave work orders and directions until he was satisfied the ship would be readied in the shortest time. He passed the command of the ship to his sergeant, allowing himself the shore bound duties of expropriating the required food and the water stores. It would not be as fast a deployment as a prepared ship could, but as he left the pinnace it was already appearing in order. As he was rowed ashore he could hear orders shouted, and answered by men in the rigging. The smoke was curling from the aft master's cabin and galley stoves. Yes, he thought, the Vierge was going to be battle ready.

The *Vierge* made way for Port Saint John two days later. d'Aulnay stood on the aft deck with his legs apart, knees slightly bent, his face a grimace keeping everyone scurrying around mostly avoiding him. d'Aulnay would demand the fort when he got there.

As they approached the harbour they could see the fort in the distance. He was mentally preparing his speech to the meager garrison, capitulating forfeiture of Port Saint John. LaTour would return to complete destruction providing he managed to return if not thrown in prison. His arms gestured and facial expressions were in orchestration with his mental speech resulting in a bizarre spectacle for the crew. Remy bristled with raised eyebrow if a crew looked too long at d'Aulnay's wild gesturing. He wanted the crew to focus on the attack and seizure of the fort, anything else was a distraction. He could now make out the LaTour banner flying beside the Fleur-de-lis knowing the hostilities were upon them. The crew had a nervous silence with many looking towards the fort making individual assessment of fortifications.

d'Aulnay looked at Remy breaking his silence and said "What did Burdett say of the fortifications?" Remy stood full height unfolding his arms and adjusting his sword sash reported; "He babbled about LaTour having reinforced cannon placements and enhanced parapets and the palisade wall were reinforced with rammed earth. He apparently left his Lady in charge of the fort. If Burdett had stayed a day or two longer and sketched out the fort plan with gun placement along with a thorough head count, we may have been a little better prepared."

d'Aulnay replied anxiously "LaTour should have left someone in charge capable of command. He most likely planned on being back here before I would come in the spring." He was smiling now and said contemptuously, "It was a fatal mistake on his part, for they have no choice but surrender or die. Load and run the cannons out Remy, and have the entire compliment of Musket loaded and trained on the fort. Give order that Lady LaTour is not to be harmed in any manner for I have need of her knowledge."

With orders given and the pinnace within distance, the anchor splashed on its way to the muddy bottom. There was an eerie silence as the only sign of life were small fires around the inside perimeter of the fort and the odd movement on the manned parapets. The ship murmured with comments about the forts state of readiness. The artillery guns were all trained on the ship as they had been adjusted to track the *Vierge's* progress to the fort. d'Aulnay realized he had the incoming tide swinging the pinnace broadside allowing use of all portside cannon. The advantage also provided an easy target. The flow would change in a few hours allowing a quick departure if needed, he looked at Remy and said "give the men some time to prepare with a little cognac and food. We will send a shore party with the King's order to surrender the fort. Choose a few good men for the task, and I will get the documents."

15 Pistole

Port Saint John,

March, 1642

The *Vierge's* long boat came ashore in front of the gate. After securing the longboat they walked up to the gate and shouting loudly asked for the gate to be opened in the name of King Louis for official business. After a long silence a rasping thump indicated the crossbar was being lowered from the fort palisades main gate. The men were surprised by the sight of ten kneeling musketeers all aimed at the invaders as the gate swung partially open. Francois had approached them using the palisade wall and gate as cover from the ship while staying clear of the musketeer's line of fire. She stood with a one hand on her hip and brandished a sword in her other. When she had stopped, she gently stood the sword on its tip beside her foot. "What is your business?" she said firmly.

The men had grown nervous at the obvious lack of intimidation they expected from the fort. The leader of the five men summoned a brave voice and loudly announced she would release Fort Saint John to France at once under the care and discretion of Charles de Menou d'Aulnay de Charnisay, Governor of Acadia.

Francois was unmoved and said sarcastically "You have *my permission* to enter." The men advanced through the gate watching as the gates were swung closed and the crossbar replaced. "You will show respect in this fort. I will not tolerate any further disrespect such as you have shown" said an irate Francois pointing her rapier at the leader. "Sergeant!" She commanded, "Remove their weapons at once and bring me those papers!

After reading the papers, she looked up at the five men to inspect their individual demeanor, saying to the meekest one "You will return to d'Aulnay with my response." Turning to the others she said "I hereby place you under arrest, Sergeant; get these blockheads out of my sight."

Stepping to the young terrified messenger, she laid the sword on his shoulder with gentle pressure against his neck said "Tell that devil d'Aulnay that he has one hour to leave or we will commence attack on your ship. The disrespectful manners of your crewmates have cost them their freedom and I have not decided their fate. We do not acknowledge d'Aulnay's authority here and the time will commence countdown once you are aboard."

She hollered "Louie!" And as magic he was at her side. "Take him to the ship, and be careful... please" she asked quietly. Turning away she commanded her musketeers to the parapets. While the gate was opened she said "if any harm comes to Louie, open fire on that ship with everything we have and don't stop until they are sunk." As she strolled in small circles in the center of the fort, she was swinging the sword in a loose circle keeping time, humming *Sur la Pont D'Avignon*.

The designated watch from the parapet soon shouted out "Louie is returning." Francois ordered the women and animals to safety. The infirmary to prepare for wounded and the lone Jesuit to lead in prayer, and lastly the fires were stoked for canon torches or cauterizing wounds. Francois was indeed in her element with command, seeing to details had left her with a feeling of apprehension; they were running out of time and there was nothing left to do but wait.

She climbed the ladder to the parapet as the closest man turned to her smiling and said jubilantly "By Grace of God, they are making preparation to raise anchor!" She looked out between two of the sharpened palisade ends, and seeing the anchor chain moving upward, ordered everyone to hold their guard until d'Aulnay was out of range. "STEADY, keep your canons trained on him and musketeers choose a target. Shoot the windlass men first to stop their departure if they fire on us."

 The joyful nature immediately was replaced by a demeanor of purposeful resolve worthy of any garrison. Her excellent eyesight served her well as she looked across the water to the aft deck. An immobile d'Aulnay was standing rigid with both hands grasping the railing. *He is facing a concentrated, withering fire and he knows he does not have an advantage or any chance of surviving,* she thought.

At twenty minutes past her given deadline, d'Aulnay was abreast Partridge Island on a Southern course for Port Royale. Francois turned away from the sea view and for the first time accepted that she had forced a retreat. She felt suddenly weak and winded realizing she had held her breath too long. Her hands started to tingle and shake so she began flexing her fingers. As she drew a deep lung full of air, the men were shouting cheers and clapping each other on the back in elation. By the time her feet had hit the main stone walkway, the women had joined in and even the young Jesuit was beaming at God's salvation from certain doom.

She felt like a shout for joy, but Francois knew it was a small victory against a determined d'Aulnay. There had been no denying the King had sealed and notarized the document. She was certain d'Aulnay would return in strength, the only hope she and the others had was LaTour`s success with the King and returning with both restored honor and his holdings. It was not the time for celebration yet she thought, *not yet.*

Louie had been watching her from a parapet. He had chosen his position carefully to cover her defensively. His arrows were standing on their points in a crack between planks as if at attention awaiting his bow. He gathered the arrows into his quiver and sat legs dangling over the edge of the walkway amazed at

Francie's stalwart composure. When she walked

slowly to the stone walkway she appeared in

thought, and began scanning the parapets anxiously.

She turned suddenly and her searching eyes first

found Louie, then the gate and back to him. Louie

was gently nodding his head, lips pursed tightly with

a look of approval on his face. She raised her hand as

if to give a small wave, but slowly dropped her hand

while acknowledging him with a faint smile and

gentle nod. She quickly lowered her eyes, turned and

hesitantly began walking towards the lodge.

16 Pistole

Le Havre, France

February, 1642

The small northern port was a necessary port of call for LaTour. The Northern port facing England was once a bustling seaport that had been newly built to replace the nearby silted in harbours of Harflour and Honfleur. Le Havre had once been a popular site for launching many expeditions because of its close proximity to Paris. The religious uprising fifty years earlier and resulting siege of La Rochelle by the Crown meant occupation was required and the now secure south western seaport had grown more popular to keep order. The port of La Rochelle was the home port for The Company of One Hundred Associates and all fur pelts traded through them alone.

For LaTour, the ability to slip undetected into France to trade his pelts, win political influences quickly while restocking his fort were his primary objectives. Secondary objective was to allow rapid departure. He could not repair d'Aulnay's deceptions if he was in prison or his ship seized. He had been fortunate to have earned several well placed allies in the Royal Council. Over the past few years they had built a network of messengers and discrete traders to allow LaTour access to his supporters, replenishments or financiers. Lines of credit had been established, and money was being made, so many could and would look away from scandal.

He knew someone would contact him once his feet hit the wharf boards. The contact was unknown to LaTour, but the proper pass grip, or hand shake, would identify him instantly. A pass was an excellent form of communication in that a friend could be found in the dark or noon day sun without detection. True to form, as he stood in the brisk winter air looking at his ship *L'Amitye de la Rochelle* at anchor, a man approached him and said "I see you are a travelling man. May I welcome you to Le Havre?" He had put his hand out, so LaTour removed his gauntlet and folded it over his left arm while taking the man's hand. They stood for a silent moment looking at each other their hands slowly shook with visibly undetectable pressures applied and answered. "I wondered if you would ever come here" said the beaming the man suddenly.

LaTour broke to a faint smile and said "I trust my ship is safe here?" The man replied "Charles, my name is Jean, Jean Bouyer" giving a slight bow. "I am at your service, and yes you are safe in this harbour. Just last week an unidentified stranger, having the proper pass grip, told me you may come here this winter. He told me to tell you that you are not to go to Paris, you will stay here and send for him, that he may apprise you properly." Turning towards a long stone building that appeared to be the main warehouse Jean whistled.

LaTour could see a man leaning against the door frame set into the thick stone wall. When Jean had whistled he began walking towards them. He had turned slightly and left the large wooden cudgel he had been holding behind his back in the doorway. LaTour felt reassured his trip was going well when a remote outpost was so obviously prepared for trouble. Jean said to the man "Etienne, take the two horses and ride nonstop for Les Andelys." Reaching into his tunic, Jean pulled a wax sealed envelope. He held it to Etienne and said "Give this letter to the Capuchin priest pointing to the front of the envelope. He will be at the only Cathedral in town" and added with emphasis "ONLY this monk." Etienne merely nodded and trotted off.

"Can I trust him?" queried LaTour. "We must" replied Jean with a good natured laugh, "he is my brother. I will leave now to secure lodgings for you and your crew in Honfleur" said Jean pointing to the south across the bay. "If you will sail across the bay and move with the high tide you will have the old wharf to yourself. Hopefully your associate will return with Etienne, regardless sir, I will meet you there on the tide" said Jean with finality as he turned and left.

"Thank you" said LaTour, but Jean never turned as he waved over his shoulder.

By the time the tide had reached high slack next day they were berthed at the wharf in Honfleur. True to his word, Jean was sitting on a dockside bollard waiting for LaTour. Bouyer had done a fine job of acquiring use of a warehouse with stables on the back. After a long voyage in the cold winter Atlantic, they were happy to have the warm soft hay in the stables and fireplace in the warehouse office for hot meals and a fresh well nearby. LaTour was aboard ship for his final inspection on the third day as the sun set over the ocean. He was apprehensive at the warning he had received upon arrival and was trying to stay as busy as possible. In the stillness of the growing twilight, a long boat was spotted in the distance and reported down from the watch in the crow's-nest. It was making good time on the calm water from Le Havre and LaTour felt it had to be Jean returning with his associate.

It was dark as the boat tied off allowing a solitary passenger to climb up to the wharf as LaTour hollered down to the panting oarsmen in invitation for a hot meal. As the man approached LaTour he held out his hand and said "Charles I presume? I am your Northern associate." They shook hands, and with LaTour receiving a proper grip, nodded his acknowledgment. I am glad we were able to warn you of Paris. It was assumed you would avoid La Rochelle if you had learned of d'Aulnay's treachery with the King, and use the alternate port as planned. We must talk at once if there is a discrete place."

By the time LaTour had been apprised by his associate, he had a sinking feeling of his grave situation in France. The King had been misled by d'Aulnay enough to have been labeled as traitorous and rebellious. He was to be detained and brought before the Royal Court to answer charges. It was a close call. Had he landed in La Rochelle, he would have been taken under arrest and unable to restore his name. Emmanuel Le Borgne was but one name in the council but he had financed all of d'Aulnay's requests. To ensure a return of his investment he had lobbied hard for d'Aulnay to be sole Governor. LaTour now realized he had fortunately taken the only avenue left for escape. He had beaten d'Aulnay for the pistole shares, and he had no doubt that the battle was only just beginning. Had he not left until spring, he would have been hopelessly under siege in Saint John with the Kings blessings. He would make arrangements for the pelts to be taken to La Rochelle and trade with the Company of One Hundred Associate's office. He would have to trust his allies to soften the King. His new problems in France would make trade impossible, so he would have to rely on his allies in New England. He was anxious to retrieve the last of the pistole from their San Sebastian metalworker before d'Aulnay could sail; the extra income would be needed more than ever for trade in Boston. The King would have time to reflect and hopefully cool off while LaTour would prove d'Aulnay wrong. It was enough of a plan to allow sleep that night.

17 Pistole

San Sebastian, Spain

February, 1642

The departure from Honfleur in France had been a
hasty matter. The men were able to unload the cargo
of beaver pelts and moose hides into the secure
warehouse in record time. Jean Bouyer would
oversee the cargo's safety and shipment to La
Rochelle. LaTour had been monitoring the tides and
winds carefully and when the last of the cargo had
been unloaded he ordered the ship ready to make
way. The men obliged without complaint, knowing

the risks of capture by staying in France increased by the hour.

Favorable winds from the North pushed the *L'Amitye de la Rochelle* hard enough to surf on the rollers as they sailed for Spain. France was a distant, brooding, grey line on the port side and the apparent wind was almost nil on deck. The only sounds aboard the ship were creaks and groans, and rushing water from the ship as the somber men realized the implications of LaTour's inability to meet with the King. They were all fugitives now, with all the uncertainties of being in flight from arrest. They were still watching the distant land on the port bow as they neared Spain. As the crows-nest was relaying information to the helm, the ship was soon quartering towards land.

L'Amitye de la Rochelle was flying a red flag with three LaTour crests as they entered the calm harbour of San Sebastian. The same strong winds from the North that carried them swiftly south, diminished in the leeside of Mount Urgull. Warmth enveloped the pinnace along with land smells from shore bringing smiles from the crew as they looked up at the massive statue of Jesus on the mountain top. Relief was palpable as the tension of sailing the coast of France had past. For LaTour, there was never a chance for relaxation until they were back in Acadia. He ordered watch set and offered liberty to the crew before he went ashore.

LaTour went directly to the Basilica of Santa María del Coro. The old stone church was both weathered and empty. His boots thumped on the aisle with small echoes as he walked reverently to the altar. He had carried his hat in his left hand and once kneeling removed the plume. He had been instructed by his associates in France to this clandestine display, but felt foolish with his hat in one hand and plume in another.

The old stone church was silent as he prayed. He had been kneeling so long that as he opened his eyes realized he was swaying. He was tired and anxious, but mostly uncertain if he had made a mistake in proving himself to this messenger. He mentally began counting time and allowed two more minutes and he would leave. He felt drained when he arrived at his decision to leave. Something was wrong. He wobbled upright and as he began to insert his plume back in his hat a small lattice door opened in the nave. He was frozen in place as a hooded monk approached him slowly and softly said "you are a patient man."

The monk beckoned him to the nave and opened the lattice door to reveal stairs to the bell towers. As they walked into the bell tower LaTour could see the *L'Amitye de la Rochelle* at anchor among the many ships in the harbour. The monk lowered his hood calmly and said "I was certain you must be LaTour by the flag on your ship with three crests. The hat and plume trickery was just a chance to be certain of your identity and occupy your hands." The monk removed a small dagger from his robe sleeve and set it down while holding LaTour's incredulous stare.

"You appear shocked at a priest with a dagger, yet your partner d'Aulnay was here and was most violent! Do you know of his treachery in San Sebastian" he asked while pointing at the wharf. "I watched from here and could not prevent him, or at least I think it was him, from murdering the lighthouse operator named Hernando Galeana." LaTour's face was twisted in rage as he remembered the Spanish name on the telescope box in Port Royale.

"I regret not stepping forward, but it was dark and I could not be absolutely swear it was d'Aulnay" lamented the monk before lapsing into silence. "He was also extremely brutal with Cellini at his shop" he added while turning and pointing down Agosto Street. "Your partnership with d'Aulnay is like dealing with the devil" sighed the priest.

"Thank you for your honesty and observations" said LaTour sadly.

LaTour was feeling sick with anguish. It was a long silence before LaTour finally spoke saying "I wish I had never entered business with him. For what it is worth to you Father, it is over between us. My arrival here is but part of my revenge for his deception.

Worse, I fear I may have become all that I despise in him" added LaTour solemnly.

"It would seem that you have been able to monitor his every move here in San Sebastian from this tower" stated LaTour while looking down the long Agosto Street. The priest watched LaTour's face as he confirmed his clandestine observations and then proceeded to give directions to Cellini's shop.

Later, as LaTour walked into Cellini's small metalworking shop, a man at a workbench stood. Cellini looked the man up and down and walked over. LaTour smiled and said politely "I am at your mercy Sir, as we have not met formally. You have performed some incredible *engraving* for my partner and me." Cellini faced LaTour and stared at him impassively. A small pink scar on his cheek was evident in the dim shop. Before Cellini could speak

LaTour said "I hope you speak French, I am afraid I never learned Spanish well enough to be fluent" as he offered his hand. Cellini was becoming uncertain of his instant distaste for all things involving d'Aulnay. He sensed the difference in both manners and demeanor between the partners. He put his hand out slowly and accepted LaTour's handshake.

Cellini remained quiet, allowing LaTour to reveal the purpose for his visit. LaTour's sincerity was evident as he divulged his betrayal and d'Aulnay's brazen lies against his honour in France. Only when LaTour was finished his rendition of events did Cellini speak.

He cleared his throat and said "I am sure you realize my initial hostility towards you was in consequence of dealing with d'Aulnay. It is said that a good business partnership is formed from opposites in personal opinion… it is clear you two are unusually opposite."

"I thank you Giovanni, it is unfortunate that we cannot continue to do business" said LaTour ruefully. Cellini gave a faint smile as he stood and said "I will have all your completed work ready to ship in an hour… please return and we will complete our business."

True to his word, Cellini had sealed a small wine keg containing the coins as promised and was waiting at the door for LaTour in the allotted time. LaTour was soon on his way back to the ship along Agosto Street with his keg in a wheelbarrow supplied by Cellini. Cellini had felt compelled to help as much as possible when LaTour had given him a sizable fee for his troubles. The *L'Amitye de la Rochelle* was soon under way with all hands looking to the west in anticipation of landfall in Acadia.

LaTour retired to his cabin mentally exhausted. This had been a voyage to restore his honour with the King and collect the last of the re-minted coins. One of the two objectives met, LaTour was still reeling from all he had learned from his associates in France.

He had learned that the King's health was failing and he had given Cardinal Richelieu a great deal of autonomy in the affairs of the kingdom. The arrangement was perhaps solely responsible for all the animosities towards the Protestant LaTour. He now understood why his father had been in good standing within the Royal court, as he had become comfortable in Catholicism and could assume either allegiance as required.

LaTour was now certain of major conflict with d'Aulnay. The only chance for immediate aid would have to come from New England, as d'Aulnay would be formidable with Emmanuel Le Borgne backing him. LaTour also had learned the frigate Grand Cardinal with twenty cannons was to be assigned to d'Aulnay in Port Royale.

The only good news from France was that La Tour's agents were sending, despite the royal embargo against him, twenty-six tradesmen to his fort, including: a baker, a cook, an apothecary, an armourer, an upholsterer, a tailor, a cobbler, a salt-maker, a slate-layer, and a ship's carpenter. His trade with pelts and settling accounts with gold coin in Rochelle had bought him some measure of loyalty even if it came from balanced ledger sheets.

18 Pistole

Bay of Fundy,

April 1642

A warm sun did little to quell cold northern winds or
brighten spirits. The atmosphere on board the *Vierge*
was as cold as the early spring weather. d'Aulnay's
foul mood had persisted since his failed attempt at
claiming Fort Saint John and the weeks since had
been calamitous to the crew. d'Aulnay had brooded
for a month before he ordered crews to prepare for
sea. He had drilled the musketeers daily until he was
satisfied of their skill. His pinnace the *Vierge* was
scrubbed and provisioned. All seamen were drilled
for hours running guns to their gun ports and back

simulating the loading procedures for the small ship's cannons.

Despite the high level of proficiency shown by the crew, d'Aulnay was always complaining and berating someone to be faster or more efficient despite his ship captain's glare for undermining his command. d'Aulnay owned the *Vierge*, but his captain was usually treated as the last omnipotent word. Remy could see the obvious, and yet knew it was pointless to try and reason with the irate and now brooding d'Aulnay.

As the Vierge heeled and nosed into the brisk North wind, d'Aulnay finally turned to Remy announcing his intentions to capture LaTour and return him to France. "We will create a blockade to stop all ships and search for the traitor LaTour, and seize any aid to his rebellious wife."

"If we capture the traitor LaTour as he returns we can forego the effort of siege on his Fort" he continued on speaking quickly. "I will then break his bitch wife and execute everyone in Port Saint John!"

Remy was battle hardened and had seen the atrocities in combat even asking Devine forgiveness for his own violence, but as he looked into d'Aulnay's dilated eyes felt what could only be described as a foreboding dread for the future. His experience of the civil battles in France with countryman against countryman was one he hoped would never happen again, yet here he was preparing for battle once more.

"Post a continual watch in the crows nest for LaTour's *L'Amitye de la Rochelle,*" said d'Aulnay passing Remy a paper showing the LaTour banner.

"This will help identify it" he added, turning back to the rail.

Remy didn't salute or confirm his orders, he merely walked away. d'Aulnay wasn't paying him any attention while staring at the distant thin grey shore, to where Remy knew was Fort LaTour.

The daily rhythm of ship life with watches cycling, meals and endless drills served to bolster onboard camaraderie with everyone. The captain was happy to run the endless tacks with soundings being provided in the less known areas to build his map of the Bay of Fundy more accurately.

After a few weeks it was almost time for re-provisioning the *Vierge* when the watch cried out from the crows nest "ships! Port abeam!" All hands raced to the port rail and some ran up the ratlines for a better look. It was so far away that it was only a small square of white. The watch had been issued

the telescope marked Hernando Galeana and were

able to determine it was not the *L'Amitye de la*

Rochelle.

Undeterred, d'Aulnay ordered an intercept course

and a boarding party organized. The *Vierge* was

ready in record time as testament to their relentless

training and as the two vessels closed, d'Aulnay

learned they were the *St. Francis*, and the frigate

Grand Cardinal flying a Le Bourgne banner,

Interesting he thought. Once alongside, close enough

to communicate, d'Aulnay was informed they had

been sent as reinforcement and the *St. Francis* was

sent from France to arrest LaTour. It was determined

they would proceed to Port Royale and to re-

provision and inspect this new frigate.

For the first time in a long while, d'Aulnay smiled broadly. As the three ships later cleared the narrow gut from Bay of Fundy towards Port Royale with their full attention focused on landfall, they missed the billowing sails of the *L'Amitye de la Rochelle* to the south west heading for Fort Saint John. Never, was disaster so closely averted by an unknowing LaTour.

19 Pistole

Port Saint John,

April 1642

Tensions were high aboard *L'Amitye de la Rochelle* in the Bay of Fundy, no doubt in part because of LaTour's comments and edgy demeanor. He was expecting trouble from forces with unknown strength. Before he had left France he had learned the frigate *Grand Cardinal* was to leave Rochelle for Port Royale under the Le Borgne banner. He had expected a blockade here in Bay of Fundy, yet as he set anchor to cheering crowds at his fort in Saint John he had met no resistance.

Upon solid ground, LaTour knew something was wrong. His beloved Francie looked exhausted as she if had not slept, and unreadable. It was also evident to his first glances about the fort that all was well if not improved since he had left so abruptly. The expected passion was not evident in her approach and LaTour, with his smile fading, felt it may be better to not push too hard. She simply walked up to him and said "come... we need to talk in the lodge." As they walked away, she was still commanding orders to the affairs of the fort. LaTour knew to leave well enough alone. It seemed she had efficiently earned her command of the fort.

"What is going on Francie?" queried LaTour evenly. She was still in command mode and ordered "Sit!" firmly. Perhaps it was the look on his face or reality had started to settle, but she immediately apologized and with softened features murmured "please Charles, have a seat. There is so much to tell."

The full debriefing for the couple was strained and not without tears and anger on both sides. It took most of the day to exhaust memory with the frequent interruptions at their door with daily operational issues. The first knock had both Francie and LaTour yell "enter," but by the last light, command had been restored to LaTour.

As their fireplace danced to life and a late meal started, LaTour stated "we have to believe we are at war here in Acadia." He continued thoughtfully saying "now, news for our future... we have been granted support from our agents in France. There was a ship to sail with supplies and twenty six tradesmen. We should have what we need for the coming year at the fort, including: a baker, a cook, an apothecary, an armourer, an upholsterer, a tailor, a cobbler, a salt-maker, a slate-layer, and a ship's carpenter." Francie asked quickly "what if the blockade is in force when they arrive? What if d'Aulnay's *Grand Cardinal* is on the picket? LaTour's response was a sober "we are finished... We won't know when the *Grand Cardinal* will be here, so we must move quickly." After a period of silence, he finished his thoughts and said "you are leaving on the next tide for France. These are dangerous times here and you stand a better chance of securing a pardon for me. I would be imprisoned on landing as I explained earlier. The best reason I can think of, primarily, is the voyage will give you some respite." The meal was finished quietly and as the table was cleaned, Francie spoke gently "Mooin can take the last of the coins to the upriver cache. He found the location and is of course trustworthy." LaTour could not help notice her switch to his Native name since his absence.

The early morning was shattered by shouts of ship approaching and loud banging on LaTour's door. Francie and LaTour were in the parapet watch tower in moments. LaTour studied the masthead banner as the ship approached and while nodding he said "the banner is flying the three fleur de Lis and star of the trading Company. They are here with our supplies and new recruits!"

With two LaTour partners as commanders on the ground, work to unload supplies and settle the new tradesmen was completed in record time. LaTour spoke with the captain of the ship advising of the potential dangers that may occur with a blockade. Time he had stressed was of the essence as evidenced by their clear passage. The winter trade had been excellent and the stores were full for transport to France. LaTour was quick to add that Francine and her maids would be returning to France with him. The Captain listened to LaTour without interruption until LaTour finished.

He broke his silence with "the Company in Rochelle has always been up front and paid for my ship charters. I am most distressed that I have sailed into this mess without warning. I will return with your trade, but I cannot guarantee your wife's safety in France" The irate Captain then snapped "are we clear." LaTour nodded his assent and advised him a rapid departure could be made on the next tide change using the advantageous outflow of the mighty Saint John River. LaTour felt the weight of the world on his back.

The solemn colonists watched as the laden ship swung around her stern anchor once the bow anchor cleared bottom. Once the outgoing tide carried the bow around, the ship was soon heading for the open Bay of Fundy and beyond. For the first time in recent memory, Francine was dressed in all her finery and had allowed herself to be attended by her maids. She *felt* regal and with tears not far away, she could not bear watching the departure from *her* fort any longer. Eyes darting, she searched the fort and then the hillside rising behind the fort for a glimpse of Louie. He never appeared, and so gathering her gown went below decks to her hastily prepared cabin with eyes streaming. One of her most prized possessions was her glass and silver mirror imported from Murano. Her mother had always been conscious of fashion, fine looks and culture, giving her the mirror along with comb and brush saying "here is something you can always use to reflect how you

appear to others! Never lose yourself daughter." She

smiled at the memory, but sighed deeply as she

decided the quality mirror did not lie... The lines were

thickening, her eyes had dark circles, and was that

grey hair appearing? She most definitely had to rest

before planning her husband's Royal pardon in

France.

20Pistole

Port Royale,

May 1642

The settlement was shocked by d'Aulnay's transformation since his departure to sea three weeks earlier. His foul mood had kept everyone on edge and avoiding their commander at all cost. He was returning with smiles and jovial laughter towards all. Colonists concluded d'Aulnay was just as excited to receive mail and new supplies from France as they were. The Colony around the Port was talking of d'Aulnay's new ship the *Grand Cardinal* at moor in the Port with its impressive twenty carriage gun compliment and professional crew. It was new and represented all the very best in small modern frigates for the period.

A feeling of purpose, vigor and wellness came from the fresh early spring air coupled with the last of the melted snow. The long winter nights they had endured were fading from memory in the sun's warm rays. Green patches were forming around the buildings foundations and the gooey mud was firming to soil again. The *Grand Cardinal's* crew was treated as only royalty would. They were the first people with stories of France in months. There was a great deal of celebration in the Port with d'Aulnay's return. Music, feasting and plays into the late night had continued for several days until d'Aulnay grew restless wondering of LaTour's return.

He needed a blockade at the harbour mouth beyond the reach of LaTour's cannons in Port Saint John. It would be easy to intercept any ship in the Bay of Fundy with the *Vierge* and *St. Francis* on patrol and *Grand Cardinal* blockading the harbour approaches. d'Aulnay ordered the naval ships provisioned and remaining small trader ships loaded for his export of furs, salt, fish and wood back to France. He was feeling the financial burden growing. The Frigate could remain at sea for six months and the provisions for the *Grand Cardinal* were staggering. Le Borgne had been advancing him funds for the colony, but d'Aulnay had been building fortifications and buying arms.

He had been delivered a letter by the *Grand Cardinal* captain written by Emmanuel Le Borgne personally, suggesting d'Aulnay was indebted for a great deal and he was feeling nervous with d'Aulnay's growing requests without the expected return on investment.

d'Aulnay was desperate to get his pistole that he had counted on earning with LaTour. It infuriated him that he couldn't report the gold coin theft and LaTour's deceptions when he too shared responsibility. His largest angst however was learning previously through LaTour that Françoise was the only one who knew where the gold was cached upriver. d'Aulnay had strolled to the bluff looking over the Port while weighing his options. *LaTour the lovesick fool! How could he trust the bitch with such important matters? LaTour was ensnared in a legal partnership that had been brokered by Françoise's father, the Doctor, an arrangement to guarantee his personal investment. A Partnership with none other than a woman was ridiculous.* He realized suddenly with a start that he was angry with himself. He had thought he could have everything in the long run with help in France, but chose an easy path to take all holdings and make extra pistole by scheming with LaTour.

If she betrayed them, the loss would surely ruin LaTour and cripple d'Aulnay for a time. It all came down to the oldest of military principals... divide then conquer. He would enjoy breaking her!

d'Aulnay turned away from the vista overlooking the Port and was forming his plans on the brisk walk back to the fort. Remy had been summoned and as d'Aulnay sat at his new desk and chair a soft double tap announced Remy's arrival. The last few months had been difficult working with d'Aulnay and Remy never knew what to expect. The last week had been a time of relaxation for Remy, being suddenly called upon left him apprehensive as he stood at attention before his commander. d'Aulnay was once again all business, soon giving Remy his instructions for the next phase of his plan to place Port Saint John in siege.

"I want Father Burdett, the *man of God*, back in LaTour's fort to gather information. I need to know what is going on." He followed with "We are going to establish a blockade again, and attempt to starve them out. There must be a weakness we can exploit before LaTour returns. We will wait and see what occurs, but he may have gone to his small outpost at Cape Sable Island. If required, I may need you to sail there and determine the forts strength."

Taking out his map of Acadia, d'Aulnay pointed where patrols would cover the Bay of Fundy while the frigate would block the harbour. His battle plans drawn, d'Aulnay told Remy "LaTour is a traitor, he will face charges in France or he will die here in Acadia in defiance. It is of no consequence to me whatever happens, but Remy, we must never harm his wife. I have need for her to be kept safe." Remy nodded his affirmation of the order and stood silently. "We leave Port when you have everything attended to. You will advise me when you are provisioned." He finished by saying "that will be all for now" without looking up.

21 Pistole

Port Saint John,

May 1642

LaTour was exhausted yet first light had beckoned him from a restless slumber. Francie had given every detail of her confrontation with d'Aulnay, including the obvious deceit or espionage by the missionaries. Her rapid departure had not left them personal time, but he felt her affection growing distant. He dressed in his "rags," as Francie had called them, smiling as he found newly made wool socks in his moose hide moccasins. Apparently she did understand the comfort they provided while hunting. LaTour grabbed his bow and checked the arrows for trueness. He straightened three of the shafts using the gentle heat from the old fireplace coals and bending them in his hands. After rolling them on the table top once more, he found they all passed his standards.

He wanted time alone in the steep undulating hills that rose behind the fort to a ridgeline and purge his mind with hunting and meditation. Gardens were all planted within the fort and fresh game was needed to supplement the abundant salted fish. He missed Louie, having not spoken to him in months. Francie had dispatched him upriver to deposit the last of the pistole in the secret cache as soon as LaTour had arrived. It troubled LaTour not knowing precisely where the cache was located. He never questioned his wife, or Louie's loyalty and honour, but his whole future depended on a gold cache that he had never seen. d'Aulnay would fight for it as well. LaTour knew it was a loss d'Aulnay would not tolerate the defeat in deception or wealth. He would be ruthless with the entire LaTour Fort.

Looking from his favorite spot on the sparse ridgeline, LaTour realized the panoramic view offered an excellent position for a cannon battery. Naturally smooth granite ran northeast /southwest allowing wheeled cannon to cover the approach to the harbour facing east. He would place a small force here once he had procured armaments from Boston. He felt desperation at being so vulnerable to a large scale attack. Recent additions had secured the fort to small scale attack, but the *Grand Cardinal* changed everything with both her firepower and manpower. Trouble would come from the east very soon.

On the trek down from the ridgeline, details were forming for the forts future. There would be a gathering in the main lodge to allow input from his subordinates and ultimately delegated more responsibility. On top of myriad military details, he wanted to focus on the primary purpose of his fort... trade. Local Mi'kmaq had filled his storage with pelts during the mild winter, but Francie had departed with a majority of the furs aboard for trade in Rochelle. It would not be unusual for the contemplative to feel anxious at the depleted storage building with mounting debt, but an endless daily trade had already begun. Shortly after the ice had cleared the river and tributaries, laden canoes began appearing at the fort.

The mighty reversing falls around the first bend upriver was a raging torrent when the thirty foot low tide occurred. Saint John River then fell over underwater ledges in the narrow gap to the Bay of Fundy, with a dangerous, impassable cauldron of roiled water. When the Bay of Fundy slowly rose above or fell to the level of the Saint John River a calm slack tide resulted, allowing easy passage. It was during these transitions that the waiting Mi'kmaq would paddle through the gap downriver to the fort. This gap he knew was also a natural deterrent to flanking maneuvers on his fort or for that matter free passage. He watched the river flow moving slower on the incoming tide and knew it would not be long before the Mi'kmaq would arrive. He wondered if Louie would arrive in the next wave.

Two days later a shout of "Sails approaching!" came from the watch tower. The fort sprang into motion securing the fort as the bell rang. As the gate bar dropped into place LaTour turned to the assembly within the fort and exclaimed as calmly as he could muster "stand down, stand down... it is the small shallop flying the black flag and white cross of the Jesuits." Relief was evident as people of Fort Saint

John slowly returned to tasks, relief to everyone but LaTour. He knew the little shallop was a tempest before the storm.

22 Pistole

Pickwauket Mountain,

May 1642

Louie had left immediately for the gold cache when approached by Françoise. He had carried the heavy canvas satchels of gold coins to the canoe along with his fish spear and bow. He travelled light because of the gold weighing down the canoe, but he knew he could fish and live well off the land. Louie had learned from his local brothers that striped bass, salmon, shad and trout were migrating upriver to spawn in the fresh clean water, leaving their winter saltwater habitat in large schools. Helping Tia'm conveniently placed him in the Kenepekachiachk (little long bay) at the best time for netting. The Kenepekachiachk ended abruptly by transitioning into marshland. The large river feeding the brackish bay was split by the marsh further inland, leaving deep narrow channels on either side of the tributary. He would be filling his canoe with as many fish possible for a safe return trip.

It took two days to arrive at the brook leading to the mountain and another day to proceed upstream to the cache. He rolled a boulder back from the small entrance revealing a natural cave that had once served as an animal den until discovered by Louie as safe repository for the gold. It was a cigar shaped den measuring thirty feet long and ten feet wide. With a slight uphill grade, the cave formed in consequence of a fissure opening in the natural granite. Thousands of years had effectively sealed the back of the fissure leaving a reasonably dry cave. It was barely standing headroom midway through the cave. Louie knelt, waiting a few moments to let his eyes adjust to the darkness, after wriggling through the tight entrance. The only light was from the south facing entrance allowing sun light into the depths of the cave.

They had made "shelves" from the flat rock strewn about the rock face outside the cave. The shelves where piled high with small canvas sacks seemingly unaffected by effects of the past winter. His local Native brothers did not understand the European desire for the useless soft metal. Iron was much better; it had strength for spears, arrowheads, knives and tools. They had claimed the area was full of gold... it was in the stream leading to the mountain they had said while bringing that first large deposit. Louie had kept that fact from the Frenchmen. He had seen firsthand how gold could lead good moral men astray. He would just keep that information to himself.

Having arrived at the last thin beach before the inland bay on his return, Louie threw his fishnet from the canoe into the incoming tidal current and paddled ashore. He pulled the ropes into the shore and was rewarded with several salmon in the mesh. He soon had a fire using dry driftwood to cook his salmon along with freshly foraged fiddlehead ferns, arrowroot, and cattail roots steaming in seaweed. He would smoke the remainder of his fish dry for transport during his evening fire. His day almost over, Louie molded a dished out area in the sandy bank matching his body and then laid his heavy wool blankets into his "custom recline furniture" to tend his fire. While a pair of loons called, he reflected; *This! This is real wealth! What a man needs. I have all I could ever want here, now, in this place. Why is there so much desire for coins?* With eyes growing heavy from his day's labours, he could only see Francie smiling and laughing while sharing his yellow birch tea as his eyelids closed.

23 Pistole

Port Saint John,

June 1642

Whatever Father Burdett had thought would occur upon arriving inside fort LaTour, seeing LaTour was not one of those options. Remy had told the old fellow to draw maps of the fort and more importantly he was to learn the whereabouts of LaTour. As he walked through the main gate he was shocked to see LaTour in command. LaTour immediately approached the missionary and commanded "Come with me."

"I must attend to my young priest here first, and I will meet with you after I have settled" replied Burdett firmly. LaTour was in no mood for insubordination or contrary arbitrations with the old spy. LaTour stepped closer and raising his voice slightly said "I will see you now! Follow me"

Once inside the Lodge, Father Burdett was feeling nauseous and starting to shake as LaTour turned to face him. "You are now in *my* fort. You report to *me*. You do not have *my* permission for full access to this settlement. *You* are here only for God's work and administer to matters of spirituality."

Father Burdett's mouth opened as if to speak, but was dismissed with a wave of LaTour's hand. "I know you are not to be trusted and serve d'Aulnay with intelligence" he continued. "You talk of God and your visions of his will... but I assure you I have a vision of your demise if you attempt to betray me again. Do your work for God and remember... you only have complete freedom within your altar."

After a moment to collect his thoughts, Father Burdett asked benignly "am I your prisoner?"

"Prisoner? No, you have merely been relieved of all your duties other than salvation of souls. That should be enough for a man of God would it not?" queried LaTour with a smirk. LaTour paused a moment and finished with "you will leave this post only with *my permission* when it suits *both of us.*"

Father Burdett having witnessed Governor d'Aulnay's unadulterated rage felt relief at not having to endure a similar spectacle, so bowing slightly, turned and left. LaTour strode to the door eyeing his bow and arrows longingly filling him with memories of a much simpler time.

24 Pistole

Boston,

Autumn 1642

Nicholas Gargot was proud to have been in a position of the trust with LaTour allowing this mission. He had fourteen good men in the cramped open shallop. Before leaving Fort LaTour, Gargot had asked to paint the name *Providence* on her, and LaTour had been enthusiastic enough to paint the name himself. Once in the Bay of Fundy they were able to ride a strong Northerner all the way to Boston allowing *Providence* to surf down larger swells beyond hull speed. The trip did not take long making the cramped open confines seem bearable. They were charged with lobbying help from possible allies to supply military aid to the Port of Saint John. Gargot had met many of LaTour's contacts while on the last trade mission and was looking forward to the sights and smells of Boston. He had worked all summer building defensive additions to Fort LaTour and the effort had made everyone feel secure from attack. LaTour reasoned he should command the fort and await the outcome of efforts Francie was making in France for his pardon.

Gargot secured the small ship and went ashore only to discover that Richard Bellingham was no longer the Governor, having recently lost elections to John Winthrop. Gargot quickly determined that he needed to speak with Bellingham and learn of any allegiances. Gargot knew John Winthrop was one official not sympathetic to LaTour's aid. As he prepared for the trek to Bellingham's estate, a carriage stopped on the docks. There was a driver and a large man that obviously was a guard for the carriage occupant. A polished door was opened and Richard Bellingham sprang out, standing in the late morning sun looking in the Frenchmen's direction. Gargot knew Bellingham was looking for LaTour, and waved his hat once with flourish to draw attention. Gargot extended his hand as he walked up to Bellingham and bowing slightly shook his hand.

LaTour had been careful to demonstrate exact hand placement with a series of pressures from his hand in the grip exchange to show a pass. Bellingham searched Gargot's face impassively and then returned the pass grip to show acknowledgement. Gargot's relief was evident as he smiled saying "I am here seeking aid. Mr. Bellingham, can you help Port Saint John?"

Bellingham sighed while pointing at the open door to his carriage saying "come, we will talk and see what can be done." During the ride to Bellingham's estate Gargot learned of the politics behind Winthrop's return as Governor, much to Bellingham's frustration.

"The Religious animosities here are similar to the problems of Protestant and Catholic for the French" said Bellingham evenly. Throwing his hands in the air he added "There will be *some measure* of aid here in Boston, but I will direct you first to Robert Compton. He is a good man, and his estate sits far enough away to allow a more indirect and larger trade for you... Compton will make it happen, he is a good ally for us both" finished Bellingham.

Gargot was given a hand drawn map of the coastline with instructions how to find Compton to the south in Plymouth. He had set sail immediately upon setting foot aboard *Providence* and was soon looking for the telltale landmarks and estate at the edge of a seaside cliff overlooking the Atlantic.

Gargot and his men were met at the cliff edge once they had trekked up the long traversing pathway from the shoreline. It was a natural crevasse that had been reworked as needed by stone masons to create the pathway leading to Compton's estate. Gargot had found himself nervously bumping into the stone wall several times as a natural reaction to avoiding the steep drop on the outside of the pathway. Gargot kept one eye on the edge and one on Compton as he advanced toward the last incline.

Compton held up his hand suddenly shouting "Halt and state your business!" Gargot shouted back "we are here seeking aid in the name of Charles de Saint-

Étienne de la Tour with direction from Governor
Bellingham in Boston."

Compton replied "you there, advance and be
recognized, but your men remain where they are.
You are all in grave danger if you do not comply. Do
you understand?"

Gargot realized that Compton was still holding his
hand up, and for the first time realized that he had
walked steadily uphill into a natural trap. Raising his
eyes slowly he saw armed men looking straight down
at them from edge of the cliff. Many were holding
large rocks ready to launch a barrage. Gargot
immediately placed both hands in the air as a show
of surrender and ordered his men to stay. He walked
slowly with purpose up the last incline to Compton
and after a slight bow extended his hand. As with
Bellingham, Compton confirmed the proper pass grip,

his demeanor changing immediately. He lowered his hand at once and the armed men at cliff-side turned away from their defensive position.

Compton was now smiling and said affably "I saw your banner with LaTour's crest on the masthead, but I had to be certain. There have been marauders from the south seas that have begun to terrorize and loot the colonies...we live in dangerous times."

Gargot turned and waved his men to join him and turning back to Compton saying "you have created a formidable fortress here. I never realized the potential for attack until it was too late. May we speak in private that I may give you an update on Governor LaTour's situation?

Compton turned and began striding towards the massive house saying "Norma will love the company and I am sure you could use a real meal!"Any trepidation the Frenchmen had felt soon dissolved as Norma Compton had her staff prepare and graciously serve a full three course meal in a civilized and very proper manner in the main dining room.

As daylight receded, Gargot and Compton retired to his study and formed a list of all required supplies LaTour had specified. Compton began writing at his ornate desk. In the ensuing silence of the study, only steady ticking could be heard from a mantel clock. Compton had written two pages and sealed them with wax using his ornate ring to place his crest.

He exhaled long and with a low moan rose from his desk to stretch saying; "Gargot, you may stay here as my guest for a few days until this letter can be sent to Boston at first light. I have a fine lawyer there who will assist us with this list. I have a merchant shipping headquarters there as well. You can resupply and I am sending this letter of reference with you. It will unlock several doors for you there in Boston."

The evening closed with everyone enjoying mugs of steaming hot chocolate. Having not tasted it before, Gargot learned that Compton was shipping chocolate to Europe for the privileged and royalty. Chocolate was a new export from South America with Compton as sole provider to a new demand.

 Three days later, true to Compton's word, Boston was indeed prepared with a list of supporters lead by John Paris. Paris was first on the list with funds and influence. When *the Providence* arrived, the first man on the dock to greet them was John Paris demonstrating support.

The dry wit on John Paris' part was not lost when he had said to Gargot "if you cannot receive proper aid from your countrymen in Paris, then another "Paris" will come to your rescue!" Gargot learned quickly that rescue was not free after reading John Paris' terms.

Before leaving Boston, Gargot learned news from an arriving French trader ship that Cardinal Richelieu was not expected to survive the winter and was essentially on his death bed. The most troubling news was that King Louis XIII had also fallen gravely ill. It was devastating news for Gargot... *how could LaTour be exonerated if the King and his first minister died before a pardon could be given?*

25 Pistole

Rochelle, France

Summer 1642

Françoise-Marie Jacqueline was rested and ready to challenge anybody including Louis XIII to battle for her partner's honour. It had seemed daunting at the beginning of her Atlantic crossing, but the unfairness of d'Aulnay using the church and religious leaders to sway the king had hardened her resolve. She had landed in Rochelle in the warm summer, vigorous with energy and an itemized list in hand. Her hands had smoothed and dark circles under her eyes were erased, her face a warm glow.

Upon setting her feet on the dock the gnarly man called Tourneau, the New France Trading Company Agent, spied her and approached quickly.

"Madame LaTour! You look radiant. How are you this fine day" he queried with his round face smiling. "I am surprised to see you here in France" he leaned forward and continued, with lowered voice at barely a whisper said "tell me Charles is not on that ship."

She did not answer for a moment, without losing eye contact said evenly in a voice loud enough for anyone in earshot "I am here on business for my husband who could not make the voyage. Are you ready for our cargo?"

Tourneau nodded imperceptibly with a twinkle in his eye saying loudly "we will unload you shortly, we are happy to assist you in the absence of your husband.

Come to my office that we might complete your paperwork."

When settled in the cramped office between orderly stacks of papers piled between curios and trinkets from traders he began; "I gathered you understood the gravity of LaTour's situation here in France. Le Borgne is said to be watching the docks. It would be his advantage if your husband were rounded up by the king's garrison here in Rochelle. I am certain eyes and ears all about the dockside are looking for a reward."

Françoise was fairly certain Tourneau was first and foremost an honest man beneath the gnarly veil that commanded dockside trading. She was also certain he was ensuring trade for his company by remaining loyal to the LaTour banner. 'Business' she had learned was always just that... business.

"Thank you for your care and concerns Monsieur Tourneau" she said graciously. Then sitting forward slightly spoke evenly; "Your attention to 'details' have kept us from certain ruin in Acadia and we are grateful. However, we now need your help even more. I must go to Paris immediately to seek atonement for my husband, but my biggest need is a ship and men to break the picket that d'Aulnay has established. We are certain of a major battle with him.

Tourneau nodded and with a sigh tossed his hat on a small model of the leaning Tower of Pisa that was a trader gift. Running his hands through his hair, he looked up and ruefully commented "of course that is why you are here. I should have guessed your purpose, but I am afraid you are missing the current news here in France."

As he continued with his revelations of the King's imminent death and Razilly being no better, Françoise was aware of her heart beating almost out of her breast. The room was spinning and Tourneau was now background noise.

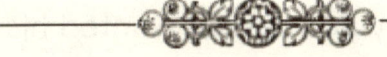

Port Royale,

Autumn 1642

d'Aulnay had already decided he wanted his hands around Father Burdett's neck for not returning intelligence of LaTour's whereabouts. It took a few months to receive news that LaTour had somehow evaded his blockade and was now securely in his fort and immediately restricted the Jesuits, his Lady was in France seeking pardon and he was still trading with France and Boston. Having no use for Burdett, he decided he would most likely have to terminate his missionary services permanently. He would have been far angrier but trade was good, he was moving thousands of pelts and hides, salt, fish iron ore and giant logs through Port Royale. His time had been divided between trade duties and occasionally joining in the blockades, but now that fall was here he decided his best effort was to keep his search active for Lady of LaTour as she returned to Port Saint John. LaTour was trapped in his fort by a ship at anchor in the harbour just beyond cannon range.

d'Aulnay had boarded the *Vierge* again when the ship had returned to Port Royale for provisions and repairs. There would be no mercy for her until he had the location of all the pistole in the secret cache. LaTour was no longer of consequence to d'Aulnay as he would eventually surrender, be captured or starve.

He knew the storage warehouse in Saint John would

be full of pelts that would pay handsomely alongside

his Port Royale trade.

27 Pistole

Port Saint John,

Summer 1642

Thick enveloping fog had settled into the port as expected during the night. Visibility was down to a few meters until the late morning sun had created enough heat to lift visibility. There had been a morning incoming tide and the fort watch in the parapets was not expecting traffic from upriver or the blockade in the Bay. Watches were told at the beginning of each shift of the treachery at hand and to be vigilant. When fishermen at the shore heard rhythmic splashes drift in and out of earshot in the fog they were certain it was a boat. A younger man ran to the palisade wall, raising his voice only loudly enough to be heard informed the watch.

Fort LaTour was instantly transformed from trade post to fort in moments after the bell rang three times. Drills were a part of life and each person knew their task. LaTour and Louie were first to the shoreline to listen and determine the threat. The challenge of sound in fog is determining direction. Louie had his eyes closed listening intently. He suddenly opened his eyes and pointed straight out saying "THERE". He was quickly nocking his arrow when a grunt was heard clearly by all from the fog. Everyone was frozen in place until LaTour calmly said "to arms." Louie was already at full overdraw on his bow, iron arrow head touching his bow hand, standing motionless as a statue. La Tour had his sword out, his first line were all bow and arrow. Wet fog could not guarantee powder would light muskets and at close quarters the bow was faster and more accurate and being lighter allowed them to attack and retreat quickly.

A large swirl of fog cleared the water in front of the shoreline showing a shallop heading past with oarsmen pulling hard against the out-flowing currents. A single figure was kneeling in the bow in front of the lone cannon, he was using a sounding line with lead weight to determine water depth and bottom content. An oarsman looked up at the suddenly visible shoreline mid stroke and shouted loudly, pointing at LaTour and company. The lone figure in the bow whirled quickly to starboard and began reeling in his sounding line to join in cheers with the others in the longboat. Gargot had returned with *the Providence*.

The men from *the Providence* had carried Gargot on their shoulders into the fort, tired as they were. Gargot had evaded the *Grand Cardinal*, in thick fog with brazen luck; delivering them to safety... he had performed the impossible. By the time *the Providence* was anchored securely in the harbour and being unloaded, fog had lifted allowing ten mile plus visibility. The *Grand Cardinal* was once again visible in the distance at anchor.

LaTour ordered a feast prepared for the weary travelers in the main lodge. He could tell Gargot was more than merely tired and carrying a mental burden. He invited him to his lodge for a debriefing. Gargot was concise beginning with Bellingham's loss to Winthrop and produced the letter Compton had provided for trade in Boston.

He told of his run up the Bay of Fundy until they were able to ease through the small notch in the coastline leading to Musquash harbour. "It could prove a useful landing site to avoid the blockade" offered Gargot. "We watched for the roaming patrols and when we could continue late in the day, we used the darkness to conceal our approach. I used the sounding line to stay just offshore and slip between the *Grand Cardinal* and shore."

After a moment he said "All good news yes, unfortunately there is bad news as well. I regret to have learned that Cardinal Richelieu is on his death bed and King Louis is gravely ill. I do not think this will help your desire to clear your name. Madame LaTour has gone to France seeking aid, but there may not be an audience! It is presumed that Cardinal Mazarin will assume Richelieu's role, and the King's son will inherit the throne. Obviously his mother, the Queen, will be Regent with Mazarin as her adviser."

LaTour had remained silent throughout the debriefing. While indeed pleased to have found aid in Boston, LaTour knew the Queen would be sympathetic to the Catholic Church. Cardinal Mazarin would give preference to d'Aulnay in consequence of LaTour being seen as a Protestant.

Of all possibilities LaTour could imagine for Francie to battle, he never contemplated a complete change of power. With events running out of control, he had to beat d'Aulnay back to Port Royale and return to France and clear this name once and for all.

Early next morning LaTour trekked up to the ridgeline behind the fort. He had Louie join him to plan a new overland route to Musquash. The small sheltered harbour was hidden from the Bay of Fundy and would allow LaTour passage avoiding the blockade. As he stood on the ridgeline surveying the fort below him he felt the weight of the world on his shoulders watching *the Grand Cardinal* slowly emerge as fog dissipated.

"Louie, Gargot used the small hidden harbour down the coast to evade d'Aulnay's patrol. He had watched the traffic and tides choosing his moment to continue on using fog as cover past the frigate. The gamble paid off because a small shallop can be rowed... he got lucky" he had continued thoughtfully.

He slowly turned away from the harbour and facing southwest pointed, saying ``we need a safe route from the fort to Musquash Harbour to bring Francie home. She could come at any time, but I am hoping she has learned of the blockade. She will certainly go to the safety of Boston if confronted and can escape. If you can make a trail, I will send Gargot back with the instructions for Francie in Boston."

There was a barely imperceptible nod from Louie. LaTour looked at Louie solemnly and offered "I am fortunate beyond words to have a friend such as you. I trust you more than anyone in the world."

Louie appeared almost sad and finally said "I have been to the waters you speak of. I will mark a trail with two cuts on the trees and use a large stack of flat rocks to mark the trail start there. The trapping is good for fine pelts so I will make use of the trip. We will await her safe return that she may send for you Tia'm. I will leave today."

LaTour, sensing Louie was holding back implored "what is troubling you? You have a heavy heart Mooin, is there anything we need to talk of?"

Louie searched LaTour's face before softly saying "Tia'm, the creator watches over us all and knows the evil and good in all mankind. You know our creation stories; we learn them to guide our lives, and be worthy. She is far more than a partner... focus on good--wealth is not only gold my friend."

He added portentously "you must remember all this in your quest for *wealth*" emphasizing the word. He finished solemnly "you *were* a man of the forest... don't get lost in your quest through this *new* forest" as his hand swept along the view of the fort below them.

28 Pistole

France,

Autumn 1642

Françoise had never suffered such incredible emotional highs and lows since her collaborating with LaTour. She had been prepared to speak with everyone including Royalty, but only managed a meeting with Grand Council. The majority of its members were Catholics kowtowing and deferring to

Cardinal Mazarin`s opinions. She had done an admirable job defending her husband, but only enough to spurn an adjournment for further debate and study.

Cardinal Richelieu was not in attendance and she had learned he was now on his death bed. They ordered her to remain in France, but graciously spared her from prison. Realizing her situation was dire, she formed a plan to learn more intelligence from the misogynistic council.

She remembered the obvious lack of security around the Council meeting chambers, using it to her advantage by later slipping back into the chambers and then into an adjoining anteroom to eavesdrop and learn more.

Listening quietly, she learned her case was pointless without senior Catholic supporters to cajole other

Council members and ease Mazarin`s anti protestant views. Her face was red with both rage and embarrassment to covertly learn their contempt towards her and LaTour. All doors for support were slammed shut and would remain closed for possibly years while Grand Council stayed proceedings. It was all designed to aid d'Aulnay and his Catholic support.

Françoise, despite her Royal sanctions left France immediately with Tourneau`s help aboard an English trading ship *the Gilly Flower*. It would take LaTour and his key supporters to plead his case in France. She had to get back to Port Saint John and advise Charles of the dire situation in France. Tourneau had quietly drawn the captain and Françoise aside before leaving to advise them of a possible blockade. The captain had merely shrugged saying "a fee to deliver is a fee to deliver…"

Tourneau, his face as tight as a closed fist had immediately faced the nonchalant captain saying "you *will* ensure the Madame makes a safe passage to Acadia. You *will* treat her with full respect. You *will* do this for your own safety and future here in Rochelle... and for *me* personally."

He stood glowering at the man until the captain smiled faintly and bowing slightly said "I am at your disposal Monsieur Tourneau, we will continue to do a prosperous business here in La Rochelle and I will guarantee the Madame's safety."

He meant every word; Tourneau was able to ruin his trading in France and after all was said, she was a paying passage. He was going to sail first to England to load a cargo destined for Boston and drop her along the way. Françoise and her entourage quietly boarded *the Gilly Flower* late that afternoon, discretely in the growing dusk, with cold air whistling about the dock scurrying the first yellow leaves in their wake.

29 Pistole

Acadia,

Autumn 1642

d'Aulnay was drained from all of his attempts to maintain Port Royale, trade, and keep his blockades in force. He was due for a break, and realized France with all its modern conveniences would be a fine respite to revitalize during the winter. His storerooms were filled to capacity with hides, furs, kegs of salt, fish and iron ore. He would settle accounts and winter at home in La Rochelle with his beautiful wife, but most importantly he had learned Françoise-Marie Jacqueline was sequestered in France. She would not be hard to find and he would gladly break her for the gold cache location before returning in the spring.

The Grand Cardinal was beginning to look jaded with barnacles growing thick from inaction over months at rest. They had recently been given fresh supplies by a shallop dispatched from d'Aulnay and the captain returned a letter asking for a return to port for caulking, paint and crew leave. d'Aulnay realized his embargo had only reached a partial victory against LaTour by making trade all but impossible as well as keeping him in Port Saint John.

He quickly decided to relieve *the grand Cardinal* for refit and then take her to France. His other ships could maintain a smaller picket and secure the harbour entrance to Saint John as best they could. He concluded he was less interested in LaTour for the time being, he wanted to get the pistole location from Françoise, then simply bombard Fort Saint John into submission or destruction.

It took only a few weeks to make ready and head down the Bay of Fundy towards the Atlantic and home. As he had cleared the gut from Port Royale to the Bay of Fundy he looked back at Port Royale once... otherwise his eyes never left the direction of Saint John in the north. Turning away from the thin line of indiscriminate land, d'Aulnay suddenly laughed and looking to the land mass on his port bow said "we have a quick stop in Cape Sable. LaTour will only have the use of that impregnable fort if it is standing. LaTour cannot be in two places at once!"

d'Aulnay knew LaTour could make an effort to relocate from Saint John if he was overrun and would have an overwhelming advantage with a superior Fort called Fort Lomeron. d'Aulnay arrived at Fort Lomeron and discovered two families maintaining the fort in LaTour's absence. They were spared, the fort was not, and as d'Aulnay sailed for France the smoke of the ruined fort rose high above Port Sable like a huge exclamation mark. *Fitting display* thought d'Aulnay smugly.

Charles LaTour was feeling the effects of his confinement by blockade. He knew what to expect from a siege as he had repelled the English and of all things his own father. It galled him that he was seen as a traitor with France and his father had tried to change his allegiance to England. He held fast and repelled their best efforts, at least this time the trade had been brisk and stores were almost full. There was plenty to eat and he was better fortified. He worried incessantly about Françoise in France and her efforts. LaTour's panic of her capture in the Bay of Fundy had Louie blazing a new trail following the ridgeline leading ten miles to the west along the coast. Musquash was a hidden harbour where he wanted Francie to anchor and await a messenger sent to the fort. His enmity with d'Aulnay was costing him great effort and great anxiety. He knew d'Aulnay wanted the gold cache as badly as he did, but LaTour had a distinct advantage in this regard and he would get the actual cache location. It always seemed that Louie was not around to guide when he did have a day or two to take the journey. Louie had been spending less time at the fort and he missed him. *He needed to regain his freedom and maybe that was Louie's thought as well* he mused.

Lieutenant Gargot had been dispatched to Boston once again using the cover of fog to row his shallop out to the Bay of Fundy past the frigate guarding the harbour. He prayed Gargot would get word to Francie about the blockade, averting her capture. Gargot was also given LaTour's letter of guarantee to secure an armed ship and as many mercenaries possible for a very short battle. It was time to turn this conflict around and give d'Aulnay a show of force by driving him back to Port Royale.

30 Pistole

Boston,

Spring 1643

It had been a voyage through hell. Françoise had been fighting obstacles at every turn in her rocky road from Port Saint John. She had arrived in the Bay of Fundy months after leaving France, her captain having seen to trade in two extra stops in England and Ireland before heading across the Atlantic. She had finally given up, resigned to stay in her cabin and deal with him once landed. It was late morning when the captain suddenly appeared with a troubled expression on his face. He informed her of a ship flying the French flag altering course to intercept them.

 They stared at each other until the captain nodded his head towards the front of the cargo hold and said "gather up everything you have in the forward section, we will have the crew stack sails and cargo to conceal you... GO, stay quiet and let me deal with this!" She could only comply and pray that *The Gillyflower* captain would actually protect her from capture.

The Gillyflower was genuinely loaded for trade in Boston with manifests showing cargo destined for merchants there. The quick thinking captain decided to remain neutral and assume a role of innocent trader. As the two ships turned into the wind sails were furled away and they slowed alongside each other. High on the raised aft decks, the two captains could speak with raised voice and the French captain immediately challenged *The Gillyflower*.

The captain stated his trade mission and when asked about his presence in the Bay of Fundy, he explained his desire to seek additional trade in Port Saint John. There was a long silence as the Frenchman considered his options and then asked if there were any passengers from France aboard the *Gillyflower.*

Françoise was actually warm for the first time on her return voyage to Acadia. The hastily stacked barrels and crates had made a small cave and with all the sails enveloping them had made a cozy den. Françoise could feel her hands shaking. She could barely hear a sound, but the ship was gently bobbing in small swells. The motion was barely perceptible but gave her something to focus on other than a raw fear of being captured by d'Aulnay. Eventually she could hear muffled voices as small beads of sweat trickled from her brow down her temple, her eyes closed. Disorientation in the congested darkness soon had her head spinning and a sense of calm had begun to envelope her. It did not seem possible; another warm layer of darkness was descending over her. She was reminded of Apollo, her Percheron gelding at her father's stable, his big warm smooth nose nuzzling her cheek. At 15.3 hands he was a formidable mount with muscles rippling and boundless energy, and now she was riding him again.

Françoise checked his lowering head with a firm response back on the reins as he happily ran full out on an emerald green field. Exuberantly they raced along as one, she responding to his instinctual raw power and his response to her urging. She was in a dark forest suddenly, branches whipped her face, faster and faster Apollo ran, her face burning from branches slapping her. She could hear someone calling her name as a large branch suddenly struck her and she was falling, spinning... Her eyes snapped open and with a scream she was awake. The captain was looking over her with grave concern on his face. She was weak, and her clothing soaked in sweat as she sat up panting for air. The Captain in a relieved voice said "I apologize for slapping you several times... you apparently fainted from the lack of air and I could not waken you." Her scream had served to awaken her maids and while they all gathered their wits in the cargo hold gloom, the captain eyed her intently advising she stay below for a while longer, but all danger was past them.

Françoise asked the obvious "where are we and where are we going?" "Why Boston of course-- we have been denied landfall in Port Saint John, so you will continue on with our voyage" said the Captain smugly.

Clear crisp air blew in the late afternoon as the outcropping called Nahant appeared in growing dusk off the starboard rail, its lone house on the rocky crag had a lantern in the window. It was almost as lonely a sight as Françoise's heart as they approached Boston.

Françoise was eager to get off the vessel she had begun to despise as a prison. In the day of travel from the Bay of Fundy she had channeled her anger into purpose again; she decided first to deal with her ridiculous passage time from France as an unfair transaction, and find passage back to Saint John somehow. The crew had deposited Françoise and her maids unceremoniously with their belongings and walked away. As the three ladies rearranged her trunks and baggage on the strange dock in an orderly fashion, word began to spread of the exiled Lady on the dock.

Richard Bellingham was not surprised to see a clearly defiant Françoise in full control standing regally with two morose maids at her side. He had been on the watch for a lady and two maids with each new ship since Gargot had arrived months ago with LaTour's letter asking assistance. They had not formally met but he was going to change that immediately.

As his carriage door opened he locked eyes with Françoise and he began walking across the dock towards her. "Governor Bellingham I assume" said Françoise politely, extending her hand. It was Richard who now showed surprise with his arched eyebrows as he bowed and took her hand formally, he had underestimated her guile.

He smiled as Françoise applied the appropriate pass grip as Charles had taught her. Bellingham inverted her hand immediately and kissed it once before saying "welcome to Boston Madame LaTour, you and I have so much to discuss. You shall be our guest as long as you require my assistance. Now come, we will get back in time for dinner... and we do not want Mrs. Bellingham waiting."

31 Pistole

Rochelle, France

Spring, 1643

Emmanuel Le Borgne looked into the dark unflinching eyes d'Aulnay was staring through. He couldn't read him and never could, or for that matter really would. Le Borgne decided it was time for an attitude adjustment and if possible knock d'Aulnay

265

down a notch. He had attempted to unsettle him by the classic stare down. It wasn't going well.

"Pierre! Come in here" said Le Borgne softly without breaking eye contact. An impossibly large man stooped through the doorway into the room. He was dwarfing a small elfish man who stepped in front of Pierre once they had stopped at the desk.

With a smirk Le Borgne said "meet my associates, Pierre and Marcel." It was d'Aulnay who finally broke his owl-like blank affect and looked at the pair beside him. Marcel smiled with yellow and brown stained teeth and pale green eyes. One hand was wrapped around the hilt of a skinny long dagger in his belt. Pierre just stood looking straight ahead balefully. As d'Aulnay began to turn his head back to Le Borgne, Marcel set his dirty scarred hand on d'Aulnay's shoulder, startling him.

Le Borgne raised one index finger from his folded hands on the desk. Marcel removed his hand after a squeeze. "You PISS ANT!" roared Le Borgne, his face now reddening. "You have tried my patience to no end. You ask for money and ask for help. You take the Associations money and mine, and you offer nothing but contemptuous attitude! I ask for you to give me a report and some return on our investment and you ignore us. You went after LaTour and asked for help again! Even with Richelieu's signature and Louis' decree you did not deliver him. With Richelieu's death, we have to reposition ourselves with Cardinal Mazarin and new Royal Council members. I am informed as of yesterday our King will not survive the month... Are you any good to us here in France? Maybe you feel you are above us all... Is that it?

Le Borgne looked at Pierre and said "I think he wants to be above us all, yes I think he does..." Pierre grabbed d'Aulnay by the lapels and pulled him to his feet. The giant slowly raised d'Aulnay off the floor, over his head, and suddenly straightened his arms. Dust shook down from the boards above the ceiling beams and d'Aulnay's wind was almost knocked completely out as he lay pinned to the ceiling. Pierre flexed his arms lowering d'Aulnay and straightened them quickly again crashing d'Aulnay with even more force into the ceiling over his head. d'Aulnay went limp.

d'Aulnay tried to focus his eyes until he realized he was looking at the floor boards in front of his face. He sat up groggily wiping drool off his chin and got shakily to his feet. After straightening his clothing and surveying his surroundings quickly, he noticed Pierre and Marcel were no longer in the room.

At length he finally asked sardonically "do you treat all your business associates in this manner?"

"Be thankful you were saved further abuse by fainting, like a little girl" said Le Borgne evenly before adding "Pierre is a pussy cat; it is Marcel that you should concern yourself with. If you fail to meet me again and give account of your actions... well let's just say you will never forget a lesson by Marcel." Charles de Menou d'Aulnay de Charnisay looked at his feet and nodded.

As Le Borgne listened to d'Aulnay he paced back and forth with his arms behind his back. When d'Aulnay was finished his verbal report he sat back in his chair and closed his eyes with a gulp and swallowed.

"You shall have our continued support" Le Borgne finally replied thoughtfully. "You shall leave as soon as *the Grand Cardinal* can be prepared. She will be leased to you until further notice and you should be able to apprehend LaTour with the extra fire power." Picking up a quill and ink he set it down in front of d'Aulnay saying "Sign here and here and here and you take one."

Le Borgne poured a small glass of wine for them and sat down at his desk before continuing. "We had LaTour's wife here in Rochelle and she managed to evade us. When she disappeared there was only one ship heading west at that time. No one saw her board *the Gillyflower* or any other ship for that matter, but I wager she made a run for Acadia despite her order to stay in France by the Grand Council."

After a sip of his wine he said softly "If she can evade me, I must extend you some latitude as well. Now, your bills are mounting Charles; I recommend you increase your trade shipments this coming year... no more excuses." He finished his glass of wine and said lightly "we will get the

Grand Council to deal with LaTour here and request another ship for his capture there."

d'Aulnay rose from his chair and downed his wine in one toss and set the glass on the table slowly, precisely, and then with one finger adjusted it to the center of the desk. His eyes never broke contact with Le Borgne as he placed his large hat with plume on his head and grabbed his walking stick. He turned abruptly and left without saying a word.

Ernest Le Borgne exhaled long through pursed lips and watched d'Aulnay brashly walk through the crowds towards the dock. *That is one little ass* he was thinking as he walked back to his desk.

32 Pistole

Boston

Spring, 1643

The *Saint-Clément* lay at anchor in the harbour. She was a stalwart vessel with fore and aft cannons for protection, making her a perfect ship for remote trade. Françoise looked at the mast head and imagined the LaTour banner flowing in the breeze. She smiled and realized this vessel would take her to

Port Saint John after all the troubles she had endured.

The captain of *the Gillyflower* had been ordered to forfeit her passage fare by the court tribunal in Boston after she had sued him with Bellingham filing the lawsuit. She had demanded damages and was awarded that as well. The exasperated captain complained he had two thousand dollars aboard his vessel and could not cover the award. Françoise had immediately agreed to settle for that amount.

She now had the ability to trade and lease a ship. Bellingham had given her a letter written by LaTour once she had settled after dinner on her first night. Gargot had personally told of his mission and hazards in the Bay of Fundy to Bellingham that he may apprise Françoise if she arrived in Boston. It was Bellingham, as a lawyer, that had been instrumental in exacting an award from the *Gillyflower* by influencing and lobbying in her behalf. The money was being spent in Boston ultimately so it wasn't a hard sell to the tribunal.

The *Saint-Clément* appeared ready for deployment and by standing at dockside with her hands on her hips Françoise was soon approached by the ships long boat and captain. She gave him a list and promised to be back at first light for final preparations. She learned the tide was favorable to a noon departure and she nodded acknowledgement and in all her finery climbed back into Bellingham's carriage.

First light found Françoise rooted on the dock with hands on her hips once again. She was wearing leggings under her basic work dress. Her hair was pulled back under her hat and she wore a wool cape against the cool morning air. She had borrowed a carriage horse with saddle and rode to the docks in the gathering light.

The captain was summoned by the watch and as he rubbed his eyes and looked again, he ordered the longboat ashore. True to his word he had prepared the ship to her list. She inspected the vessel once aboard and was shown her austere owners cabin. She crossed the small cabin and took the fine rapier from atop her berth. The sword was of basic construction, but well made. The humorous smirk on the captain's face slowly faded as she wielded and thrust several times before sliding it into its scabbard. She looked at the flintlock pistol and cocked the hammer back, holding the flint in one hand she pulled the trigger and eased the flint down a couple of times and shrugged. "Get me another please. This one has a weak spring and the frizzen is worn out. I expect you to procure proper equipment for me." She passed the worn flintlock pistole back by the barrel.

The captain smiled and nodded. "You are a savvy lady, and I see you do know how to handle weaponry properly" he added admiringly. He extended his hand and said "pleasure to serve under your leadership Madame. Come and inspect the rest of your lease. You won't be disappointed." Françoise smiled as she shook his hand firmly and while shaking said "Only if you call me Françoise."

As she walked on deck, she carried her trademark sword as a cane, and for the first time since Port Saint John she hummed along to Sur La Pont du Avignon.

Her hands on the raised aft deck railing she said solemnly "We leave on the noon tide tomorrow, I have business to attend before I leave. Have the longboat ready for mid-morning to collect me." Before she stepped into the longboat she passed her rapier back to the captain and said "your ship Captain."

As she marched along Market Street she thought of Charles' letter again. It was emblazoned word for word in her mind having read it until the paper folds separated. Every step to get back to the fort was fraught with danger... now she would have to evade roving patrols and wait for Charles in Musquash harbour. A runner would be sent overland to the fort ten miles up the coast.

Across the cobblestone street from the market, she saw the non-descript building with a sign proclaiming the Law offices of Percival Henderson. A small brass bell on a spring over the door tinkled twice as she opened and then closed the door behind her. The din of Market Street subdued, she could hear the old German brass clock ticking on a desk, brass orbs slowly spinning back and forth. A door opened at the back of the room and a grey haired man glided into the room. He looked at her expectantly without saying a word. She cleared her throat gently and said "Mister Henderson I presume?"

"And you are?" he asked politely. "Madame Françoise-Marie Jacqueline... oh, LaTour" she stated firmly.

"Of course you are! Welcome to Boston, and my humble practice" said Henderson cheerily. "WE" he emphasized, "have been waiting for you! Come" he said as he turned around and headed for the door at the back of the room.

She entered a room with a large plank table that filled the room with chairs around it. Richard Bellingham sat at one corner. Papers were on the end of the table and at the other corner sat a smiling stout man in finery. "Robert Compton, may I introduce Françoise-Marie Jacqueline. This is LaTour's lady that we have been expecting" said Henderson formally. Compton beamed as Françoise offered her hand in formal handshake and applied the proper grip for identification. Compton gestured at a seat and said cordially "please have a seat and we will get on with it. There are a lot of details to sort out, but we have some relief for you folks in Port Saint John. Money it seems can solve almost anything."

Later, bitterness had formed over the sweetness of aid as she walked back to the dock to retrieve the horse she had left that morning. She was indeed more than thankful for the ships lease and all their

279

aid. She was thankful for Bellingham's protection and mentoring, but it had cost her all the money she had with her, and the money she had won through her lawsuit. *They knew I had money and would also pay with the lawsuit settlement they had provided in the tribunal. It truly was bittersweet. Everyone had plans it seemed. Despite her ability and planning she was always a half step behind.*

Mounting the rested and fed horse, she thought of a steaming cup of yellow birch tea and a simpler time, a happier time. With a start she realized there were only two people who knew where a wealth of pistole laid waiting in a dark cave...

Her green wool dress wrapped around her legs as she sat astride a powerful gelding, she bolted down the road at full gallop. Her hair spilled out as her hat flew off making her smile and flick with the crop faster.

33 Pistole

Musquash Harbour

Autumn, 1643

Charles LaTour almost swam across the harbour to start his long trek to Musquash. Two Maliseet had arrived at the fort with a letter in Françoise's handwriting. She made it! She actually had made it despite all odds and was waiting only ten miles away.

LaTour quickly prepared for his excursion and packed for an extended visit to Boston. He was restless and most of all tired of being trapped for over a year. He had worried incessantly about Françoise and hated not knowing anything. Her letter was his only proof she was both fine and had received his letter.

He had planned to go to Boston when she returned and procure enough military strength to repel d'Aulnay back across the Bay of Fundy and under the rock he had slithered from. Now they would travel together. Nicholas Gargot had been given command of the fort with orders to repel any who dared a show of force and continue trade.

Louie had marked the trail well, allowing an easy hike as the limestone ridgeline simply faded into the west with intermingling beautiful vistas of the Bay of Fundy. The smooth lands edged red muddy tidal flats along the shoreline. The fairly open land with copses of trees, their leaves starting to change colour, intermittently displayed Louie's marks. He had marked on trees facing the desired direction by gouging two small slabs of bark off. They were following the coast which would make easy navigation, but Louie had provided the most expeditious route with fewest obstacles and therefore straightest.

The small group had left at first light with LaTour pushing hard. He carried his share of the load to best gauge when to take breaks. Each load was placed on an A-frame made of springy green poles. A yoke on each person allowed the load to be carried and towed easily.

As the level spruce forest began to thin in the late afternoon dusk, LaTour caught a whiff of wood smoke and stopped immediately. He motioned silence and squatted down listening intently. As they sat in silence the young Maliseet guide behind LaTour began to fidget and asked LaTour what was wrong. The similarities in Mi'kmaq and Maliseet were close enough that LaTour soon understood from the guide they were approaching the campsite Louie had established with these Maliseet locals. The Maliseet suddenly laughing, stood and started forward again. Within moments they arrived at a vista overlooking a beautiful sweeping arc of beach. LaTour dropped his yoke and travois as he stood transfixed on the ship at anchor in the harbour.

He ran past the wigwams and bewildered looking Maliseet and raced down the narrow path to the beach. He stopped when the shock of 45 degree water reached his knees. "FRANCIE!" yelled LaTour. He could see activity on deck and with hear their voices travelling across the water, it meant they had also heard him. The feeling was leaving his feet forcing him stumbling back to the beach, but his eyes never left the ship. He had promised himself he would stay composed, and he tried, but tears ran freely when he saw a figure in a green dress go over the side and join the longboat alongside the ship. Francie looked like a figure head on a ship as she leaned out over the bow of the longboat and screamed "Charles!" When she held up her arms towards him as the boat drew nearer he made every effort to keep from an actual sob and with tears flowing waded slowly back into the surf to land the longboat and his long lost bride.

As with any ship, large or small, there are no secrets. Everyone aboard the *Saint-Clément* knew of Françoise's tribulations. The four men rowing the longboat got caught up in the emotional meeting. It wasn't hard as Françoise kept laughing, giggling, shrieking and crying at the same time, her hands slapping the gunwales to will the boat faster and then reaching towards her partner.

LaTour caught the longboat two handed and with oars held straight up the men could only look down to stay composed. Francie jumped into the waist deep water beside LaTour with a shriek and they held each other for the first time in sixteen months. The uncomfortable silence was broken when LaTour said brightly "I can't feel my legs any longer in this ice water!" Laughing as they turned to wade ashore, he stepped on Francie's dress and as she lost balance they splashed down in the frigid water laughing like children. Everyone was now laughing loudly as the longboat grounded on the beach, the soaked LaTour couple on each side pushing. At the small encampment on the hillside overlooking the beach, the Maliseet stood agape at the unfolding spectacle and decided they couldn't understand white people and their strange humor.

As the six figures on the beach laughed in the growing darkness with over animation, imitating Françoise falling into the water, high on the rocky coastline a lone figure leaning against a tall black spruce straightened and walked inland. Mooin had to get back and settled into his remote hunting camp before it was completely dark.

34 Pistole

Boston

Spring, 1644

The winter had been harsh yet somehow tolerable with all the modern amenities Boston had to offer. The main landing site for colonists had been Charlestown, but it was John Winthrop and eleven others who decided to settle on the Shawmut

Peninsula. Of the three distinct mounds the largest called Trimountain had a large abundant water spring at its north side and made Boston far more suitable for growth. The Puritans, after signing the Cambridge Agreement, were prime shareholders answerable only to the English crown.

From the time the LaTours had reunited they remained inseparable. From their first night, in a wigwam in Musquash, with unrivalled passion, to their small room in Boston, they recounted their tribulations and planned. It was relief for LaTour to be free again and be without the daily burden of the fort operations and it was only now he realized how brittle he had become.

The LaTour's were popular with Boston's social elite, and dinner was the venue for gleaning accurate information on the warring Frenchmen. LaTour now understood why fifteen years after the settlement had begun to flourish, that challenges were part of Governance.

Richard Bellingham had made a successful run, only to be ousted a year later. It was all familiar to the French, the religions differed-- but it was still religious wars for domination. The LaTours had talked intimately at length about what to say or omit when interacting with Bostonians, as he could not afford to alienate his only support. Trade was a necessity here as France was so far away and far too volatile against him.

The past winter had been a time for rebuilding allies and preparing for battle with d'Aulnay. LaTour had a zest for life like a teenager. Everything was exciting. The couple would sit late into the night with planning discussions. LaTour was always asking her to apprise him where the pistole cache was hidden, and she would always reply it was secure and too complicated to explain. Françoise had been busy with her list informing him that they were finally ready.

"Francie," began LaTour delicately. "I am worried about you. I have heard you being ill almost every day lately. Will you see a doctor here and ease my fear? Please, I don't want anything to happen to you."

Francie looked at him anxiously and nodding at the chairs smiled serenely while softly saying "please sit down, we have to talk... I am with child." Charles responded after his initial silent shock by saying quietly, "I see...this changes everything does it not?" Françoise anxiously searched his deadpan serious face for clarity, but nothing betrayed a crossroad had just been reached in their relationship.

After sharing in their future and all it now held for them, Françoise noticed an immediate change in LaTour's attitude towards her in the next several days. *They* had been ready to take the battle to d'Aulnay and now a few days later the battle talk was gone from LaTour. He now began ordering her to rest and what to eat and most definitely was no longer confiding in her.

She was also aware of his continual queries for details on the pistole cache location.

When she had asserted her thoughts on the Fort in Saint John, LaTour had turned on her sharply and said "enough of this! Your place is to rest and be healthy for *your* child and prepare for that battle not d'Aulnay. Now! No more of this talk. You are staying here and I will take care of that devil incarnate myself. I will also get the pistole to finance this enterprise, and you will give me a map with details. No more of this Françoise! We are finished talking about it."

He instantly saw it in her eyes, a sort of detachment or withdrawal. She was anything but melodramatic; she never replied, cried or displayed any emotion and simply analyzed him like a stranger. Whatever had been was gone in a one ice cold heartbeat. Françoise felt her world drop out from under her, feeling alone and once again a man had made every effort to control her. She had been through hell and back since her partnership with LaTour. She had gone the distance to fight for his honour in France and been his lover and now it was all about leverage and pistole. Since maturity she was continually dealing with a misogynistic world where she was underrated. Françoise had enjoyed her partnership, even feeling she was in love, and with a child they would have been complete. However, LaTour like all the rest had seen a weakness and was attempting to capitalize on it. It was the last straw to break her back.

She had studied music and as a student of the modern *air de course* had developed through all eight volumes of monophonic music... she could ride horses, perform on stage, shoot any weapon, handle a blade and proven her leadership. She had learned to dress and act civilly, read, write and most important was her understanding of legal matters. In short, she was comfortable with solo activity and had all the skills as a leader.

It seemed legal was the skill set she would draw on now. And with the full knowledge that LaTour was always looking for his best interest first and foremost she began…"Who do you think you are talking to?" with a Royal air of a queen.

LaTour was a formidable size and was seen by most men as capable, but Françoise only saw an obstacle. As he seemed to puff up and ready to answer, she cut him off with raised finger, and continued evenly "you will talk to me as your partner and if you have forgotten our legally signed partnership I will remind you of my *equality* on these matters. I will also remind you that this is also *your* child that I have to carry. It is *my burden* for us, but it is not a burden to my mind."

LaTour had stepped back a pace, and she had stepped forward a pace and continued through clenched teeth "you will accept what I have to accept, but not for one second presume to order me like a servant or one of your charges."

LaTour's face began to harden and his eyes grew dark as looming storm clouds. His mouth was forming words when Françoise, who had stepped even closer, raised her voice saying "Now, being that we have apparently returned to formal names, Charles de Saint-Étienne de la Tour, you will provide your legal partner with an account of your actions. Your *failures*, as well as your *successes* are also mine" she finished sarcastically.

"Now *we* are finished talking about it, and do not bother to ask me again where the pistole are hidden. I know what your real intentions are, and what I actually mean to you" she said firmly. She crossed the room and jerked the door open and turned. "Get out and deal with d'Aulnay" she said as she stood at the open door. Pointing at her belly she said

laconically "I will deal with *this* problem here *on my*

own-- as usual" When he had walked through the

doorway he turned as if to say something, she closed

the door quietly and he heard her walk away.

He cursed under his breath as he walked down

Market Street angry that he had not gotten a map to

the gold cache before she had obviously shut him

out. As he imagined the coins in the cache he

realized he could get Louie to take him there. All the

pistole, instead of half, he decided would fix

everything and to hell with both her and d'Aulnay.

35 Pistole

Bay of Fundy

June, 1644

His mind was clear as he stood on the bowsprit with the dark indigo water rushing beneath his feet breaking into white froth. Looking up and over his shoulder he smiled at the long red banner with a

298

LaTour crest fluttering from the mast head. It was like a matador's red cape before the bull.

The warm summer air held myriad land smells as they surged along close to land in the Bay of Fundy. LaTour had commissioned the *Saint-Clément*, over two hundred men, and two loaded shallops with fore mounted cannons. His battle plan included the element of surprise and he had previously sent another shallop to Musquash with battle plans for Gargot in Saint John the month before. It was brazen with so many unknown variables, but surprise would have to be the key weapon. Not knowing if Gargot would get the message and prepare in Saint John for his moment to launch into battle, made him unsure of the outcome but no less compelled to attack. This was his last stand to drive d'Aulnay back and allow trade again while he returned to France and dispelled d'Aulnay's preposterous charges against him.

His enthusiasm was what led him to the bowsprit on the front of the ship looking for the fight. The *Saint-Clément* was prepared with every cannon loaded and prepared to run out the ports. Muskets were now being loaded and with cool efficiency, the mercenaries were gathered around the treadle grinder to sharpen swords, daggers and knives. The two smaller shallops were being towed on short warps from each aft corner, their masts removed and stored alongside the oars. The eight crewmen on each vessel were laying about the small open vessels resting as the coxswain steered along. Two gunners at the bow of each shallop had prepared their cannons and were now sitting on either side of their guns waiting. Small size made a harder target for enemy cannon and with good oarsmen allowed fast and maneuverable attacking. Tucked in close to the stern of the *Saint-Clément*, they would be invisible until an approaching ship got extremely close. Their small cannon would merely bounce shot off a battleship, but they could maneuver quickly into position to inflict damage to the rudder and fire grape shot onto the deck. LaTour's plan was to allow d'Aulnay's ship to see only one respectable ship and at the last possible moment launch a classic three ship pincer flanking maneuver to disable or destroy. He would destroy d'Aulnay, but wanted to mitigate the injury to his fellow Frenchmen if possible.

"Ship to the North East" shouted the watch in the crows nest. With his French accented English, LaTour ordered his men to the main deck for his rally speech and as they all gathered and grew silent looking up to the raised rear deck he began; "Brothers in arms, I thank you for helping me restore what is mine. I promise you I will fight harder than any of you in this battle. We have surprise on our side and with God's blessing we will do this without injury. Now, to keep this element of surprise, stay below decks and prepare to earn your wages." The mercenaries were all hardened men and gave their assent with little fanfare as they scurried below.

In short order the intercepting ship was bearing down on the *Saint-Clément*, and it was obviously not d'Aulnay as the ship was too small. The ship was called *St. Francis* and LaTour had learned previously in Boston it was the ship assigned to his capture from France. A year had made the patrolling crew complacent from their mundane task of stopping ships and turning them around or directed to Port Royale.

They were not expecting a fight, having never seen any resistance to their policing efforts. The captain was watching the *Saint-Clément* from the raised rear deck. His experienced eye swept the deck and rigging and then fixed on the raised rear deck to learn and anticipate orders from the captain. There was calmness aboard the ship and it seemed a small crew was operating with precision without commands. They approached head on and the captain matched the *Saint-Clément* and began lowering his sail to slow his speed and heave to alongside. All the commands were shouted back and forth as the vessel slowed, but not on the alien ship with the red banner.

The calmness bothered the captain as he realized there was no sign of fear or nervous activities as expected aboard this closing ship and it was his nervousness that kept him at the rail watching a man obviously in command, walk to the ships bell. He then rang the bell loudly five times very slowly and deliberately.

He had never heard a slow five bell communication. He had no idea what an answer should be. As his mind worked hard to process what was happening and the ship slowed to a mere crawl. His eyes widened as two shallops fanned out from behind the *Saint-Clément*. He grabbed the helm and spun the rudder over hard a port to bring the sluggish ship around while also screaming to raise the sails again.

In the moments it took to get the shocked crew to react, their chance to fire on the first shallop passed as the little vessel threw a small bow wave with each coordinated pull of the oars. With a boom, the shallop fired broadside into stern of her prey. The *Saint-Clément* lay perpendicular and could not bear cannons onto the other ship, but they could not be fired upon with cannon either. The second shallop cleared the bow on the *Saint-Clément* and was pointed straight into the rear of the patrol vessel.

They were so close the gunner gleefully laughed as he touched off his cannon and blew the rudder completely off the small ship. The shallop crew roared as one in delight as they were showered in splintered wood.

The sound of a bugle peeled softly over the side and the shallop crews returned to the rear of the *Saint-Clément* and tied to the warps again. LaTour ordered the men waiting below topside, and grabbed a large brass megaphone commanding the disabled vessel to stand down.

The vessel was disabled and could offer no fight, LaTour ordered their cannons scuttled over the side and all weaponry surrendered to him including two small swivel cannons. He personally inspected the ship and explained his situation to the captain. He also explained that harming his countrymen was not in his battle plan if it could be avoided.

The captain bowed politely and thanked LaTour for his salvation on behalf of the crew and advised with a twinkle in his eye that he was out of the fight for some time with required repairs and armaments. LaTour nodded and before long was looking for sails on the bay again. He had just learned d'Aulnay was aboard the *Grand Cardinal...*

Within the next hour, LaTour was once again on an intercept course. There was still an element of surprise, but the two small cannon shots had alerted and brought the wolves in to hunt. Two ships were coming this time from port and starboard bow. LaTour sent the mercenaries below and took station once again beside the helmsman.

The *Grand Cardinal* was a modern frigate with cannons and trained soldiers. This was not a simple armed trader doing patrol duty. The frigate was fitted with two fore and two aft mounted small cannon on swivels. Their purpose was having firepower on both ends to defend or assist in a battle. Where the patroller had a blind spot on the bow, this frigate was able to fire 360 degrees.

The other ship was approaching from starboard having been on patrol at the mouth to Port Royale`s bay. LaTour ran to bow and scanned the waters behind *Grand Cardinal*. He was praying for a miracle and as if on cue, sails were seen now seen in the distance, leaving Port Saint John in pursuit of the frigate. Gargot had got the message and battle plan! His primary orders were to prepare the *L'Amitye de la Rochelle* for battle, load the cannons and muskets and stand at the anchor windlass until the *Grand*

Cardinal pulled anchor in the harbour. The *Grand Cardinal* would lead Gargot to the battle LaTour was bringing to the Bay of Fundy.

Outsized, and out gunned with overwhelming odds, LaTour stood at the port bow with his arm around a rung in the ratlines. His mind screamed retreat; it was a logical maneuver in such situations. LaTour realized suddenly what his element of surprise would be. He ordered a white banner run to masthead and then advised the crew of his plan.

Gargot had already altered course to intercept what LaTour believed was the *Vierge*. Gargot had advantage as his few cannon were able to fire broadside at the *Vierge* which approached on a perpendicular course, trying to fall in behind the *Grand Cardinal*. Gargot had the advantage and he was seething from his entrapment for so long, it seemed all four ships were converging on the exact same spot in the Bay of Fundy.

d'Aulnay was confident of the warships ability. Having heard the two cannon reports earlier he went to action, he knew LaTour was on the *Saint Clement* because of his banner flying at the masthead. He also knew there was a distinct advantage in his favour with surrender the only option for LaTour. He was hoping LaTour would foolishly fight back and give him a reason to bear all guns on LaTour. His death would save a lot of problems for him in France and also leave little contest for the pistole cache.

He intently watched the *Saint Clement* as they closed in. As the white flag began running to the masthead, a shout rang out from the stern watch of an approaching sail. d'Aulnay spun around and saw the *L'Amitye de la Rochelle* bearing down on the *Vierge* behind them and said with a toss of his hand "we will deal with them later. We take LaTour first. The *Vierge* is on her own."

d'Aulnay was surprised to see so few men and then he saw LaTour making way to the rear deck. There were four cannon per side on the *Saint Clement,* and d'Aulnay noted the ports were all closed. The sails were only half furled and the *Saint Clement* was slowly making way. He saw the sails being fully furled and ordered the same. LaTour it seemed had no fight in him. The heavy frigate slowed to a sluggish stop almost immediately.

LaTour watched the fore gunners on the *Grand Cardinal* and when they finally left their guns to prepare for boarding at the rail as the two ships glided towards each other. LaTour launched into action.

The *Grand Cardinal* crew and d'Aulnay were caught completely by surprise. LaTour had shouted something indiscernible, brought a broadsword down on a rope at the back rail and then grabbed at the steering wheel on the helm spinning hard to starboard. What had appeared as a minimally crewed ship was replaced with musketeers bursting out of the holds and more crew to redeploy sail. As the *Saint-Clément* lurched forward, LaTour had made his ship a difficult moving target. The muskets boomed out, their mission to provide withering firepower and keep the Frigate crew pinned down.

LaTour was determined to once again mitigate injury to his countrymen, but d'Aulnay was a different matter. Two men ran up to the aft deck and dropped a small swivel cannon into a hole on the deck and struck a fuse for LaTour. The sound was deafening with muskets continually firing, their muskets reloaded and passed back to them for another shot.

Acrid gun smoke billowed as LaTour scanned the frigate for d'Aulnay, as he would only get one shot he needed it to be a good one. Ropes were hanging and wood chips flying, he spotted d'Aulnay cowering low behind the foremast just as the little falconete cannon bellowed and spit out its one pound ball. LaTour had aimed it as well as a swivel cannon could be managed and was rewarded with a direct hit on the mast above d'Aulnay's head.

It was his only chance and he had not damaged the *Grand Cardinal* other than a hole in the mast and d'Aulnay had survived unscathed.

Withering musket fire had kept the frigate crew pinned down and unable to raise sails and give chase. As they sat dead in the water the shallop crews went to work with their small two pound cannons from low on the water. They had fanned out and began firing up into the gun ports causing more damages along the sides of the frigate.

LaTour had studied the battle plans of recent history had come to the conclusion that rapid small fire, like Gustavus Adolphus had used against superior forces in the Battle of Breitenfeld, had indeed worked equally well here. He saw the musket fire was becoming less effective and the frigate crew was coming alive again. He bugled a retreat for the shallop crews while turning broadside to provide covering fire with his cannons. LaTour had not taken the *Grand Cardinal* out of action. He had only given the crew resolve for revenge. Worse, d'Aulnay was still there and mad as ever.

Gargot had fired several rounds of cannon fire at the *Vierge* and her captain, without returning a shot, beat a hasty retreat. The *Vierge* captain and crew had been witnessing the spectacle of the *Grand Cardinal's* abuse and were having none of it.

The sails were all out and tight. LaTour would have to retreat and make a stand in Saint John. With the shallop crews no longer a surprise, they had stopped long enough to raise mast and sails and make a fast sail to Saint John. For LaTour, the battle was over. The Frigate could now bring the fight back to him with two levels of cannons on each side. There was an air of quiet acceptance aboard the *Saint-Clément* as the mercenaries all slowly sat where they stood for a rest, a look of abandon on their faces. Sails began to unfurl on the *Grand Cardinal* and they knew the LaTour expedition would not survive the hour.

36 Pistole

Bay of Fundy

June, 1644

d'Aulnay almost cracked the *Grand Cardinal's* first mate with his walking stick. He screamed with spittle flying "Get these cowards moving! Raise the sails and get that traitor LaTour! MOVE … NOW!"

The first mate stared incredulously back at him and said "this ship has been fired upon; we have damages and a hole in our foremast. We out-gun and we are faster. Wait until we have checked over the ship and prepare, or you endanger us all."

 d'Aulnay was in a complete rage and he swung his walking stick at the man. The gnarly first mate merely put one hand up and with a loud smack caught the ornate orb on the stick, holding it in mid air before tossing it to one side. In the sudden silence d'Aulnay screamed "get his rat trap moving!"

The men nervously eyed the standoff unsure of who to obey. "Now!" roared d'Aulnay breaking the spell. Sails began falling and with creaking moans, the Grand

Cardinal was moving once again in chase of LaTour's expedition.

The winds increased with both LaTour and d'Aulnay willing more speed for opposite reasons. The *Grand Cardinal* was gaining fast in the rising wind and as they closed in a loud snap rang out from the fore deck. A man shouted, pointing to a large crack in the damaged mast. The first mate cursed out loud and with a glare at d'Aulnay ran forward to the mast.

He ordered some crew to gather short planks and rope to reinforce the damaged mast with vertical staves tied around the mast like a barrel. The first mate roared back at d'Aulnay "reduce sails! You are losing the mast, my God man, are you insane" he further implored. d'Aulnay ignored the mate and enjoyed the closing half mile gap, LaTour was about to fall.

They would tell the tale of what happened that day for decades. As the crew with planks and rope got back on deck, the mate had turned to see if the crew were returning and never saw the mast explode from bearing the load of sails around the hole and the jagged broken mast shot down and sideways catching the first mate above the hip bone and tearing down into the deck in less than a second almost ripping the man in half. d'Aulnay ordered reduced sail and rushed forward to the bloody macabre scene. The mate was in his last breaths as death approached, he looked up at d'Aulnay with hatred and spit red foamy spittle at him. He stopped moving, his sightless eyes glazing.

LaTour never heard the mast snap or see the man killed, but he saw the mighty mast with sails and rigging fall like a felled tree. He whooped and ordered 180 degree course change. All hands startled, they looked up and thought LaTour mad as he laughed and danced on the aft deck. They all looked at each other and back to LaTour not realizing that their fate was not sealed. LaTour yelled out gleefully "I did it! I took the mast out after all!" All hands ran for a look at the rails and saw the *Grand Cardinal* floundering with the foremast laying across the ship and sails in the water. As the *Saint-Clément* came about, LaTour rang the ships bell five long tolls to signal *L'Amitye de la Rochelle* and the shallops to attack.

d'Aulnay sensed the attack coming and while wiping the mates spittle from his face ordered the broken mast, rigging and sails cut away. Once cleared, any remaining sails were set. Now he would have to run for the safety of his fort in Port Royale. The heavy ship with one mast was not able to continue in the fight.

He was closer to Port Royale and was now on the downwind run, so he could match the smaller ships speed and stay ahead. He would soon have the fortress cannon to help defend the frigate.

LaTour had learned before leaving the previous fall visit that Port Royale was more fortified than ever, and did not want to test the gunners precision. He could not gain on d'Aulnay and could see the fort in the distance. d'Aulnay it seemed had beaten him again. As he stood watching d'Aulnay fall into the forts cannon range he cursed. He turned his head and spit over the rail into the small bay and swore again. Lifting his eyes he saw stacks of lumber on the shore opposite the fort and smiled. *Yes, that will do fine as a secondary target* he thought instantly. He called the mercenaries to attention and said "we have missed our opportunity with d'Aulnay, and he lives to fight another day, but he will need repairs and that mill will be the source of his materials." He stood looking expectantly at them and waited in the growing silence. A man yelled out "burn it to the ground!" All hands cheered and LaTour bowed graciously with a smirk and said "as you wish."

The entire mill and all lumber were ablaze as the LaTour expedition set sail for Saint John. The smoke could be seen all the way across the Bay of Fundy.

The celebrations at fort Saint John that night were unforgettable. LaTour received a hero's welcome and the stories of the battle for Bay of Fundy went all through the long summer night with feasting, music and merriment. LaTour was feeling like he was finally getting things in order. He had paid for the lease in Boston and paid the mercenaries a little extra before sending them back to Boston with the *Saint-Clément*. It felt good to have beaten d'Aulnay back, and now he could freely go to France without interference.

37 Pistole

Port Saint John

Autumn, 1644

Françoise-Marie Jacqueline had given birth to a healthy boy while LaTour had been fighting d'Aulnay in the Bay of Fundy. She later felt relief when the *Saint-Clément* had sailed into Boston and learned the expedition had reasonable success without injuries or death. The blockade had been broken and the overfilled warehouse could now be traded. She had also grown irritably restless in her surprise new role of motherhood.

She had immediately relegated her maidens to attending on the child and only when her breasts filled did she hold and nurse him. She had no desire to stay in the small rented home any longer than was necessary, preferring to walk through the streets and market in Boston or stare out to the ocean from the docks. Gabrielle was her maid in charge of her new son and she accepted the role with passion.

Françoise missed the responsibilities of running the fort along with the entrepreneurial building of an enterprise. LaTour's words still stung in her mind as he had inferred she was a mother now and not a serious business partner. Everything she had worked for was now dismissed as trivial by the 'great' Charles LaTour. The significant age difference between them was now the hammer driving the wedge of contention. He would soon find her resolve much more than he had signed for in his contract of marriage and business partnership. Françoise would head back to Saint John and see what LaTour had accomplished. She had now firmly decided to withhold the pistole location from LaTour until she knew more of LaTour's intentions. She wanted to see what other revelations would surface now that she was seeing her partner under a microscope jaded by the light of scorn.

It had only taken a day to make arrangements for ship passage to Saint John and close up the small home, piling her belongings, maidens and little Charles-Françoise into the ship. She had everything packed and settled all accounts checking items from her list. One last item remained, and it said 'Louie.'

She informed the captain of the small trader schooner that she had one last business item to deal with saying "please prepare and I will return shortly. I hope to leave Boston once I am onboard." The captain dispatched a rowboat and oarsman to take her to the dock and await her return and within a half hour Françoise was walking quickly down Market Street to the market. She walked directly to a small stall where an East Indian merchant was selling blades of all sizes. She had loved the wavy patterns in Damascus steel blades and when she spotted the ten inch knife she had thought of Louie.

Damascus steel was known to be extremely tough and hold an edge, but the East Indian was not having much luck in sales, so there sat the knife. She haggled as animatedly as the merchant and unrelentingly chipped at the man until he finally sat back on his stool with a long "ayyayaya." He was almost glaring at her as he said "it is yours" and put his hand out, palm up. Françoise held out her hand with a gold pistole and opened her other hand for the knife.

The midsummer trip had not taken long for Françoise to arrive in Saint John harbour. She could see the fort was bustling with activity, canoes coming to the fort loaded and going empty, piles of logs, barrels with goods, and stacks of furs. She had planned this voyage and her return carefully. She wanted to assert her authority and place LaTour as a business partner. She had changed into a plain grey wool dress and her hair pulled back into a long braid, her trusty sword hung at her side while she stoically remained by the captain and helmsman. The captain had been stealing glances at her to see if the lady was emotional on her return, but not once did she unclench her jaw or show emotion. She was ready. Ready as she ever would be to take control of her life. The thoughts of one more day with someone prepared to take advantage of any weakness only sharpened her resolve. She gave explicit orders on dropping anchor in front of the fort. She would remove her banner at the mast head and go ashore. Only when she sent the tender back, were the maidens, Charles-Françoise and belongings to come ashore.

As the little tender scrunched up onto the rocky beach familiar faces ran down to the shoreline with warm greetings. They gathered around her and began asking questions all at once. She held up her hands in mock surrender and said with a gentle smile "I will answer you all in good time. For now, Please show me all your fine accomplishments... I have missed you all so much."

She walked along taking in all the sights and waving back to the other well wishers. She learned LaTour had gone in search of Louie and was not at the fort. They looked at her intently as she had merely given a 'so what' expression and kept walking and then said "send the tender back to the ship for everything." After two long years she walked back into the lodge she had left so hastily for France.

Within an hour the lodge was swept out, a fire laid in the fire place, water on to boil, a meal underway and little Charles-Françoise had been nursed. Françoise was out the door and ready to inspect the storage area and read the tally sheets reflecting trade. Nicholas Gargot gave a brief report on the Bay of Fundy battle and current state of the fort. By evening she felt all was running smoothly and had a good operation.

It was dusk when LaTour walked through the door of the lodge and looked apprehensively at Françoise sitting at the table in the now tidy and spotless lodge. He had obviously been apprised of her arrival. "Francie—"was all he could say before she cut him off with "Charles LaTour, Françoise is my name. I will thank you to use it correctly with due respect."

LaTour turned and closed the door slowly before turning back to face her. "How are you? And the health of the child?" he asked pensively looking around the room. "We are fine since you left us in Boston" she said sourly. "We have more important things to discuss-- other than I suppose the weather next. While you were out looking for Louie, in an attempt to discover the pistole cache I am sure, I have inspected the storage, our records, and Gargot has given an account of operations. We need to discuss what we require upon your return from France" she concluded, all in a smart, businesslike manner.

LaTour's eyes narrowed and he said sharply "I never said *when* I was going to France."

"Oh! you are going for certain, as soon as we can get *L'Amitye de la Rochelle* loaded. I am here now and I will run the post while you are gone" she said firmly while standing. Her trademark sword and scabbard clinked on the table leg as she turned.

"As my business partner, you have become a great liability. A liability that can and will be corrected and this you will do at once" she stated firmly. "Listen to me" said Françoise, interrupting as LaTour tried to speak. "I have tried to be your wife, lover and business partner. I have been revoked free passage from France for attempting to speak on your behalf. I fled my own country and became a rogue traitor just like you, became pregnant and birthed your child. All you care about is more wealth and that damn pistole cache." In the following silence that came from realizing an impasse had been reached, LaTour saw the truth in her convictions.

"It was a boy" said Françoise quietly in the growing silence. "Pardon me" said LaTour uneasily, "what boy are you talking about..."

Shaking her head sadly she said "unbelievable. *You* have a son." Arching her back to remove the strains, she stretched with a yawn and straightening her dress she gently massaged her breasts a moment with a pained expression. Staring into his eyes she said "his name is Charles-Françoise, if you were curious."

"*I see*" said LaTour the hurt evident in his voice. "After *our* names I suppose" he added drily, his voice rising.

"Good night Charles. Nadine and Gabrielle tend Charles-Françoise, but I must nurse and it is always during the night when he cries. Be quiet, so he isn't awakened." With a rustle and fluff, Françoise was in bed. LaTour stiffly sat down at the table with the flickering candle and stared at dying embers in the fireplace.

LaTour was a man on a mission at first light the next morning. He was uncharacteristically harsh and demanded an extremely fast preparation for the

L'Amitye de la Rochelle to make passage for France.
The small trading post was buzzing with hushed,
confused gossip surrounding Françoise and newborn
Charles-Françoise returning to Saint John with total
indifference towards LaTour. His sudden departure
on the next tide was a quiet affair for Port Saint John
and the few who came to the shoreline stood
huddled in small quiet groups without fanfare. There
was suddenly something wrong at the trading post
and no one could understand the sudden enmity.

High on the ridgeline behind the fort, Louie
Membertou was watching the ship fade into the
distance. His father had told him how White man
loved gold and would follow an impure path to have
more, never happy. He cautioned young Louie to
never fail in the creator's eyes, to hold value in real
wealth as their nation had for thousands of years.
He could not understand at the time and Henri

Membertou could only hope the Louie would remember and make the proper choices.

Louie had also watched LaTour's distant naval battle from high on the bluffs at Musquash Harbour to the south west and concluded LaTour was fighting his way back to Saint John. Details were unclear at the distance, but Louie learned latter he had guessed correctly.

He was troubled at Françoise's whereabouts until learning she was with child. He envied LaTour and in the great creator's eyes he knew envy was wrong. He decided his time in Port Saint John had come to an end and broke camp, loading his furs and meager possessions on his travail for the ten mile excursion to LaTour's fort.

He had only just returned to Port Saint John in time to witness the few silent people on the quiet waterfront and departing ship. Louie had stood on the western ridgeline watching the ship disappear and decided to answer his curiosity by crossing the mighty river and return with his furs to learn more.

There was still a small amount of out flowing tide to pull Louie's canoe downstream to the fort. He did not want the birch bark to become damaged and jumped into the frigid back eddy in front of the fort. He pulled the heavy loaded canoe broadside and began throwing the fur cargo as high as he could manage. He stopped for a moment when he realized the fort was almost silent. He looked around and saw people walking about inside the fort and the occasional clunk or a rattle, when he realized what was wrong... no one was speaking. There was a lifelessness that had descended over the fort in an unsettling, eerie manner.

He finished unloading his canoe and hoisted it over his head to carry it to safety along the fort wall. Nicholas Gargot had seen Louie approach and was now walking his way with three others to help cart the furs to storage. Louie looked at Gargot and saw sadness in his eyes. The other men were silent and downcast. As the last bale of furs thumped down in storage, Louie said "what is wrong here? What has happened to take the life from the fort?"

Gargot sighed and said "sit down Louie, and I will tell you all I know." As he finished the story with LaTour leaving for France, Louie understood what his father had cautioned him about in his younger days. *LaTour had undervalued his real wealth.* The weight at the fort was fully transferred on Louie now and the two men sat on their fur bales staring out the open doors with the same doleful expressions as everyone else.

Louie sat contemplating his future and his conflicting emotions until he could not stand being in the fort any longer. He rose quickly and turning to Gargot said "tell Françoise... tell her I said... ahhh, tell her it is good to see she is safe and strong."

Louie was out the gates before Gargot could respond with powerful legs propelling him up the slope to his campsite overlooking the fort.

As the fall evening air dropped cool, a large yellow moon appeared on the Bay of Fundy as if it was incredibly close, filling the horizon with every detail visible. He tensed as he saw a shadow coming up from the fort steady and sure, the lone figure approached his small fire. The half risen moon was now an impossibly giant yellow ball of light, casting blue light complete with shadows. A slender figure was silhouetted in the light and stopped in front of Louie's fire.

"It is a beautiful cool evening," Françoise said softly almost reverently. "The moon sometimes seems to be able to get closer. It is magic is it not?" She asked gently as she stared at the rare spectacle. Louie threw several larger pieces of wood on the fire and as the fire danced higher he could see she was carrying a basket.

"Sit with me" said Louie suddenly. She smiled and as Louie shuffled sideways at the shelter entrance she sat down beside him. They remained that way as the moon crawled quickly into the night sky, shrinking to normal size in its place among the stars, the illusion waning. After both had tossed sticks on the fire several times, she said quietly "I missed this... I missed you."

He nodded with a barely audible grunt. She felt the nod in his shoulder. Leaning to one side she picked up her basket and reached in. Louie was on heightened awareness and as she sat straight again her shoulder and arm was once again snuggly against his. Turning to him she said softly I have thought about you, worried about you, and remembered your protection at the fort... I bought you something from Boston. It comes from a craftsman in a land where they work fine metal. She passed him a soft linen cloth with the long knife wrapped within its folds, and said "thank you... for being you." She kissed his cheek gently, hurriedly stood and scurried through the bluish light back to the fort. Louie sat and held the linen cloth to his nose and certain he could detect the faint aroma of perfume. The knife could wait until daylight.

38Pistole

Port Saint John

January, 1645

It had taken time to return Port Saint John to any sense of well being. The obvious issues with the LaTour couple had made even the most optimistic settlers feel they had wasted their time and efforts at the settlement.

Françoise realized quickly that the well being of trading with prosperity was symbiotic with their sense of belonging and happiness. She quickly set forth the Order of Good Cheer every Saturday night. There were no exceptions with attendance at the weekly music and pageantry. Dancing, skits, laughter and music had soothed frazzled nerves and had indeed brought almost everyone together with a sense of purpose.

"Reading people" was a natural skill she had adopted early in life and served her well now. There were only a few disgruntled settlers spreading negative seeds of dissention. She had caught on to their displeasure of "a woman" deciding their future and met them head on one Monday morning.

Françoise ordered a general assembly in the center of the fort, outside in the frosty winter morning. With everyone grumbling and complaining about the cold along with the murmured "why couldn't we have met in the lodge or storage house," Françoise opened the door of the main Lodge and closed the door quietly.

When she turned back to the assembly, she was wearing only her grey woolen work dress wearing her sword at her side. The crowd grew silent as she stood stoically looking at each person without saying a word. The merciless January cold had already turned her nose red, but she appeared oblivious to discomfort. Her silence was deafening and put everyone ill at ease. Only after she had looked at every person did she speak.

"Many of you came here years ago. A few were here even before I came here. My husband and I are partners in the operation of this outpost and our relationship has become somewhat unclear. It does not mean the operations of this trade post are in jeopardy. Rumors have been circulating since Charles returned to France, and I will only advise what is factual. Charles must clear his name with full absolution of the ridiculous fictitious charges leveled by Charles de Menou d'Aulnay. The charges have placed us in difficult times to continue trading, and time is what d'Aulnay is counting on. We will prevail with truth... What I cannot and will not endure is the abuse from within these walls from the few who undermine my authority and resolve."

The crowd parted around her as she began walking through the assembly towards the people in the back row. The three couples were now looking uneasily at each other and the crowd. She stopped in front of her biggest problem and said "You Gaetan, I will begin with you and your wife. You are to leave here at first availability."

Before she could continue He stepped forward and boisterously hollered "you have no authority to..." His sudden silence drew everyone to look where he stared. Louie had suddenly pulled his arrow at full draw in his bow and was aiming it at the man. A blank, wide eyed and baleful countenance spoke volumes to all that could see Louie. He would kill the man at once without remorse if he harmed Françoise. Gaetan opened his mouth and closed it again several times in an attempt to speak, but nothing would come out.

She informed two other couples they were banished as well, and as the banished couples looked about the crowd, everyone looked down and remained quiet. She had walked to one last man of Swiss descent and told him that although she felt she could not trust him, she had not heard him make disparaging remarks. He could stay but would have to prove his loyalty.

With their wives weeping quietly, and the men scowling dark looks, she quickly decided their remaining in Port Saint John would only cause further problems. She turned to the young lone Priest and said "Father Gagnon, I request you to travel to Port Royale in your shallop at once with these people and return if you wish to remain with your mission here."

Father Gagnon merely bowed his head and clasped his hands in prayer and nodded his affirmation. "That is all" Françoise snapped and walked slowly to her lodge.

When the door closed, the silence was broken immediately by murmuring. Louie relaxed his draw on the bow with the arrow still loaded and held in place with his bow hand as it pointed to the ground in the lowered bow. The crowd quickly dispersed into smaller groups leaving the outcast to themselves. Father Gagnon was quick to prepare for his journey and was leaving on the tide in four hours. The small open boat was soon a small speck heading south towards Port Royale with the disgruntled outcasts staring grimly ahead to an uncertain future.

The firm knock on the door brought Françoise into reality as she had stood staring at the fire crackling in the fireplace. She had every reason to second guess her decision as she could only rely on her own judgment without a partner on hand to second guess her thoughts. Banishment was harsh and yet she knew she had to remove dissention before negativity tore the trading post apart from within.

Wondering who would possibly be knocking at her door after the uncomfortable showdown made her stop and adjust her dress and cap before pulling the door open purposefully. Nicholas Gargot bowed respectfully and said "Madame, I would like a moment of your time if possible." Intrigued, she opened the door and offered a chair at the table.

Gargot was fidgeting as he looked up from the table and into her eyes and began speaking in a measured but firm tone. "I, indeed we, here in Port Saint John understand your desire to maintain a positive ambiance and allow everyone to feel that we are part of something worth doing. We have all committed our lives and hopes here. We have all believed in LaTour's governance and dreams, perhaps me more so than any other in this port, and by your marriage to him makes you the Lady in command during his absence. This is clearly understood..." he said trailing off.

When she gestured him to continue he said "I feel you have earned the respect due a commander as your skill at leading us in battle against d'Aulnay proved your ability. You also understand the concept of leading by example and your courage is legend. The port is working along finely..."

Françoise interrupted him with a hint of impatience "please make your point, and are you speaking on behalf of this settlement?"

He continued with a nod, "I speak freely from my observations and thoughts and I represent no one but myself. What I wanted you to clearly understand is my loyalty to you personally. What I came to speak of, relates to this morning's confrontation. Your husband asked me to enhance fortifications and indeed I returned from New England with extra cannons for that purpose. I have created modern defense designs in the parapet walls that can withstand cannon fire and repel infantry charges. We had a certain element of surprise against d'Aulnay if he attempted siege again, now you have now enraged Gaetan and the other banished settlers sufficiently that they will offer d'Aulnay all the information he requires to take this port... you have given up our element of surprise in your haste to remove undesirable opponents to your command. They should have been sent from Acadia to anywhere but our enemy" finished Gargot quietly.

Françoise sat composed with her hands clasped on the table and in the growing silence thought carefully of how best to respond to Gargot's heartfelt and honest reflections. She sensed Gargot had wanted to say more to her and was withholding something bigger. "Is there anything else I should know?" she queried calmly. "I feel there is something you are uncomfortable revealing. I think it is a perfect time to advise me of anything I should be doing to better the settlement."

Gargot sat a little straighter and began with "very well Madame." He fidgeted a moment searching for the right words and then he looked her in the eye and said "there are many here that feel you have grown too *close* to Louie. It is clear he has feelings for you and is very protective towards you. You have been seen going to his teepee, in the night as well... this subject makes me uncomfortable." He squirmed a little before continuing "I want to believe that it is a matter of friendship, but the best thing Louie could do now is move out until LaTour returns."

Françoise was too stunned to speak, but remained composed. Her heart hammered in her ears as she stared into her hands on the table. For the first time she was being forced to examine her feelings and while she was not about to divulge anything personal to anyone, there was a truth emerging that she realized had been obvious to everyone at Port Saint John. With incredible clarity, in an instant she knew what lay ahead in her future and it did not include Charles LaTour. There was a small fortune hidden in *her* cache and Louie was the only man she had ever met who had shown her respect and protection when it was needed. With all the thoughts and plans filling her mind, she realized the silence had grown even more uncomfortable for Gargot.

Clearing her throat gently she said "Thank you for your insight. I will take all your counsel under advisement. I realize it is difficult to speak your mind on these matters and I thank you for your courage. I agree I have reacted to Gaetan harshly. It may cost us our advantage in defending the fort, but we must maintain a quality of life that is not being undermined. The obviously outrageous charges filed against Charles in France should be proven frivolous and his honour restored from his efforts and thus d'Aulnay will have no authority here and it is of no further consequence. As for Louie... he gives everything he has and asks for nothing. Charles relies on him and so do I, perhaps more so, but he will not be asked to leave and I will not tolerate anyone who treats him unfairly... are we clear on this?"

Gargot knew it was as far as he dared push and yet when he arose from the table he "I pray Madame Jacqueline, pray that you have made the proper decisions and yet I came to you because I feel we are doomed. Charles may be in prison as we speak and will never return here. It will take a great deal of time to learn of his success in France... d'Aulnay however, *will* return and he will return as soon as possible now that he knows Charles is in France *and* now knows our defenses. " With a flourish he bowed, then swung his large hat to his head, and left with a brisk stride.

Françoise respected Gargot and his opinions since meeting him years before, his loyalty was beyond doubt and it troubled her that a decision made by her would have such grave consequences. He had said "doomed" and it now rang in her head like a church bell. If d'Aulnay came to Port Saint John it would be to attain the gold coin cache, the trading post was a secondary goal yet there would be nothing for LaTour to return to. The pistole that had promised to make the two governors a comfortable profit and build prosperity had proven to be their downfall. Françoise was never more certain at that moment of her plans. She would never allow either man have or share the pistole. She would forge her new life with the very metal that had enslaved the barons with its luster. Louie would be part of her new life, if he could learn what wealth could give him and how much easier life could be as a nobleman, perhaps he would agree to leave Acadia with her. *There was no turning back now* she thought. Time would be critical as d'Aulnay rebuilt and prepared to battle, and also LaTour's return from France was inevitable after the harsh winter conditions of the Atlantic passed allowing safer passage.

The cave will be accessible by mid-April she reasoned, Louie could retrieve enough pistole to allow discrete passage from New Netherland to the south and into a more civilized culture. If she prepared, she could be on her way to a new life by the first of May. In a few years she reasoned, she could slip back to the cache and retrieve all the pistole, and perhaps to settle upriver around the cache where fertile land promised a rich life. That would depend on who ultimately governed the land, and she could never be free from looking over her shoulder after fleeing Acadia.

Her deep thoughts were shattered as the back room door bounced open and in wobbled little Charles-Françoise heading straight for Françoise yelling "mama." Gabrielle had followed him with a little smile and said "I thought you might want a little distraction from…" but before she finished speaking, Françoise had glared at her and turned Charles-Françoise back towards her.

Françoise said haughtily "I was busy planning my affairs and you are charged with his care. Please do not interrupt me so rudely again" and pointed to the back room again. Gabrielle looked down at the floor and turning quickly, led Charles-Françoise by the hand out of the room. Françoise had already turned back to the fire before the door closed with anger evident on her face from the interruption.

Gabrielle had become increasingly concerned as Françoise seemed even more distant from little Charles-Françoise than ever. He had become her sole responsibility and Françoise seldom saw or inquired of his well being. Little Charles-Françoise had become a typical toddler, but his mannerisms and "firsts" had become Gabrielle's joy and accomplishments. She had heard and seen enough to know that Françoise was definitely not in love with Charles any longer and it worried her that Charles-

Françoise had no love or attention but Gabrielle's. She couldn't understand the complete lack of maternal instinct. Charles barely regarded the boy and had not given him so much as a nod before leaving the previous autumn for France.

Despite his estrangement, Charles-Françoise was a happy little toddler, never straying far from Gabrielle. It bothered her that Charles-Françoise had become just as indifferent towards Françoise. *It is a strange relationship* she mused. Within seconds they were laughing quietly in the primitive nursery playing peek-a-boo. She was happy to be rewarded with his giggles.

39 Pistole

Port Royale

February, 1645

Charles de Menou d'Aulnay de Charnisay seldom ate

or left his lodge and rumored to spend long hours in

bed since arriving at Port Royale with LaTour on his

heels. The lumber mill had caused him great anguish

because of the need to rebuild the saw mill outweighed repairing the Grand Cardinal. His greatest stress was the mounting debt load from trying to overtake Port Saint John alongside operating a trading post.

There would be no time wasted in getting back to Port Saint John in the spring. He wanted *his* pistole, all of it now, and it all seemed fair he rationalized after the setback of his saw mill. He would also take all of LaTour's winter stores of furs to supplement his own trade, but most important, he would destroy LaTour's fort and operate Port Saint John as his outpost. *I will become a powerful and wealthy man in France* he had thought incessantly. He still had his royal authorization to seize all of LaTour's property and assets. He couldn't believe his incredible luck when the small shallop loaded with outcasts unloaded in front of his fort. It was a gift of epic proportions to the point of seeming to good to be true.

 d'Aulnay's trepidation of this "gift" was soon eased when it became clear that the self imposed spokesman named Gaetan was of the personality that would grate on his nerves over time. His negativity had obviously been the catalyst to his expulsion. But whatever the reason, Françoise had made a grave error. It was not difficult to gather intelligence on Port Saint John from the dissidents. He merely treated them like the prodigal son returning, and they excitedly divulged details without being asked. He was drawing maps and making plans for his attack within days of their arrival. LaTour getting a pardon was irrelevant to him now. By the time he came back to Acadia with his absolution of charges, d'Aulnay would have already reduced his Port Saint John to rubble.

Gaetan had provided all the details he could dream for including the gossip that Françoise was now estranged from LaTour. *Why* she was estranged from LaTour caused d'Aulnay the most anguish... *had the pistole been retrieved with LaTour double crossing him and worse Françoise?* He would know for sure, as she would suffer until she told him everything including the pistole location.

Remy Martin had found life easier since the now famous retreat from Port Saint John by steering clear of d'Aulnay. He was summoned occasionally for new work details and debriefing his ongoing tasks, but his heart was not in it. His personal opinion of the ongoing war with LaTour had soured. He could not understand why d'Aulnay was so incensed with LaTour and Port Saint John to the point of Port Royale being affected adversely. There had been a history of conflict in Port Royale throughout the previous decades, but nations warring over the rich new resources found in Acadia differed greatly with battles between countrymen. His distaste grew as d'Aulnay was now on a renewed vigor to claim Saint John. His orders to have the Grand Cardinal ready for battle by spring had meant re-masting and repairing planks damaged from cannon fire.

The giant mast was the most difficult task. Scouting the woods for a reasonably straight black spruce had been tasked to the local Mi'kmaq and once found, the retrieval had been epic event through the deep snow and frozen ground. A jig had been constructed to hold and allow debarking, then smoothing the tree. It was clamped with wedges to ease out irregularities allowing a straight true mast. A tent over its full length allowed work to continue in the cold winter. Planks were also being sawn off logs over a pit by hand until the mill was rebuilt.

Despite the grueling work the only person to display excitement was d'Aulnay. Remy, like the others, felt a foreboding of the upcoming siege on Saint John. It seemed pointless for the good of France. This month was his last as d'Aulnay's lieutenant, he had decided Port Royale was so beautiful and he wanted a piece of Acadia as his own to settle. Time for a family was as good a reason as any for tendering his resignation, but he was tired of the fighting and wanted to finally beat his sword into ploughshares. He hoped the demons from the many campaigns he had fought, would take the painful twisted memories they brought into his sleep every night and melt away like an early morning summer mist.

He felt as confident as any man could be that he would fight until death to protect the settlement from invaders, but he could not believe that God would sanction the battles against LaTour. *If God would not*

agree with d'Aulnay's plans, what divinity would?
Remy had mused many times. The only answer that would come to him made him uncomfortable, but could explain the source of d'Aulnay's demonic rages.

"I need you to lead the land attack in Saint John, you cannot resign on me now" snapped d'Aulnay as Remy informed him of his impending resignation. "You know I will give you whatever land you want here in Port Royale for your loyal service, but I need this war with LaTour to end and his fort must fall as soon as possible. I need your expertise and firm hand on my soldiers in this last battle..." he trailed off. Remy had stood looking as stoic as ever and without emotion obviously not listening to him.

 Remy finally spoke after a short silence with measured exact words "I have served you and my time has come to relinquish my command. I have had Gilles as my replacement in mind for some time. He will serve you as I have and will have my counsel as needed. Catherine and I are ready to settle into our piece of Acadia and my life is her life. I will be your militia captain to maintain our security here in Port Royale if you wish, but that will be my only military service." After a long pause he walked to the wall where a rough map of Port Royale was hanging and traced his finger over a land tract he desired and said "this would be my choice for a farm, with of course your permission."

Without looking up, d'Aulnay said "Very well, I will draw up the land in your name and you are relieved. Please send in Gilles when you leave..." Remy Martin, land owner and free man had been dismissed, and thus turned and walked out the door without a thank you or handshake, nor did he offer one. He was conflicted with the joy of being clear of

d'Aulnay's plans and resulting clear future with

Catherine to the uneasiness of the unknown as a

farmer. To be clear of the battle with LaTour would

be a blessing.

40Pistole

Port Saint John

April, 1645

The early spring warmth had given the winter's

heavy snow fall no respite with the ground bare by

the first week of April. The dreaded meeting with

Louie had taken place only a few weeks before.

Françoise effectively managed Port Saint John

without fueling any gossip by keeping her distance

with Louie until he finally asked if he had offended

her somehow. *He really does know me well; I cannot keep anything from him* she thought with a smile.

He deserved truth. She had walked to the ridgeline behind the fort to clear her head and think of the proper way to break her plans to Louie. She was startled when Louie just appeared in front of her. He nodded when she said it was time to explain everything. Louie had sat down and stared towards the thin ribbon of land 85 kilometers across the bay remembering his fathers strange words. Neither his father nor he had understood the vivid old visions, but the fact that gold was in the forefront confirmed his future was unfolding as the chief had said it would be. He was no longer waiting for his signs.

Françoise had made detailed plans to flee everything and Louie was flattered that she wanted to spend her life with him. He had taken all the pistole to the cave as asked and never saw it as a means to his survival. When Françoise had told him that the pistole would provide the means for travel to foreign lands and have special possessions like his Damascus steel knife he was intrigued. What sealed it was when she turned to him and with hopeful countenance she said, "I am leaving all this. It all means nothing to me. You do. I cannot live without you... if it pleases you... come with me and we will start over... together." Louie said quickly "and what of little Charles-Françoise? Is he not part of your new life?" Françoise's face reddened and with tears starting to form she said quietly "I did not want a child. Charles never wanted a child. My sister in France cannot have children... he will go there with Gabrielle where he will have a proper life with caring parents. I am preparing Gabrielle and Nadine to take the baby to France with the first ship to France."

The silence was deafening. They were both staring at the bay, but with different perspectives. Louie rose to his feet and asked firmly "you will go with or without me... I am correct--yes?" Françoise merely nodded slowly.

Louie's mind now was made and it felt right. He gave her his large hand and she put her hand in his. He lifted her from the rock she sat on and said "I will go to the cave and bring as many sacks as can be travelled with. I will leave with you, *because I did not influence you to leave*. Your decision was already made. I too want to be with you, but remember, I have all I will ever need in the forest. We cannot live in the great cities you describe forever. I hope you realize my time in the forest is my life... there must be a balance." The embrace signaling acceptance on both parties was held so long they felt each other's heart and warmth.

As they walked down from the ridgeline she laid out the plan to leave May first for New Amsterdam in New Netherland, a mere three weeks. Louie would prepare for their first leg of the journey where they would follow the coastline south with his large canoe until they could travel by land. She would have to skirt Boston and all other usual sea ports as LaTour would learn of her whereabouts. She had no doubt of both LaTour and d'Aulnay coming for her to get the pistole wealth. All plans made, Louie stopped at his encampment and gathered his needs for the trip to the pistole cache. Françoise went directly to her lodge and tried to conceal her joy while preparing to slip away from Saint John.

Two weeks later there was a great shout and people began running and hollering. Françoise felt her heart flutter with butterflies wondering if Charles had returned only a week before she planned to slip away. As she ran out the door, Gargot was already heading for her lodge. He pointed to the harbour and said melodramatically "Now you will see how wrong your decision was! I told you he would come..." Message delivered, he ran to the parapets and began shouting orders. Françoise's butterflies were replaced with a solid fear as she saw *The Grand Cardinal* flanked by a ship on each side approaching the fort in the harbour. She had not even given a thought that she would have to defend the fort before leaving it. She was not mentally prepared for the battle, but she would adapt and overcome d'Aulnay again. She ran back to her lodge and grabbed her faithful trademark sword, then back to the center of the fort. She bellowed to the people running around the grounds to prepare for battle as they had before.

Fires were lit, ammunition and powder passed around. Cannons were prepared and manned. And by the time all three ships were close enough to see the men aboard them, Françoise Jacqueline felt prepared. She looked around for a glimpse of Louie and finally had to ask if anyone had seen him. It was confirmed that he was not inside when the main gate was barred shut. She was on her own with Nicholas Gargot, her second in command.

If there was any doubt of their intentions towards Fort Saint John as the ships cleared sails and dropped anchors, the answer came without warning. The silence was broken with a blistering roar as *The Grand Cardinal* discharged her cannons one at a time until they every cannon on her starboard side had fired. The first cannon balls hit the canted walls and with a thud flew upwards over the fort. Some landed in the courtyard, some went over the opposite wall.

Before Gargot could react *The Vierge* then delivered her cannon balls in similar fashion. Before the next volley, Gargot commanded all cannons to fire on *The Grand Cardinal.* The cannons from the fort fired in staccato as the ship began its second volley. Françoise swore she actually saw cannon balls colliding over the water. The fort took some damage to the walls, but the withering cannon fire plowed through the main gate, and shattered upper portions of the palisade walls that did not have the benefit of rammed earth behind them. Gargot ordered grapeshot fired on both ships and the shotgun like cannon blasts sent splinters flying and screams rose from the ships.

Françoise surveyed the fort and saw the gates dangling and bodies in the courtyard. Time seemed to have stopped and now moved in slow motion. Gargot had given d'Aulnay a surprise with the use of grapeshot, but they had battered the fort. She

ordered the gates sealed and re-barred as best they

could. Before anyone moved, another volley from the

ship tore into the fort. She felt and heard the swish of

a cannon ball passing inches in front of her before

smashing into the storage warehouse. It had been a

close call with the hole in the warehouse telling of

forces capable of obliterating flesh and bone. Gargot

raised a red flag as he stared at the ridgeline behind

the fort. Immediately a mighty roar erupted on the

hillside and the four entrenched twelve pounders spit

forth mayhem on the ships below. It was obvious

from the activities aboard the ships that the hidden

guns had been a total surprise to the invaders. The

mighty cannons kept the barrage going until anchors

were being raised to allow a retreat from the

withering firepower. There were no cheers as the two

ships drew away from cannon range.

The third ship had earned everyone's attention as men were seen transferring to longboats. They were heading for shore below the fort and beyond range of the cannons. Gargot now realized what was in store for the fort. They would take the ridgeline overlooking the fort and silence the large twelve pounders. If Gargot sent enough men to battle the expeditionary forces on the hill, then he would not have enough manpower to repel another frontal attack on the fort. He cursed then climbed down from the watchtower and hurried to the center of the fort to break his bad news to Françoise.

She accepted his information graciously and calmly, and then asked what he would do. "I will take six men and attempt to repel the attackers on the ridgeline, leaving the main force here with you. Madame... If we fail to defend the twelve pounders on the ridgeline... well then Madame you might well want to consider surrender. He can, and will pound this fort to the ground." Françoise considered his words and said "you do what you can and I will defend as best we can here." Gargot stared at her with accusatory eyes and said "well, I guess that is the best we can do now with situation we have been placed in."

Gargot gathered his battle hardened six and left as the gates were being restored. The old feeling of doom was heavy on his shoulders as he sensed he would not be returning. He paused only long enough to look one more time at the fort and turned back to trot towards the ridgeline.

The ridgeline defense was established in scattered groups of two behind the plentiful large boulders. It was a gallant defense that managed to keep the invaders from reaching the cannons for that day. The skirmishes had cost one man an eye from rock chips and three invaders fallen to the accurate musket fire. They held their ground for most of the next day until more men had been sent to overwhelm the defenders. With a roar the invaders charged and Gargot was first to stand from his crouched position behind rocks as he yelled "I will fight on my feet a free man rather than grovel on my knees!" The gruesome hand to hand combat played out with swords flashing, men screaming until blood ran on the rocks. By the end of the second day of the siege, the ridgeline cannon crews lay dead with the remaining invaders waving d'Aulnay's flag on the ridgeline amid the bodies of the defenders. Nicholas Gargot had fought his last battle.

The ships were once again moving back in range for the next attack. The silenced cannons on the ridgeline battery were useless against the fort by their clever placement in the rocks against the possibility as Gargot had predicted.

d'Aulnay's men on the ridgeline however were now free to form up and advance with ground attacks. Françoise was for the first time in her life terrified beyond words. Her world was falling apart in front of her eyes. Gargot's failure to repel the land forces would give d'Aulnay the advantage of charging the fort at the most opportune time. Wounded and bodies of the fallen were her reminders of how grave her situation clearly was. The young priest, with the saddest expression and most loving manner Françoise had ever seen had just given last rites to a dying man. When she touched his shoulder he looked up at her with tears in his eyes and said "what is wrong with those people? Do they not realize it is Easter Sunday in the morning? In the name of God why do they want to harm us? I just don't understand... we are all Christian countrymen under the flag of France. *Countrymen*—not soldiers. Let the Crown sort this out in due time and surrender before more good people are lost..."

"It is a complicated situation Father" began Françoise slowly. "We have put our whole lives into this settlement, and it is easy for you to give away, what is not yours without a fight."

"What is not *yours* to give away so easily is the lives of these *people* for your goals... how many lives are worth this settlement?" replied the young priest.

Françoise turned and walked to the parapet again to survey her situation. She had lost the element of surprise and defense with the ridgeline battery along with Gargot and ten good men. The fort had taken direct hits on the closest defending cannon positions with injuries and two more deaths. The main gates had been ravaged again and needed to be bolstered with more lumber. In the now silent twilight of the second day of the siege on Saint John, Françoise called everyone to center of the fort. It was time for her to rally them and stiffen both spirits and courage... including hers.

"There are armed men outside these walls" she began in the most authoritative voice she could muster. "We must be vigilant, there will be a double watch established on the parapets and watch towers. We can expect attack in the night. We have taken losses, but we are still strong!"

Before she could continue, the settlements cooper stepped forward into the bonfires brightness and said quietly "why not stop this siege? If d'Aulnay is truly wrong in this siege, could we not await the Crowns decision and live to enjoy this settlement?"

Murmurs arose sporadically and at once she knew the Priest had been the voice of opinion. She was losing them. Driving her sword point into the partially frozen ground for effect had silenced them all. "I have been to France. I have tried to right the wrongs of the man who wishes wealth over our safety... It is deeper than man against man. d'Aulnay is but the spear point of the sentiments in the church against all who are not Catholic. Our new King is but a toddler, in his place Our Queen has been ruling with Chief Council Mazarin. This is all about freedom from the church! Charles LaTour is in the fight of his life against his artificial charges in France where loyalties are hidden."

Driving her sword forcefully into the ground again, she spat the words "I will defend this settlement because it is righteous! I make my stand in remembrance of the St. Bartholomew day massacre!" The speech had arrived in her head as she spoke and its effect was immediate. A cheer rose into the night sky as one. She did not know yet how she would get clear and find Louie, but he would have her pistole and the means for ultimate escape. She just had to get through the next day.

Aboard the *Grand Cardinal*, d'Aulnay heard the great cheer inside the fort. The sound had travelled clearly in the cool air across the water. It made his eyes narrow and his hands tighten into fists. The surprise of the cannons overlooking the harbour had been effective. Had he come with one ship he would have felt defeat again. His plan to include a ground force had been his best preparation. They were ordered to attack at will and he had no doubt there would be skirmishes in the night from his forces on the ridges. *I will take the fort by nightfall tomorrow and she will surrender the pistole* he vowed to himself as he smashed his fist into his hand. "Get rest and prepare

for landfall before dawn" he ordered to the men as

he went his cabin.

41 Pistole

Pickwauket Mountain

April, 1645

Louie had picked his way carefully through the floating chunks of ice. The upper river ice was only just breaking up and clearing to the open areas of the large waters. A week previous would not have allowed passage on the ice surface and it was impassable until the warmth of the early spring coupled with warm day breezes working with the tides broke ice into large chunks and sheets. He had hiked up to the small cave and made camp. He needed a small respite from his canoe trip and the game was plentiful enough to allow his bow and arrows earn his meals. The cave gave a dry place to sleep and he had thought perhaps a day would be enough rest. The next morning had started the same as any other in Louie's life until he heard the distant thumps down river in the direction of Saint John. Louie spun on his heel and cupped his ears with his hands and listened as yet another series of thumps was heard like distant thunder claps. His heart froze as he knew at once what was happening. As his mind tried to function, the third round of thumps was the largest and most prolonged.

Louie threw his gear together and began carrying as much pistole as he dared carry in the large canoe. He had hurriedly placed the two rabbits he had taken earlier on a makeshift roasting spit while preparing to leave. After sealing the cave again he grabbed the cooked rabbits and ran down to his canoe in the stream below. The twenty foot canoe was making a small wake as he cleared the brook into the river and he was on his way back to the fort. He had the incoming tide to battle for most of the downriver journey, until he was back in the large lake- like expanse of the lower river. Louie was in a blind terror as he fought exhaustion and only stopping for a drink of water and quick bite from his meager supplies. Louie had paddled almost non-stop for that first day and night. By the next morning Louie could hear muskets on the ridgeline behind the fort. He was upriver but prevented from going through the now massive reversing falls. The massive tide was not cooperating with his journey as it would take hours for the huge tide to equal the height of the river and negate the outflow of the Wolastoq River. *The*

Wolastoqiyik people of the river called the river Wolastoq, meaning beautiful river, and any other time Louie would have agreed. Today he cursed the twenty foot tides and the falls together as a curse.

He had grabbed his knife, bow and all his arrows, and then hurriedly hid his canoe above the high water mark. He ran until he could only walk. He could now clearly hear the shouts and occasional musket shots, as he neared their position the odd musket ball could be heard whooshing by him.

He looked to his right and was shocked to see the three ships in the harbour. He could see the fort had taken punishment, but withstood the attacks so far. His eyes searched frantically through the running figures in the fort until he finally spied the grey dress with a sword scabbard. She seemed to be in charge and without injury bringing a sigh of relief. Battle sounds had intensified on the ridge bringing Louie back to the task at hand. He dropped lower and advanced carefully as if hunting from boulder to tree and occasionally crawling under thick brush until he was in bow range. Voices could be heard with swords clanking and men groaning. A united howl went up from the men on the ridge and as Louie drew his bow and leaned gently around the tree he had just hidden behind to prepare, he saw strangers, invaders waving the d'Aulnay flag towards the harbour. He had been too late despite his gallant efforts.

He gently eased back around the tree while relaxing his bow. He was shaken to see Gargot among the fallen. He respected Gargot as a decent man who had been a brave soldier and wise leader. He was a devoted settler and fought to the end defending it. He knew him as a warrior and that meant these invaders were skilled soldiers as well to have beaten him. They had been overwhelmed by greater numbers, but Louie vowed he would avenge the deaths.

As the day drew to a close he could see the fort below him and a gathering around the central fire. Françoise was evidently building them up with a rousing speech with her sword point thrust in the ground. The invaders on the ridge had sat pointing at various locations around the fort and Louie knew they were only resting while planning attack. Dark would be on them soon and Louie's hand was on his large Damascus steel knife as he watched them. Some would not see morning.

As the half moon rose into the frosty early spring night, the invaders began to prepare to leave. Louie knew they were planning on breeching the main gate as it was heavily damaged. They never heard him slip almost into their midst in the darkness. He knew their plans and thoughts and when he had heard enough, felt so reviled that he almost spat on them before withdrawing back into the darkness. He now knew they had spied his wigwam and talked of checking it out in the daylight.

There would be nothing of importance by the time they got there as Louie would have cleared it all away. He was still in awe that they knew his name and were looking for him. Why would these strangers seek or know him? Henri Membertou had told him of the evil that the coins garnered. Was d'Aulnay aware of his involvement in hiding them and brought the evil to him? His heart fell as he realized the truth boiled to the top of his questions.

As the invaders began picking their way through the rocks and brush downwards toward the fort, Louie was long gone. He would deal with them later in the night when they tried to attack the fort.

It had proven more dangerous than Louie anticipated. When the invaders tried to the breech the main gate there was concentrated musket fire from within on the gate. He also was outside the gate in the dark, now dodging friendly fire.

He was able to move quickly and dispatched two invaders before they withdrew into the night in retreat. The next two attacks in the night cost them three more men and they never knew the danger that was within their ranks. Louie was able to counterattack and use the musket fire to conceal his movements. It would be the next day before they would realize that death had been by a knife and not musket. The invader that had spoken the most and waved d'Aulnay's flag on the ridge fell last to Louie's knife just before a graying yellow light hinting at daylight.

Louie withdrew to concealment in the rocks on the ridgeline after seeing movement on the water and realized the ship was landing men on the shoreline. The attack was coming at first light and he was in no position to help with the overwhelming numbers of armed men. By grey dawn there were armed men surrounding LaTour's Fort.

Louie could see Françoise commanding the fort from the parapets yelling and directing those people running back and forth with their tasks. The priest approached her from the main lodge. What happened next confounded his every thought... she had obviously just ordered everyone to leave their stations and go to the lodge... Louie could not believe his eyes. A lone figure on the parapet by the gate against two ships and ground forces and Françoise had taken everyone to the Lodge. Louie determined with his sharp eyesight that the man on the parapet was the Swiss settler Hans Vaner.

As his mind swirled with how many things were wrong at the fort, the ships broke the morning silence with their barrage. The cannon fire was like nothing Louie had ever seen or heard. Cannon balls slammed through anything that was not earth reinforced and designed to absorb or deflect the blows. Holes began to appear along the tops of the sharpened palisade logs like broken teeth. Over it all Louie could hear voices singing in the lodge and he then he understood.... It was Easter Sunday and Fort Saint John was seeking divine interference from a certain doom with prayer.

From where Louie sat in the rocks overlooking the battle, it would only be God who could save them now.

42 Pistole

Paris, France

April, 1645

Charles LaTour had been in the fight of his life since landing in Honfleur France. Although he had landed without conflict and made contact with friendly allies, he learned his wife leaving France had not been taken lightly. His opponents had used the LaTour couple's flight from France as admission of their guilt to treason.

Mazarin, he had learned was a clever strategist who had beguiled the Queen by giving her fifty thousand écu from his winnings at gaming... his favorite pastime. His calm demeanor had garnered a crowd as he went "all in" and won. Commoners and Royals alike were impressed with Cardinal Richelieu's prodigy in the Council of State. The Cardinal Mazarin, now Chief Council, "advised" the Queen serving as Regent in governing France. His anti-protestant views were not lost on the Queen who shared his views.

There was always reason for more income in any dynasty and France was very needy in the current campaigns on foreign soil. LaTour had reason to believe that raising the income for France would speak volumes for him and had brokered a deal with his associates in Paris to prepare a meeting with Mazarin to plead his case. He felt that he would fail any attempt to climb the ladder and address each level of government would fail. No, he reasoned freedom would come from the top down.

Mazarin had agreed to a clandestine meeting that allowed LaTour to refute his false claims laid by d'Aulnay with proof. He then proposed a surcharge on imports to allow France more direct profit.

Being a clever strategist, Mazarin immediately saw that LaTour had just given the best defense he could have made... a strong offense. There would be fallout from the agencies that operated in Acadia, but La Borgne had already dirtied his hands with d'Aulnay and the Company of one hundred Associates would have to surrender more of their profits. Mazarin could see that France would govern Acadia in the coming years, but the fact that LaTour was embroiled in false charges had obviously hurt trading. He promised that he would see the Queen forthwith to have his charges stayed and allow LaTour and his wife the freedom he needed with royal assent to operate Port Saint John.

Mazarin genuinely was impressed with LaTour's brazen maneuver and felt his courageous lifestyle coupled with loyalty to France should reflect some form of compensation. He smiled as he stood and putting his hand out he firmly shook the calloused weathered hand and said "it will take time for writs to be drawn, old charges dropped and your new charter to operate as Governor in Port Saint John. I will send an emissary to Acadia with your authorizations and Charles d'Aulnay's desist orders towards you. It will take time, but I'm sure you can find your way out of France again and await our emissary... most importantly Monsieur LaTour, you will avoid conflict if possible."

With a bow, and one corner of his mouth curled up in an attempt to stifle a grin, Cardinal Mazarin wheeled around and was gone in the night. LaTour felt as if the weight of the world was lifted from his shoulders. He would travel for Honfleur at daybreak and make way to Boston on the first tide. He would finally have d'Aulnay off his back and he would win Francie's heart again. *I am going to win this war after all* he thought smugly.

43 Pistole

Port Saint John

Easter Day, 1645

There was not a dry eye in the main lodge as the young priest led the congregation of settlers and soldiers in a rousing rendition of 'Soldiers of Christ, Arise' as cannon balls flew and cannons crashed aboard the ships in the harbour. The young priest had begged Françoise to allow a quick service in hopes of God's grace. She was certain that unless a miracle occurred Fort Saint John would fall and acquiesced as the lodge was probably the safest place with the withering cannon fire.

She grudgingly allowed Vaner to keep watch as they had a hasty service and communion. Trust was something she had trouble with and had posted another watch outside the lodge to give her piece of mind. The moment the canon fire stopped, a cry of alarm and anguish followed by the door banging open. The watch announced with a great shout "Hans just waved them in and opened the bar before I could stop him!"

As people spilled out the door of the lodge, invaders were spilling in the shattered front gate. The skirmish began as soon as the occupants could arm themselves and meet the attack. Cannon were now useless and the advance had come inside the fort making musket fire useless. The gallant efforts of the retired military men held the first wave of attackers and from a fierce sense of ownership began to push the fight back towards the gate.

Françoise was prepared with sword drawn to engage as she defended the women while commanding her ragtag militia. As the fight reached the gate she ordered half the men to the parapets and crew a cannon with grapeshot to clear the gate of invaders. The next few moments began to see the fight waning in the invaders as Fort Saint John fought for their very existence.

As Hans cowered on the parapet by the gate watching the battle for life and death at his feet, Françoise climbed to the parapet and started walking down the narrow plank walkway towards him. She could envision herself running her sword through him. As she started walking towards him she had glanced over the palisade wall to look at the harbour. What she saw stopped her in her tracks and caused her stomach to roil.

Charles d'Aulnay stood on the grounds outside the walls with walking stick in one hand and a smile. He was flanked by soldiers and in front of him were ranks of musket carrying soldiers. The ranks were an impressive three deep and had been arranged in an arc to place their firepower in the gate. Four small mortar cannons were crewed behind them to lob cannon balls up and over the invaders and palisade walls to rain death on the fort occupants.

At the shoreline she could see men using the rocks as a shield were prepared with breeching ladders. This was it. She knew it was over. The precision that d'Aulnay used was overwhelming on her ragtag settlers. Where he commanded a polished army with all the weapons, she could only try and repel. There would be no counter attack, no surprises or secret weapons, and not even God could prevent the destruction that d'Aulnay was happy to deliver. As the men fought for their lives, they had no idea that the main battle group was on the other side of the fort walls... waiting, not even in the fight yet.

As she turned and looked towards d'Aulnay again through the sharpened logs of the palisade walls, d'Aulnay having spied her, bowed with great flourish after removing his hat. He stood erect and after replacing his hat carefully, turned and spoke to his bugler. Stepping up beside his commander the bugler sounded a long tone followed by a short, and the well trained squad in the fort disengaged their battle to run through the shattered gates.

The men of the fort, not understanding what lay outside the gate, were baffled why Françoise suddenly screamed to them and ordered retreat, followed by "seal the gate as best you can!"

As the men exchanged confused looks, she looked over the wall as d'Aulnay appearing like a Cheshire cat with a mouse stood mocking her by clapping his hands in mock applause for her actions. The sounds of gate barring and the lack of faces on the parapets emboldened d'Aulnay to simply stroll towards Françoise on the wall.

Looking up at her he spoke righteously "Why all this fuss Madame? We are going to seize this settlement in the name of the King. I have the Kings petition to seize all in his name. We do not need to fight over what is not yours or mine. Spare our countrymen any further bloodshed. I will do what is necessary as a servant to France." He held the official writ up with one hand and the other was raised as he said "see, it is not hard to surrender. Do what is right and honourable... surrender Madame! And you will surrender all to me including anything hidden away" and then having spoken the words he waited so long to say, he stared at her in silence before nodding and strolled back to his place in his battle group.

Without turning, d'Aulnay lifted his walking stick and the cannon crews on the mortars held their torches over the flash holes. When d'Aulnay lowered his stick to the ground all four cannons went off with thumps. Immediately cannon balls were falling inside the fort. Miraculously, no damages were incurred. The mortars were all adjusted minutely and then d'Aulnay shouted out "shall I send you another volley? Perhaps that will help you to decide."

Françoise realized that d'Aulnay was actually enjoying the carnage and mayhem. He would not relent until he had all the pistole, but he wanted the fort to fall. Utter destruction would shatter LaTour's future chances to retaliate.

As d'Aulnay raised his walking stick again, Françoise shouted down from the palisade walls "Charles! Enough! This has already cost too much. These are people, settlers not soldiers. You have..." before she could say anything further the walking stick came down and she was drowned out with four thumps again. With a different charge and trajectory, one mortar found its mark by obliterating a watch tower and careened down, then across the fort interior. The other three made small craters while throwing dirt in the air again. The injured were moaning and crying out in pain.

Françoise spun back around and thrust her head between the sharpened logs on the palisade walls and screamed "STOP! Have you gone mad?"

As d'Aulnay lifted his walking stick he yelled back to her "Do you surrender as ordered by your King?" She looked over her shoulder at the carnage in the fort and then to the massed disciplined troops at her gate and realized it really was over.

"Will you spare any further bloodshed to these people?" she pleaded. d'Aulnay was already moving across the grounds towards her position on the palisade walls. He also knew it was over.

With one hand on the wall he stood looking up at her and said quietly "you will surrender the fort of course, but you know I want everything including the cache. Your militia is of no consequence to me." There they stood in silence... Françoise looking down at d'Aulnay... searching his face for a hint of betrayal and d'Aulnay looking up at her... searching for her deceit.

After a long pause she decided it was indeed over and nodded slowly. They would all live to see another day and best of all for her, Louie would have a nice stipend for her. If she lost the cache she would not have lost all. LaTour had lost everything, but that was acceptable.

"Very well Charles, I surrender Port Saint John to you... as the King has requested" she said sadly while turning away from him, and as she looked down inside the fort into the faces of the settlers, tears were forming which served her from seeing the faces clearly.

"Open the gates" she ordered with a break in her voice. "It is over. I have surrendered to Charles d'Aulnay who has official orders from the King. Drop your weapons."

As she walked slowly back along the parapet planks she returned her sword into its scabbard and climbed down the ladder. Her face was streaked with dirt and sweat. When she stopped at the gate, she adjusted her dress, attempted to flatten out the front while whisking dirt off. She placed a loose strand of hair behind her ear as d'Aulnay strode through the gate looking about the small groups of glaring settlers gathered around the gate. He noted the pile of halberds, swords, and muskets lying on the ground.

He stopped and with his hands on his hips began quickly turning his head back and forth searching faces. "Where is *your* savage... that *serves* and protects you?" he asked quickly with a smirk. He caught her hand in midair as she attempted to slap his face.

"You could never understand the meaning of *friend*. You vile animal! You come here to maim and kill and call him a savage. His name is Louie. He is Charles's friend and has been baptized by the church.

Before she could continue, d'Aulnay shoved her brusquely towards her lodge and said "shut up and get out of my sight. I will deal with you shortly. Stay in your lodge until I get there."

Deflated, she turned and walked obediently to her lodge as d'Aulnay herded everyone else into the main lodge. The young priest stood on the steps with a troubled look on his face. d'Aulnay stopped in front of him and said "get your possessions together and go to Port Royale at once. You are finished here. Take her child and maidens with you as well. The innocent need not dwell here any longer in this treasonous rebellion."

Charles d'Aulnay walked briskly in to the center of the main lodge and stood looking at the bedraggled settlers. Clearing his throat he commanded "where is Louie? The local who befriended LaTour... I want to know his whereabouts or a best guess." The room was silent, it was not that they were defiant, more that they were defeated and unable to focus. d'Aulnay suddenly screamed "WHERE IS HE?" causing everyone to jump and a few women were now sobbing.

"He is not here. He left in his canoe a week ago" offered a man holding his arm with a wound. "Which way?" snapped d'Aulnay. "Up or down river to the harbour" he further urged the man. "Why upriver of course" said the man. d'Aulnay wheeled around and headed for the door saying "You people stay here... I may have further need for you." It would not have mattered if they had wanted to leave, as the fort was now occupied by d'Aulnay's mercenaries... including guards at the door.

d'Aulnay strode across the compound with a brisk purpose, his head on a swivel and observing all. He strode through the door without knocking and as a further discourteous behavior to set the tone he left his hat and gloves on. Marching over to the table where Françoise was sitting with red rimmed eyes, he stood over her and speaking through clenched teeth said "where are the pistole?... all of them... I want a map drawn here on this table or you and this pitiful lot will all suffer until I do."

She was genuinely afraid of him for the first time since meeting him. For the first time in her life she felt trapped and without options from a certain fate. Before she could raise her eyes d'Aulnay spoke menacingly a notch higher in volume and said "I was here as plans were made for your hiding the pistole in a cache upriver with the help of savages. The biggest mistake of your life was sending Gaetan to me as your enemy. He told me of your relations with the savage 'Louie' as you call him. It was not hard to place him as your accomplice with the cache."

Her heart felt as if would explode from beating too fast. Her face turning red and the fight returning to her, she made an effort to stand. d'Aulnay shoved her viciously back to her chair with one hand and raised the other hand to strike her. "WHERE ARE MY PISTOLES YOU TRAITOROUS WHORE" he roared at her with his hand held over her to strike.

In an instant she knew she could never give him all, but she could perhaps draw any map to buy some time. She wanted the pistole to create a new life and was only days from having made good on her dreams. Mustering as much courage as possible she looked up at him and managed to blurt "he is out for pelts and hunting... he does not see any value to gold coins Charles, he is not your enemy."

d'Aulnay became composed quickly and after removing his gloves replied "if Louie knows where the pistoles are hidden, I have no further purpose for you or LaTour for that manner. You over-estimate your worth to me."

"No! What you do not understand is that Louie will be gone for months, staying wherever he feels like hunting and trapping" she said quickly. Standing over her he rolled his gloves and suddenly swung them at her shoulder with a loud smack. Then reaching down he grabbed her by the back of her neck and thrust her up out of the chair towards the door. As she staggered and flew across the room, d'Aulnay was moving and next had her pinned against the door. He looked her up and down with a look of disgust on his face. "Imagine! I once desired you as a beautiful woman. I now see nothing more than savage loving whore that will say anything to keep the pistole from me..."

Grabbing her by the throat with one hand, he reached around her roughly and opened the door. He thrust her backwards out the door and said "join the others in the main lodge, stay there until I deal with your deceit."

Wind milling her arms and legs she barely avoided falling as she was propelled from her home. Choking back a sob she straightened her dress, pausing long enough to wipe her face before standing straight before walking to the main lodge. She was ushered in by the two guards and the door slammed behind her.

d'Aulnay was methodical as he searched through the lodge, pausing only long enough to survey the room

417

for hiding spots. When he finished he was more disgruntled than ever. Not one pistole in the lodge and such little coin that he knew she was not divulging all that she knew.

Standing in the middle of the room he placed his hat carefully on his head, and using his thumbs and forefingers to level the edges of the brim strutted from the cabin.

The past months had been spent planning for the moment when he would overtake Port Saint John and become sole Governor of Acadia. It may have been enough aspiration for most, but he wanted the wealth he had helped grow from re-stamped coin. Acquiring mercenaries, ships and armaments had been costly. There would be pressure for repayment in France that would not be overlooked any longer, the additional pelts and resources in the full storage building would buy a little time, but the pistole would clear the debt load.

As badly as he wanted the pistole, LaTour would also want it. What troubled him was Françoise now acting in her own interests. It had been wise at the time to have her hide the wealth as opposed to him or LaTour. At this moment he regretted ever forming a pact with LaTour.

All the worry, setbacks, and failures were erupting in an unconscionable rage. He felt the rage in his very person, radiating from his core in waves. By the time he had entered the lodge with his battle hardened mercenaries, he wanted to hurt. He wanted her to suffer as the focal point of all that had gone wrong. He also knew she would lie to protect her pistole as long as she could... *he knew because that is what he would do.*

As he stood looking at the assembly in front of him as a hawk looks upon a small rodent, he waited and was rewarded when the silence was broken by the leather apron wearing cooper. "Why are you holding us here? We have no quarrel with you and only defended..." He was cut off mid sentence as d'Aulnay turned and spoke to his new lieutenant Gilles and commanded "we will start with him" pointing to the man, then added "Your sentence for raising arms against a representative of the King, as a traitor... is death by hanging." Several muscular mercenaries grabbed the small man while the group gave a unified wail of dismay.

"Charles! You promised not to harm anyone" screamed Françoise. As a rope was hurled into the rafters and the man had his hands tied behind his back, a small chair was placed under the rope now hanging from a pulley above. d'Aulnay strode quickly to the chair and with a violent kick sent the chair flying into the wall where the back flew off. The mercenaries looked at him with bewilderment.

Looking at Françoise and then the group he said with a maniacal laugh "*I said they were of no consequence to me.*" The hastily made noose was placed over the man's head and the mercenaries looked expectantly at d'Aulnay, unsure of what he wanted. They wondered what he would use to allow the man to fall from and break his neck.

Their bewildered looks changed to incredulous wide eyed shock as d'Aulnay said loudly "HANG HIM…" and pointed upwards. After a pause that allowed his garish order to sink in, the remainder of the mercenaries pulled the struggling man clear of the floor.

d'Aulnay turned to the mournful assembly and magnanimously said "Now as a show of goodwill, I will spare a man. You there... Hans Vaner. Thank you for help by allowing us entry. Gaetan said you would help if possible. I however, do not like deceitful people. You will earn your freedom by becoming our executioner. Do you wish to be spared?" Without looking up, Vaner mumbled almost imperceptibly "merci" and took the rope.

The macabre scene played out five more times as the strongest or most vocal of the group were read their sentence and hoisted to their death, then unceremoniously dragged outside to be thrown into a heap as if yesterdays rubbish. d'Aulnay stood impatiently looking on as if a grand magistrate until the sixth body was removed. He had set the tone, and the reaction was predictable. Nobody in the room could watch the hangings, eyes were averted and prayers whispered and Françoise pleading to stop. *Time to change the tempo* he thought.

Looking to Gilles he commanded "rope here as well" tossing his head towards Françoise. Although she fought like a trapped wildcat, she was soon subdued and now had a noose on her own neck and her hands tied behind her back. d'Aulnay held the rope in his hand and as he took slack from the rope she was obliged to rise on her toes to keep air moving to her lungs. Walking up behind her, d'Aulnay leaned in to her ear; seething "comfortable? You will give me the location, but I do not think you will be honest without some motivation to do the right thing. I must insist that you *watch* as the rest of your fellow traitors pay for your cooperation."

Two women were executed next and after being removed from the lodge, d'Aulnay relaxed his grip on the rope allowing her to stand on the floor and breathe clearly. "I am running out of patience and you are running out of fellow traitors" said d'Aulnay, strangely amiably.

Françoise spat back "You are everything evil, more evil than anything Satan could conceive..." she was cut short with a gurgle as d'Aulnay pulled the rope so far she was choking on her tip toes again. With a nod from d'Aulnay two more women were executed while d'Aulnay held the rope with one hand and her head in his other. Directing her face towards the hangings he continued "why do you make me do this? It is your entire fault. Not mine. Do you wish to tell all and perhaps draw me a proper map?"

Françoise was overwhelmed. She only wanted out of the main lodge and the nightmare playing out before her. She had read the old book called Dante's Inferno as a student, but this was real and far more horrific than fiction. She was reminded of the line *'The darkest places in hell are reserved for those who maintain their neutrality in times of moral crisis.'*

My writing paper is in my lodge, if we can retire to there, I will give you what you want. d'Aulnay gently pulled on the rope once again just enough to raise her head. Looking deeply into her eyes as if seeing her soul, he nodded and released the rope. "It is not *your lodge* any longer. You may want to remember your place here. Have you learned nothing so far? This is all mine" he said laconically while gesturing in circles.

"Untie her hands" he then commanded. As he led her out of the main lodge with his hand around her neck, he nodded towards the remainder of the group as he eyed Gilles meaningfully. There was no need for

witnesses or dissidents in Port Royale as prisoners.

44 Pistole

Port Saint John

Easter Day, 1645

Louie was at first baffled by the events unfolding below him inside the fort. He had seen everything from his niche in the rocks. He had almost jumped from cover when she had been ejected forcibly from her lodge. He had an ominous feeling as she had entered the main lodge building joining the others. The lone priest had almost run to the shore, then wading without hesitation into frigid waters to get aboard his small shallop. The maiden Gabrielle was soon carrying young Charles-Françoise with Nadine following along with small trunks. Louie noted the *brave* soldiers offered no aid.

They waited on the beach as the Priest landed the shallop to load them. He was underway as soon as he could get sails up. It all seemed wrong. When d'Aulnay went into the main lodge, Louie felt ready to run down the slopes to help. It was not a lack of courage that kept him in place, he *knew* it was all beyond his help now, and if d'Aulnay was looking for him then his best action would be to avoid capture. He thought he could hear wailing, but was unsure because of the distance and slight midday breeze.

Suddenly the door opened and Louie was stunned to see a body thrown down a few paces from the door. The remainder of the mercenaries turned away... watching for any sign of threat. After the second body, the guards never bothered to turn around for the next four. Louie was trying to decide if a frontal assault that would kill at least a few before they could kill him was feasible when the door opened and d'Aulnay was leading Françoise back to her lodge by the neck.

The disrespect coupled with her obvious discomfort caused Louie to close his eyes, and raising his face to the sky he swore to the Great Spirit that he would kill d'Aulnay and avenge the deaths of his fort comrades as soon as he was able. Finding little peace he opened his eyes and looked down as the door opened and yet another body was piled on the others. *If they can do this to their own people when they claim to love God and be Christian, then I am Mi'kmaq and my name is Mooin Membertou* he thought as a great heaviness fell upon him. Traumatized, he couldn't move as the pile of bodies turned into several piles representing the population of Port Saint John.

Mooin watched the horror unfold and was changed forever. His life goal now was retribution. He would never rest until he freed Françoise and purged the earth of these evil people.

By the time long shadows had formed on the fort, the only man left alive from Port Saint John was Hans Vaner. He was kneeling by himself on all fours and Mooin guessed that he was vomiting. It was most likely overwhelming to walk out of the lodge and see piles of corpses taken by his hands. Hans Vaner would not die by Mooin's hands. He would suffer his own misery every day that he lived, having killed all forty people of Port Saint John.

d'Aulnay had not left Françoise's lodge and the small cabin was now wafting smoke from the chimney.

Thinking of the fireplace made Mooin realize he was shaking uncontrollably. He was now suffering from being in the rocks all day. Dulled senses were his clue, and he knew he had to move... now! The cold had it's hold on him and threatened his life.

On his first attempt to stand, both legs would not work. On his next attempt, his hands were shaking and he could not hang on to his knife. He managed to get his beloved knife back into its sheath, and stand. He willed one foot after another and then he was on the ridge once again.

As he turned and looked one last time at the fort, he knew what he had to do first. There was no chance of d'Aulnay getting the very pistole he could kill over. Not for LaTour either he vowed, a man who would turn his back on his son or partner did not need the pistole. He could not decide if Françoise seemed less corrupted from the effects of the pistole because of his feelings for her or the fact that she wanted to create a new life without the trappings that existed here.

As he headed to the west along the ridgeline he forced a painful jog to ease his stiff muscles and start warming blood again, not stopping until he reached the canoe he had hidden the day before. The ridgeline dropped steeply down to a huge eddy above the reversing falls, he stopped long enough to eat from his meager rations in the canoe and was soon paddling upriver once again. With strong strokes he soon crossed the river and beached on a small pea gravel beach he had spied on the trip downriver. Huge slender rocks were layered on the upriver side of the beach like fat fingers pointing up into the woods. As the early spring daylight disappeared allowing the stars to appear, Mooin

Membertou was warming his hands by a sheltered, warm driftwood fire. As he looked into the darkness of the river his grim face was faintly visible by fire light, two streaks from his eyes formed a drop under his chin. He was too disturbed to feel it... he could feel nothing but overwhelming sadness.

After a restless, ghoulishly nightmare laden overnight, Mooin was restless to press on upriver to the cache. He had planned as he stared into his campfire and decided he would take a simple approach and merely move the pistole to another nearby hidden niche in the rocks above the cache. He had scouted the area while hunting during his previous visit and had enjoyed the view wile inspecting the large naturally stacked boulders. He decided to hide the majority of the cache and travel lighter. He knew it would be necessary to move quickly as he would plan her escape from d'Aulnay.

After a tiring return to the cave and relocating all the pistole, he was feeling the strain of the past three days. One fact kept him motivated. He would avenge the evil deaths at Saint John. Every muscle was tight and aching with cramps and hunger making regular complaint. Before moving on to step two on his mental checklist, he needed rest to recharge his body. As Mooin lay wrapped in his sleeping hides, he tortured and killed d'Aulnay in a thousand ways.

The next morning had Mooin preparing to travel. Rage, pure and raw, had replaced exhaustion. There was no time left for introspect, only action. It took a little longer than he wanted to reach Saint John, but paddling along he had an epiphany that as long as Françoise was alive she would be hunted. If she wanted to restart life, and Mooin was to be part of it, then he reasoned she would have to die to end her current life. A plan formed and he knew the method, now the means would have to present itself.

The ships were still in the harbour as Mooin eased into view on the ridgeline. He sensed human presence close by and began a stealthy approach to determine their purpose. Eventually he heard enough to know that he was approaching an encampment of local Wolastoqiyik people.

He stowed his arrows to appear less hostile and straightened tall to announce his presence as he walked into their midst. They were nervous, and though they knew each other from the fort during previous trading they needed assurances that he was alone and not hostile.

He learned quickly that the bodies had been buried behind the fort and that they had been strangled. They were genuinely afraid of the French occupying the fort and everything attached to it. They had quickly become comfortable with Mooin as he was equally troubled with the recount of horrors at the fort.

As is the custom of Mi'kmaq or Wolastoqiyik, was the unspoken code of sharing and hospitality, Mooin was soon eating his fill and relaxing with his comrades. He learned that trade had been reestablished the very next morning and that Françoise was prisoner in her lodge. He watched as the storage warehouse pelts and hides were being loaded into the ships by longboat crews. Two men guarded the lodge as d'Aulnay oversaw trading while he had mercenaries dismantling all the fort cannons for transport. Canoes were travelling to the fort laden with pelts and hides for trade unchallenged. Mooin was elated... there was a way inside the fort. Turning to his brethren,

Mooin was soon asking for assistance with his plan to free Françoise.

45 Pistole

Port Saint John

May, 1645

Françoise wondered how much longer she could survive with d'Aulnay. He had merely slapped her and thrown the first map she had drawn into the fireplace. The second map had elicited a grunt before he balled it up and threw it into the fire and said "make me something to eat."

She could hear the voices and sounds of the mercenaries working outside in the fort without any hint of their purposes. She decided to wait out d'Aulnay and not bother to draw any more maps until she was forced to do so. It irked her that d'Aulnay had been correct for throwing her useless maps into the fire, he knew she was deceiving him on the pistole cache true location.

After d'Aulnay had ignored her and slapped her a few times, the next week had turned more repulsive as he began randomly groping and manhandling her. She knew he was playing her mind as a cat with a mouse, so much so that she had become numb, almost catatonic in the same room dreading each return to her lodge.

She almost jumped out of her chair as the door was flung open and the guards allowed two Wolastoqiyik women to enter with large woven baskets of food supplies, another man entered carrying a larger basket filled with firewood. The door closed with a bang and immediately the man reached into his clothing and removed two small hide sacks.

The man spoke French poorly but managed to convey that Mooin had sent them, then looking at the door apprehensively said "Mooin says to eat these berries and the leaves next" She took the two small sacks being thrust into her hands, too stunned to speak. The Wolastoqiyik man shook her aggressively and held the sack with berries in front of her face and hissed lowly but aggressively "berries first! Wait! Then leaves! In early morning! No more food for you! Only water for you!"

As they set the woven baskets filled with meat on the floor, the guards jerked the door open again looking around the room and ordered them back out. The Wolastoqiyik man never took his eyes from her as he backed away then followed the women out. The door slammed shut and she was once again left to her thoughts in the dim lodge.

Louie is here she thought with a sudden burst of energy and hope. For the first time she felt hopeful that she might be able to survive d'Aulnay. Louie would have a plan.

She was intrigued by the sacks and allowed herself a peek at the contents. One bag contained dark red berries that smelled pungent, the other bag was crammed full of dried leaves smelling of summer hay. How these were to work into her plan she was unsure, but she would eat the berries in the early morning and wait a while then take the leaves. He had said only water so she would be fasting until morning, not that she had any appetite lately.

It seemed tomorrow would be her day of freedom with one more night to endure d'Aulnay's unending abuse and treatment. He had mostly broken her down and lately with the addition of the groping was making her feel as dirty as d'Aulnay said she was. She had refused to react or even look up when he had last grabbed her. She had started to wear her old wool work dresses and layers to hopefully not escalate his advances.

He was enjoying the fact that he had domesticated her into a house maid and broken her down. He had told her he would get her to draw his map soon and if he thought it was the correct map she may be spared a hanging like her settlers.

By looking out the opening and closing door she had seen glimpses of fort Saint John and once saw a cannon was being rolled by, another time she saw across the fort that the doors were gone from the warehouse and it was empty.

Most of her despondency resulted from the understanding that d'Aulnay was destroying the fort, looting and preparing to leave. He wanted the pistole more than the fort, she knew it with all her being that he was playing her. He would never harm her until he had all the pistole.

Now that Louie had made contact, she knew that d'Aulnay would fail... somehow she was getting her freedom. It seemed easier for Françoise to make d'Aulnay's evening meal in the hearth that evening. While alone she hummed and scurried about the lodge making a stew thick with the fresh bear meat. She had decided if it was to be d'Aulnay's last meal, why not make it a good one for the condemned.

 She had chuckled out loud to herself as she thought of d'Aulnay not getting her pistole and his rage at losing. After d'Aulnay had returned to the lodge for the evening, he informed her that he would be taking her and her new map upriver in the next few days. She never reacted and remained mute as she was ordered to her mat in the corner by the fireplace on the floor. He had commandeered her bed and treated her much like a dog to break her. Two weeks had indeed almost broken her. She lay on the floor dreamily thinking of Louie, her shawl pulled up concealing a smile.

In the grey light of dawn she opened the small sack of berries. She had drank from her water pail by the fireplace throughout the sleepless night as instructed and now placed the handful of berries in her mouth. The acrid, bitter berries had almost made her vomit. She ate them as she had been directed and fought waves of nausea.

Next came powerful cramps that forced her knees up to her bosom. It seemed that there were lights flashing around her and her ears were ringing. Panic began to sink in as felt like she was now floating over the floor. It was then that she remembered the second sack.

As d'Aulnay snored on the bed, her hands forming claws as they cramped into uselessness, she managed with extreme effort to eat all the leaves in the bag. After taking a long drink from the pail, Françoise fell back to her sleeping mat and stared up at the spinning ceiling. Louie's giant face appeared in the lights on the ceiling, then her horse in France, finally as she lay paralyzed on the floor her last vision before darkness was her mother holding her arms out to her and smiling.

"Get the fire lit you lazy whore" yelled d'Aulnay from the bed. When he got no response from her, he jumped from the bed and stomping loudly over to her said "I will teach you proper manners for not have my morning fire ready." He kicked her without response, he then reached down and felt her face... it was cold. He ran to the door and throwing it open for better light, ran back to her sprawled form in the corner.

"Get our medic NOW!" he roared to the guards outside the door while feeling for a pulse. Françoise was unresponsive and he could find no pulse.

The three Wolastoqiyik people that had brought the supplies the previous day were amongst a crowd that had quickly gathered around the door to the lodge. As the medic probed and felt for a pulse, d'Aulnay stood transfixed over her. Holding an eye wide open and looking into her fixed and dilated pupils, he let go of her hand that he had been feeling for a pulse. He looked at d'Aulnay and shaking his head sighed "she is gone..."

Charles d'Aulnay would never feel the failure and complete loss as he did now. His world imploded. He was too shocked to speak or move. The medic looked up at d'Aulnay where he was still kneeling by Françoise and watched as d'Aulnay's color drained from his face.

 Standing, he looked down at d'Aulnay and "sir, are you feeling alright?" When d'Aulnay could only kneel transfixed looking at the lifeless corpse without an answer, the medic took him by the arm and led him to the bed.

He spoke softly now and said "Why don't you lay down a moment sir? You look ill." Charles d'Aulnay was in a complete state of shock and could only nod slightly. Even as he lay back on the bed, he never took his eyes off Françoise's body on the floor.

The medic followed d'Aulnay's gaze back to Françoise's body and then looked at the people crowding the doorway and said "Dispose of this body with the others behind the fort." The Wolastoqiyik trio immediately stepped into the room and the man said it would be an honour for them to return her body to the Great Spirit.

The medic had seen d'Aulnay execute everyone in Saint John without so much as a blink, almost with joy and here was one woman who had died of apparently natural causes pushing d'Aulnay over some mysterious mental precipice. All he knew was the body had to be removed at once to give d'Aulnay any chance of peace. "Get her out of here now" he ordered with a nod to the trio.

The large Wolastoqiyik man gently picked her up and the two women placed a blanket under her. They rolled her body into the blanket, then the man picked the bundle up and with a toss she was over his shoulder. He appeared to be shifting her into position on his shoulder as he thrust her up and down a few times before walking out of the lodge with the two women singing a song of sorrow for the fallen. The mercenaries had all parted and wordlessly watched as they walked slowly out the gate and headed through the massive boulders in the foothills of the ridgeline behind the fort.

As wailing dirges grew in volume for Françoise, it had attracted more Wolastoqiyik peoples from the woods around the fort. The men had dug a large deep hole to bury the last remains in upright fetal position as custom dictated. When the fetal like form in a rolled blanket was lowered into the hole along with donations for the afterlife, the wailing had ended and feasting began. The hole was quickly filled in and soon people were heading in various directions away from the fort. They had completed their purpose of helping the "body soul" return to Manitou.

The medic had administered a heavy "dose" of cognac to d'Aulnay, the effect allowing him the effort to get dressed. He seemed to be completely lost and without energy. As the medic watched him carefully, d'Aulnay began nodding and mumbling with his thoughts coming forth.

He finally stood tall, stretched and commanded "Burn this hovel to the ground. I am returning to the ship." He stopped only long enough to give Gilles his orders. He wanted the warehouse left for trading and everything else destroyed. "I am going back to Port Royale immediately; you have a lot to accomplish before you leave. I want this fort destroyed and operated as an outpost from Port Royale... And Gilles, if LaTour returns with the proper paperwork, secure our trading pelts and skins and return everything to Port Royale. If the paperwork is valid, we are obliged to return it to him... if not, defend yourself at all cost."

Charles de Menou d'Aulnay had lost his chance at taking the pistole. He never looked back as he walked through the main gate that only two weeks before had seen his triumphant entrance. He lay down in his bunk aboard the *Grand Cardinal* and ordered his return to Port Royale as soon as feasible. His ground forces had reported that the savage Louie had cleared out of his encampment and vanished.

The information tied in with other Wolastoqiyik reports at the fort of him with a woman to be venturing far north for better furs to trade in Mount Royale.

d'Aulnay now believed Françoise had told the truth in that Louie would never be his enemy or take the pistole. *These savages never saw the value of gold. The power it held for the holder...* he lay thinking. It made his heart ache thinking of the pistole hidden away and lost to everyone. It had almost all been his! He was now in debt to Le Borgne without the pistole to satisfy his debt and the other debtors. He had bested LaTour, who could not recover financially and had lost his winter trade pelts and skins as d'Aulnay's spoils of war. Despite this knowledge, for the first time in his life he felt irreconcilable failure.

46Pistole

Port Saint John

May, 1645

High on the ridgeline overlooking the fort, Mooin had
watched d'Aulnay return to the ship in the harbour.
He stood tall feeling the exhilaration of
outmaneuvering d'Aulnay and as the *Grand Cardinal*
cleared the harbour and began sailing the Bay of
Fundy for Port Royale, Mooin held his knife up and
said aloud "I will come for you! I will finish this."

His words stirred his companion standing beside him
enough to murmur "I know you will Mooin, I know
you will." He looked down into her pale face as he
pulled her blanketed form in closer under his arm

and neither spoke. His warmth radiated into her cold body and his strong arm held her weightless. She felt nothing as her lodge inside the fort was reduced to ash with only a fireplace and chimney standing in the rubble.

Circling in thermals above the ridge a pair of osprey calling their peeping whistle to each other made Mooin look up and with a smile said softly "there is our sign... your name will be Níkmuesu... you are so much like those noble, and graceful birds." Françoise had just begun her new life with a new name. Níkmuesu.

Níkmuesu looked at Mooin and said with effort "noble and graceful yes, but a bird of prey as well." After a pause and a grunt Mooin replied "True words, but did you know they hunt and work as pairs? It was

Níkmuesu's turn for a grunt, a pause and she murmured "seems right."

It had taken extra time for travel over the ridge and down to the river above the reversing falls where the canoe laid waiting on the bank. Níkmuesu was exhausted and was fast asleep as soon as she was lying in the bottom of the canoe wrapped in furs. With only her face visible, Mooin paddled upriver with rich green foliage emerging from the brown wasteland of winter.

It had been a close call for her. He had only watched his father administer the berries and leaves to render a coma to a warrior that needed an amputation after a battle. The warrior had barely bled during the procedure and it had stayed in young Mooin's memories. He could only clearly remember the order taken and plenty of water. The ratios were a guess.

His accomplice had been instrumental in her recovery when he had given her stomach thrusts with his shoulder while inverted over his back. The blanket had concealed her disgorging the pungent mixture. Further bounces on his shoulder had worked to stimulate her heart and lungs and increase blood flow through her body. When Mooin had anxiously started work on her behind the fort in the boulders, she had a faint pulse and shallow breathing. Pushing on her chest and rubbing on her arms and legs soon had her eyelids fluttering.

The first cognizant thing Françoise saw was Mooin's grim face as he worked to revive her. As the burial continued, with a bear carcass replacing Françoise in an identical blanket, even those watching from the fort had not seen the switch of bodies. Mooin had walked slowly away with Françoise under his arm, carrying her in plain sight to freedom. Barely conscious, her long native robes concealed unmoving legs as everyone had left the burial site.

Mooin realized a lot could have ruined his plans, but what he had learned from his observations of Frenchmen was; their revulsion of death, their predictability, their lust for gold, and most importantly he learned they were ruthless when gold was involved. His plans were successful because he had exploited d'Aulnay's predictability.

Mooin had established a small encampment on the little beach he had used. There was a small spring in the woods for clean fresh water and the fish were plentiful on the river. He would rebuild Níkmuesu's health and she would learn the values of his ancestors. If she could see the value of a life embracing nature, and being self sufficient, perhaps she would see less value in the gold.

Thinking of the gold cache had presented a thought for their survival. If the cave could be made comfortable, they would have all the shelter they could want, they could survive together as she fully learned to speak his language and customs. He doubted he would have any choice but learn more of her culture as well. If the gold meant not trapping the beaver for pelts or moose for hides he was happy not to have to kill but for the very food they needed.

As he paddled along he was broken from his thoughts as Níkmuesu spoke after clearing her throat "where are we Louie?"

Mooin looked down at her serene smile as she lay wrapped in furs and replied "Níkmuesu, Louie is no longer my name. Not now not ever. If being a Christian means savagely killing comrades and

458

acting like the great evil Satan, then I will always be Mooin... just as you are now Níkmuesu."

As his words settled in her mind, she could feel his strong paddle thrusts. As the water gurgled under the canoe with each stroke, the sway was soothing and as she stared up into the evening blue sky she finally said firmly "I cannot blame you for despising Frenchmen and Christianity... Mooin it is then."

Mooin nodded and then studied her face before saying "Níkmuesu is your name. You must never say your old name or d'Aulnay's deception will fail. He also wanted me as far as I could learn."

Níkmuesu nodded and said "what did you do with the pistole? Did you move them from the cache?"

"You have been given a new life. I will teach you skills and we will be as one. If we are to be together you must understand what is important to me... and we will learn more of your desires..."

He reached into his canoe and retrieved a small sack of pistole. Holding it to her he said "this is all we need to trade and buy our needs. You must be happy without coins as your first love... Do you understand me Níkmuesu?" pleaded Mooin.

"You keep it safe, you know best" came the soft measured reply. She turned her head slightly and closed her eyes again.

Within a short time they were unloaded on Mooin's little beach retreat and lighting a warming fire for Níkmuesu. Huddled together sharing the hides, her arm was locked around Mooin's elbow and head on his shoulder. They were drinking Mooin's yellow birch tea and as Níkmuesu asked for the hundredth time since first trying it years before why his was always so delicious over her attempts; he laughed and said

"I never told you a secret ingredient is red clover."

 Their laughter wafted over the dark water and as

only friends can manage, they laughed loud and hard

for the first time in a long time over silliness, happy

to be safe and warm together.

47 Pistole

Boston

August, 1645

Charles LaTour was brimming with optimism as he climbed onto the Boston main dock. He wanted to meet with Robert Compton as soon as he could make the journey. Compton could be counted on for backing a defense against d'Aulnay's attacks and counsel the best trade contacts.

His intentions also included a friendly visit to his good friend Richard Bellingham. While it had been a while since they had visited, he would have knowledge of Port Royale and probably Saint John as well. Trade allowed information to flow along the Atlantic seaside as people made friends and gossiped at each port of call.

It had only taken minutes to secure the use of a horse and LaTour was heading for Bellingham's house on the hill. The late summer air was resplendent with the smells of wild flowers, and hay drying. He felt the sun on his back making him somewhat dozy. *I could enjoy living here in Boston* he thought lazily. Maybe Boston would excite Françoise and they could try to raise Charles-Françoise while mending their shattered relationship.

Riding up in front of the Bellingham mansion, he jumped off and had the horse hitched to the post in seconds. He bounded up the steps and tapped at the door. Not receiving an answer, he walked around to the back of the house and through the small gate into the flower gardens. Richard sat in a chair staring out at the ocean.

Charles gave a cheery greeting causing Richard to spin around and seeing LaTour his mouth fell agape, his face a look of shock. "Sorry to have surprised you" said LaTour amicably.

Bellingham composed himself slightly and replied "Charles... where did you come from? Are you alright? I have worried about you..." he trailed off as he searched LaTours face rapidly.

LaTour could not understand Bellingham's discomfort and peculiar behavior. "Did I come at a bad time?" offered LaTour cautiously.

Bellingham stood staring at LaTour until he nodded at the chair across from where he had been sitting and said calmly "I am guessing you have not been to

Port Saint John since you went to France... would that be correct son? He added gently.

LaTour blurted out "Richard, you are scaring me. I just got here from France after clearing my name from d'Aulnay's foolishness... what is wrong..."

Before he could continue, Richard cut him off with a sorrowful stare and finally spoke with a catch in his voice "I wish it was someone else to tell you son. d'Aulnay put Saint John under siege in April. She held him off for three days son. Your men were gallant and defenses were good. He was better equipped, had more trained mercenaries and he arrived with three ships."

He paused to take a sip of tea allowing him a moment to compose. Looking at LaTour he continued woefully "those that came here after the battle say that a Swiss on the wall opened the gate and brought the fight inside the fort on Easter Day... of all days man! She had allowed a special moment of prayer inside the lodge during the first barrage of the day, and it was close defense when they were already inside the palisade walls. They fought a good fight never realizing a main battle group was outside the walls waiting. She surrendered Charles, to save the lives of the settlers. d'Aulnay had promised he would spare them, but that evil demon of Satan strung them all up. He killed them all Charles except your boy and the maidens along with the Priest. I understand they went to Port Royale."

As LaTour attempted to ask the obvious, Bellingham cut him off with a raised finger and said "she was placed captive in your lodge where she survived for two weeks or so..." he trailed off and LaTour began shaking his head saying "no... no... it can't be true..."

Bellingham's expression gave his answer. He finally spoke sorrowfully saying "They figure she succumbed of despair, having witnessed all those deaths and losing everything." At length Bellingham stood and looking out to the ocean again said quietly "some of the men on his expeditionary land force were paid and they came back here saying they would not stay in Port Royale with a man as evil as d'Aulnay. My God son, those spooked lads were battle hardened soldiers. They say that he had each one pulled up into the rafters until dead. Charles, he made her watch the whole thing with a noose around her neck. You should further know d'Aulnay came here looking for support against you, and he was not well received. He left with the extra soldiers, but no other aid was given by merchants. Compton caught word of his attempts to buy arms and had an embargo placed on Port Royale. d'Aulnay was pretty perturbed at the lack of support here after Compton made his move. I will assemble those lads together for you to learn more... if you want. They are not your enemy Charles. They were hired to do a job, as you did against d'Aulnay."

 LaTour could only nod as he stared at the ground in front of him. Richard Bellingham stood with great effort from the weight of the moment and walked to his friend saying "your room will be readied and you will stay here for awhile. I figure you need a little time to sort it all out." With a pat on the shoulder, he shuffled away leaving Charles LaTour feeling more alone than he had ever felt in his life.

The shock lasted two days before LaTour could engage the world again. His world had been ripped from him. It had been rage from Françoise's rejection that had motivated him first, then slow realization that *he* needed to work on his partnership for *their* growth. He felt a need to grow his home life before a good thing slipped away, and regret had replaced rage. Everyone and everything that mattered to him was now gone. The son he had neglected, he had learned was sent off to France.

He ached for his losses, but could not help wondering where the pistole cache was hidden. He was sure that Françoise would not give him the location and her knowledge was what had kept her alive. He had a rough clue given by Francie after hiding it, the same as d'Aulnay, but neither knew the actual location which was the point of the third trusted partner.

One week after arriving in Boston full of hope and plans, a remorseful Charles LaTour was heading for Saint John in a borrowed sloop with a few men for support. He had to find Louie. It was his only hope for salvation from certain financial ruin. He could only guess that d'Aulnay was hurting financially as well. Wars cost money, big money, and it also cost big money to grow a trading post while exporting goods. LaTour had already learned of the looting with the entire warehouse cleared and loaded to d'Aulnay's ships. It would be difficult to see his blood and sweat equity burned to the ground, but he had to see it and feel closure. Louie would be there somewhere he hoped.

As the small sloop sailed into the Saint John harbour, LaTour could see d'Aulnay's banner flying above the fort. It hardened his resolve to see his own banner there again. As they neared the fort, canoes were seen on the grounds outside the fort. With the small tender tossed over the side, LaTour was soon on Saint John soil once again.

There were only six men operating the trading post. The palisade walls showing the effects of d'Aulnay's cannons were all but destroyed on the harbour facing sides. LaTour did not recognize any of the six men and their indifference shown, divulged their lack of recognition to him. He kept moving and was soon out of sight, hurrying up the ridge to Louie's encampment. As he got closer he could see a woman tending the fire with her back to him and she did not seem to notice his approach. He called out a friendly greeting and she turned to wave to at him with a wary but friendly smile. LaTour asked if Louie was nearby and looked expectantly at her. She was confused at first and then confirmed that Mooin had gone far away to the north to trade furs and her family now lived in the encampment. Mooin, she informed him quickly, had said he would never return and had given them the wigwam as it was.

LaTour nodded to her politely and quickly turned to look down on the fort. He did not want her to see his incredibly dejected countenance threatening to reduce him into a sobbing mess. To see the ruination of the fort displayed before him, along with confirmation that Louie had vanished to the north for trading, left him helpless without any hope for rebuilding. *Louie had moved on.*

The woman sensed LaTour's sadness and as she sidled up next to him and looked down on the fort said "there was great evil here. Everyone died. The Frenchman d'Aulnay is an evil spirit." LaTour could only nod his head. It took all of his being to remain calm and polite to the innocent woman who was merely trying to reach out to him. He mustered a mechanical quick smile, thanked her and began the hike back to his tender beached below by the fort on the beach.

Halfway down his hike, he could see fresh soil piled in one large mound with a smaller mound to one side behind the fort. He hesitated a moment thinking of going to what must be the graves and offer his respect.

He continued on, because his embarrassment for his failures causing their deaths was too great... even in death he could not face them. Thinking of all the people brought actual pain to his chest, and as he thought of Gargot dying for defending the fort... he groaned out loud. *He* had failed everyone and would never have the opportunity to win Françoise's heart again.

As he rowed away from the shore, he knew he would never set foot on Saint John soil ever again. He cursed and mumbled obscenities all the way back to the sloop, because he was forced to sit and stare back at the ruined fort as he rowed. He came looking for closure, and learning Port Saint John held no future for him any longer was absolute. Knowing that he could never repair the damage to his marriage and reconcile with Francie, or see his comrades again would never allow closure.

Standing with one foot on the bowsprit as the sloop sailed out the harbour for Boston, LaTour was staring straight ahead at the thin grey ribbon in the distance, reminding that d'Aulnay was close, yet untouchable in his fort. He had taken everything that mattered to LaTour without a chance of reprisal. Clearing Partridge Island, the bow swung south relieving LaTour of any more visual reminders of his rival. The open ocean lay ahead of him with the return to Boston providing an opportunity to think of hisimmediate future. In all of his planning in decades, he never thought he would be restarting life after losing everything. He did know that his only chance

for recovery would be retrieving the pistole.

He had never been to Mount Royale, but as it

seemed a logical place to look for Louie, Mount

Royale would somehow be the center of his future

plans.

48 Pistole

Port Royale

October, 1645

Charles d'Aulnay was now Governor of Acadia's western holdings. He would have been sole commander had Nicholas Denys not been given his slice of Acadia as the Governor of Canso and it extended from Isle Royale in the south to Nipisiquit in the North.

It was a harsh tract of weather beaten rock coastline and islands that Cartier had called uninhabitable more than a hundred years before. Nicholas Denys had seen beyond the harshness and created several settlements to trade Lumber, salt, fish and the abundant pelts and hides in the south.

He had returned from France only a few years earlier with his new wife and an optimistic plan for growing his exports. He had befriended the native peoples and encouraged fair trading to encourage cooperation.

Henri Membertou had deep roots in Isle Royale and when Port Royale grew, Membertou had no desire to stay there, and moved east into the rich lands on the island beyond any French intervention. Denys' cordial and honest dealings soon had a symbiotic coalition formed with Membertou's descendants.

d'Aulnay had heard of Denys' appointment with subsequent successes and had him under his loose scrutiny for the past couple of years. LaTour and Port

Saint John had consumed all his attention for the past two years and with that defeat, d'Aulnay was now free to pursue the remainder of Acadia.

Had there not been another project for him to prioritize his efforts, the depression of losing all the pistole would have rendered him useless. He knew Le Borgne would be in Port Royale in the spring. The time would arrive to settle accounts-- accounts that could not possibly be covered. d'Aulnay knew that his position as governor was at risk with a real possibility that Le Borgne would foreclose and replace him after seizing all his holdings. He needed time to recover financially and commanding all of Acadia would provide him the entire trade wealth. It had taken several years to remove LaTour as a competitor, and until he started the process of discrediting Denys as a first step in annexing the east coast of Acadia, he needed valuable time. It would be ambitious, but he knew there could only be one commander of Acadia.

He had waited until the very end of the season to send mail and his last exports for France. He would normally have returned to France with the ship any other time to winter in Rochelle, but he now actually felt safer in Acadia.

All ship leases had been returned, filled with trade goods and the mercenary forces, leaving a peaceful settlement once again. Some families had left Port Royale upon hearing gossip regarding the hangings in Port Saint John. d'Aulnay could not contain the gossip, knowing well the gossip would travel far and wide, reveling in the resulting notoriety he would receive. It would serve to warn anyone thinking of crossing him in the future.

An inspiration bloomed one frosty morning that excited d'Aulnay to his core. He had been thinking of Remy and how efficient he had been. Once he had asked for land and retirement, Remy Martin had created a farm on his new tract of land in record time, complete with a small home. He was now working on a barn foundation while also clearing the virgin forest for fields. Remy was a man who made things happen without asking for assistance or negativity.

d'Aulnay realized he had a man that he could entrust with a confidential mission without compromise. The way d'Aulnay rationalized the situation, Remy could use income and he could use trusted eyes to search for his pistole or Louie, or both, upriver from Saint John. The cryptic location Françoise had given when the cache was initially created meant he would have to entrust Remy with a certain amount of information he would never trust anyone else with.

He had never believed she would divulge the location and any maps or references during her capture were made to obscure the real location from him. It had taken a great deal of cajoling to get Remy agreeable to a meeting for possible re-employment. He was resistant to working for d'Aulnay again and it had taken a personal visit with pleading to sway Remy into at least listening in confidence to his offer.

d'Aulnay had laid out the minimal story of the hidden pistole, omitting the partnership and coin re-pressing portions, but focused on the thin details of where the cache and, or Louie might be found. Remy was intrigued, a man who wanted a hidden wealth that required clandestine operations, would have to pay handsomely. He had agreed to only listen to d'Aulnay, but as d'Aulnay left for the fort without an answer, Remy knew he had found a way to get his land cleared and a barn built regardless of pistole being found.

Early one afternoon Remy Martin rode his dapple grey workhorse through the main gate and tied off in front of d'Aulnay's lodge before knocking firmly on the door. Two hours passed with plans and deals struck for Remy. He exited the door and swung up onto the large horse. The two stared impassively at each other before Remy finally reined the horse around and left the fort without a word.

Remy Martin was once again on d'Aulnay's payroll. It had cost d'Aulnay a new barn, cleared land, a deeper well and new fences to sign Remy on. The final deal clincher was several new cattle and swine in the spring as well. *Must be one large cache of coins*

thought Remy as he plodded along his way home...
d'Aulnay agreed and never blinked when Remy
received his bounty *after* having his wages
reinstated.

The following week Remy took a sloop and two men
to cross the Bay of Fundy for Saint John. It was a
beginning to learn more of Louie and retain some
local scouts for the next spring.

Finding native people who knew Louie or his
whereabouts proved a challenge until he discovered
he was looking for Mooin and the fact that LaTour
had returned seeking the same answers according to
the lady at the encampment.

He then spent a cold week in a borrowed canoe
travelling the briny unfrozen river every day
comparing landmarks to clues before the first
threatening snow of the season chased him back to

Port Royale. d'Aulnay's pistole would have to wait for spring, and it seemed likely that he would be searching without clues to Louie's whereabouts.

d'Aulnay was in an upbeat mood for the first time since taking Saint John. With his one trusted confidant dealing with the cache search, he could finally focus on building Port Royale again, despite a dismal first report from Remy. His first step forward was getting more intelligence on Denys' settlement in Isle Royale to the south west.

Planning was the key to success and planning for d'Aulnay, usually meant suffering for someone else. As he stared into the crackling fire while the wind whipped snow outside, Jeanne passed him a warm cup of tea. He was smiling and as she turned away he patted her backside. The jump and his resulting laughter made her stare incredulously at him and say "what has gotten in to you?" As she scurried away he was still chuckling in his chair.

Epilogue

The outpost in Port Saint John continued successfully trading for pelts and hides after d'Aulnay confiscated the operation. LaTour had foreseen the value of the location and possibilities for large quantities of quality pelts. d'Aulnay was capitalizing on trading with an established presence, Wolastoqiyik people had continued to trade, however they had lost the working relationship LaTour had established. The forty deaths at the fort cast a shadow that no Wolastoqiyik person would live under.

After trading for necessities they required with their pelts and hides, the Wolastoqiyik would quickly leave the fort. Fort Saint John functioned, but it did so almost in silence. Life had been usurped and replaced by impersonal transactions with uncaring, and unsmiling traders.

Across the widening harbour, above the high tide line, a small encampment had grown from a centuries old fishing site. It now served as a meeting place for Wolastoqiyik that needed rest before a return upriver, but away from the fort. From spring to early fall, the scattered wigwams grew in number each year. Set back from the others on higher ground a wigwam was set up by a couple with obvious Mi'kmaq origin. They had just shown up and established a camp with a perfect view across the harbour to the fort.

Remy Martin was frequently based from the fort and without explanations travelled upriver for weeks at a time. Like the Wolastoqiyik, Remy did not like the cold ambiance at the fort and preferred to stay upriver or pass through on his returns to Port Royale. The fort actually gave him an incredibly uncomfortable feeling.

d'Aulnay always received Remy's reports with a nod and reaffirmed his mission asking what he needed for his success. Remy was also pleasantly surprised with each return home as fort engineers and carpenters labored at building a homestead as promised in his contract with d'Aulnay. He just kept thinking *I must be looking for a lot of coins...*

It was during a late summer return to the fort in Saint John that changed everything. While Remy was preparing to leave from the fort, a young teenage boy from the Wolastoqiyik settlement across the harbour had paddled to the fort and sought him out by name.

After Remy was summoned, the boy passed him a small hide pouch tied with gut cord, before he turned and jogged quickly to the beach to paddle his canoe back across the harbour. By the time Remy had given up trying to untie the sack and cut into it in frustration, the boy was already paddling away. Remy froze as he stared at two gold coins in his hand. He ran out the gate and was yelling at the boy to stop. He ran into the water yelling for the lad to come back, and as the others in the fort ran down to the water's edge in alarm, the lad only looked back once. Remy watched as the boy in the distance beached after his long paddle and was met by two figures before he ran off into the settlement. As the taller of the two picked up the canoe and placed it safely on higher ground, the shorter person waved once at Remy before turning and they disappeared into the midst of the settlement.

After three years of searching, Remy finally had his first positive report for d'Aulnay and verification of the coins existence. Clenching his fist tightly, he never said a word in answer to questions from the traders who had ran to the beach in alarm.

He was reluctant crossing to the native settlement where he would be both unwelcome and unproductive being unable to identify Louie. No, he would return and report as he was directed. He found it curious that he had been given what he was searching for in such a strange clandestine manner. He could not understand why Louie would suddenly make an appearance. Within the hour Remy was on his way for Port Royale in the little sloop. As he lifted the anchor, the two lone figures stood down river watching him leave.

Unknown to anyone at the settlement in Port Royale, Emmanuel Le Borgne had filed his foreclosure papers in Paris to launch his takeover of Port Royale. It had taken years in France to build alliances and serve official papers while dealing with the trading company. Le Borgne knew it was impossible to keep the legal proceedings from getting back to d'Aulnay eventually, but he reasoned that d'Aulnay would not have the revenues to honour his debts and was defenseless. It was just good business. In the end, he would have no further interest or use for d'Aulnay. He would have Port Royale by next years trade.

d'Aulnay had jumped up and began excitedly pacing as Remy related the strange story while passing him the two coins. The two Spanish coins were proof that

Louie had taken the cache for himself. With word of foreclosure and orders to return to France, he was desperate for the massive wealth from the pistole. He could almost imagine the look on Le Borgne's face as he paid off his debt in full before throwing him out of Port Royale. By the next morning Remy had restocked the sloop before sailing for Saint John with d'Aulnay.

It was late in the afternoon as d'Aulnay stepped ashore in Saint John. He gave a cursory inspection of the trade post and then walking outside with Remy in tow, stopped and stood staring across the harbour. Having arrived too late in the day he would cross the harbour in the morning and find Louie. He decided with desperation that he would arrest Louie if necessary, but he would be made to surrender the pistole.

The next morning at first light, d'Aulnay having not slept much was in a foul mood and anxious to recover the pistole. He strutted to the beach with Remy following him, a long boat oar over each shoulder. What they found next, caused d'Aulnay to curse aloud. Not a long boat or canoe could be found. His sloop was at anchor with a man standing on deck looking back at them, but no way to return to it. The sloop could never approach close enough to the beach, and the frigid water prevented swimming. "I loathe this wretched place" growled d'Aulnay.

As they stood on the shore stranded for the time being, Remy said quietly "there... those two." d'Aulnay followed where Remy was pointing and there on the distant shore two figures had appeared on the shoreline. One was a head taller than the other and the tall one was preparing a canoe. After a moment on the shore, d'Aulnay could only conclude that the two were hugging before the canoe launched and being paddled straight for the fort.

Closing the distance with powerful strokes, the expert canoeist was soon picking his way through the shallow low tide water, stopping in an eddy. d'Aulnay could see no sign of a weapon in the birch bark canoe and the lone occupant seemed to be catching his breath in the silence. After eyeing the two Frenchmen for a short time, the canoeist pointed to d'Aulnay and said "Louie says you come."

Hearing the name caused butterflies in d'Aulnay's stomach, it was true! He was here. d'Aulnay stepped forward and Remy grabbed his elbow, quietly saying "you cannot go alone. There is something amiss with all of this."

"Good point" said d'Aulnay as he turned and reached for Remy's pistol stuffed in his waist band. He then took his musket and powder horn. As d'Aulnay turned for the canoe again he said "I will send for you once I get there... I will be fine."

Remy shook his head as the indomitable d'Aulnay, resplendent in nobleman's clothing along with sword, walking stick, pistol and musket, wedged himself into the front of the canoe. As the canoe started off, the load had considerably slowed the canoeist, he bent into the paddle and was soon making way.

d'Aulnay sat in the bow with his large hat flying its long plume. He had not asked for a paddle as he had no intention of paddling himself across. As Remy watched the canoe cross the harbour, he had no words to describe what happened next as the canoe approached the distant shore in later accounts of the day.

d'Aulnay sat stoically in the front, willing the canoe faster while scanning the opposite shore. A voice, in perfect French diction, firmly said "it is time for you to pay for all your evil ways."

The canoe wobbled, almost tipping had it not been for the skills in the aft. d'Aulnay frantically tried to turn and the oscillations of the canoe began slopping water over the sides into the canoe.

"Sit down or you will upset the canoe" said the voice from the aft of the canoe. d'Aulnay froze and finally said "I assume you are Louie."

"My name is Mooin Membertou and I have denounced all that is French, all that is Christian because of your evil. I watched you destroy my friends and for that you will die. Mooin turned the canoe to point at land with gentle turns of the paddle and said "there on the hill... by the large boulder" d'Aulnay saw a slender figure in a grey dress and as the canoe glided towards her he gasped, then mumbled "no...no, it cannot be. I saw her myself..."

Mooin said vehemently "YOU SAW, what I wanted you to see. You are as predictable as you are greedy and evil. What you are fighting in your mind now is how this could happen, but you are so very predictable. WE are not the stupid SAVAGES you believe us to be, and we do not kill our brothers and sisters over coins."

As d'Aulnay sat wedged in the bow, his shock began turning to rage. He had been out witted by a savage and a woman. He slowly took his hands off the thwarts and as Mooin watched from the aft of the canoe d'Aulnay began to slowly turn to finally see his opponent.

His hand now held his dagger and as he attempted to hurl it at Mooin, it was slapped out of his hand into the water by the heavy paddle. "You are so predictable" said Mooin with a sigh.

Still standing by the large boulder, Françoise shouted out towards the canoe "Go to hell where you belong evil monster" and held her fist out. With a nod she turned her thumb down, just as she had read that Caesar had done in the coliseum. With one swift motion, the canoe was upside down in the frigid Bay of Fundy water in the harbour. The dark water made d'Aulnay panic as he was wedged in the front and now upside down. He fought to clear his legs and then clear his sword from between the seat and floor. His heavy clothing pulled him down as he finally cleared the surface and caught a breath. He felt hands on his legs and suddenly he was pulled down, thrashing and trying to kick, underwater again. The cold water and wet clothing sapped his strength almost instantly. He could see the outline of the canoe above him and as his lungs burned with their desire for oxygen, he struggled to ascend. The hands on his waist suddenly released and were on his shoulders only to be replaced by two feet that used his shoulders as a spring board. As d'Aulnay was thrust down further, Mooin's kick launched himself up to the air pocket under the canoe.

As the overturned canoe began magically moving towards shore, only the hat flowed on the surface current. Níkmuesu finally breathed again. She had questioned whether the meticulous plan would work, Mooin had said quietly *it will work, because they are so easy to predict.* As she waded into the frigid water and pulled the canoe, with Mooin still beneath it, to the safety of the rocks and flipped it over did she realize it was finally over.

"Did Remy see it all" was all that Mooin could say as he shivered uncontrollably.

"Yes, and he is still standing there now" she answered calmly. Níkmuesu kissed Mooin on the forehead before helping him walk to the stash of dry clothes behind the boulder. They changed in silence and once they were comfortable in their warm and dry clothing, Níkmuesu made a fire to warm Mooin. He had taught her well in the ways of the Mi'kmaq and they had learned from each other working as one. After warm tea and the warmth of the fire had revived Mooin, they stood and as Níkmuesu eyed the fort in the distance she dropped her old grey work dress on the dying fire. "Let's go home" she said to Mooin softly.

True to his word, Richard Bellingham was a gracious host and accommodated LaTour for the harsh winter months when LaTour had first arrived. When the season warmed enough for travel, he had ventured to Compton's cliff side mansion seeking comfort among friends. Robert's easy nature and Norma's flair for entertaining soon had eased LaTour's languid mind into gear. He knew it was time to move on to the next phase of his life and Mount Royale was all he could think of.

Charles LaTour was able to sell his faithful ship *L'Amitye de la Rochelle* to a purchaser that Compton knew. The only condition LaTour made to the new owner was passage to Mount Royale. Within weeks of the deal, the new owner loaded ship and cleared Boston harbour for Mount Royale trading. A generous southern wind had the pushed the ship at hull speed, coupled with the Gulf Stream helping, they made record time all the way to Isle Royale. As they rounded the island their new course shifted to North West on the last leg to Mount Royale.

Charles Jacques Huault de Montmagny was the duly appointed Governor of New France. He was a large man with fair sense of morality. He had been well received by the Algonquin people of the area... receiving the name Great Mountain. LaTour having heard of his rapport with the native peoples was anxious to meet the man and offer his assistance.

On arrival at the dock in Mount Royale he asked where to find the Governor and was directed to the largest building in sight. He found a suitable inn and attempted to clean up and prepare to make a good first impression. In late afternoon he built as much cultured air as his deflated ego would allow on the walk to the Governors house. He was out of options and he was "all in" on this play for his future, and his role today was of a nobleman with trade knowledge.

He was ushered into a parlor to await the Governor after politely tapping on the large door knocker. He sat straight in his chair with his broad shoulders square waiting for the unknown. The butler had summoned the Governor, who was now moving so fast the butler was almost trotting as they entered the room.

Charles Jacques Huault de Montmagny met few men who stood as tall and looked him in the eye. As he shook hands with LaTour he was impressed with his rough calloused hands. He smiled as he exclaimed loudly "The great Charles de Saint-Étienne de la Tour! What brings you from Acadia? I am so pleased to have finally met you."

His shock was complete when the Governor, who he had just met, knew many of LaTour's triumphs stating he was legend in Mount Royale circles. When the Governor and LaTour discussed the fall of Saint John and LaTour's subsequent losses, de Montmagny immediately offered a liaison position with local Algonquin to build relations and trade. The two were instant friends, resulting in LaTour receiving a lavish suite in the Governor's Mansion.

After war had erupted in the first winter after his appointment, between the local Algonquin and the English backed Iroquois, LaTour realized he had been thrust into a hornets' nest. His work to aid the Algonquin Kitcisìpiriniwak people at the fortress on l'Isle des Allumettes was heartbreaking after they had almost been decimated in Iroquois attacks with help from the English. After several years of selfless work, the Algonquin were now as prepared as possible for both winter and war.

LaTour had just returned to Mount Royale after a successful trade mission to the North and as he entered the mansion received a letter with a royal wax seal. LaTour stood looking at the letter in his hands with trepidation, he had waited years for his name to be cleared officially and assumed it was proclamation.

When he opened the seal and read the letter, he had to sit at once.

De Montmagny hustled down the stairs upon hearing that LaTour had returned and saw his friend sitting by the door with his long grey streaked hair in a pony tail, still dressed in buckskins. Had he not known him, he would have thought him an Algonquin. LaTour was staring at the letter in his hands with a bewildered look on his face. "What is it man! What has happened" was all he could ask of LaTour.

Looking up slowly LaTour replied slowly "it seems that d'Aulnay has died and Cardinal Mazarin has placed me as Governor of western Acadia with the Regents blessings."

There was a long silence as the implication settled on de Montmagny and LaTour. "Well done Charles. You have earned the Crowns respect... What is more you have earned my respect here. What a wonderful turn of events" was all the Governor could offer.

LaTour sensed de Montmagny's heart was not in the praise and it matched his own feelings. "My work is not done here. The Algonquin need my help and I have further plans to help them learn how to work iron and I..."

de Montmagny interrupted him quickly saying "you are my friend and I do not think you are replaceable here, but I will get someone to work as liaison to follow your work. You have given all your heart to this position and it shows, but you are not a young man... it is time to leave it Charles. Port Royale is getting the best possible man they could have."

"You knew all this" said LaTour sullenly.

"Yes, and it weighed heavy on my heart. If I were more selfish... I would not have recommended you" said the giant man softly.

He added with emotion in his voice "you care. You care for Native and Frenchman alike. You work hard and demand fairness. You have shown the world that you are ready as Governor of Acadia in Port Royale. You have shown me that one man can make a major difference. Your ship will leave tomorrow..."

LaTour wanted to say something, but he was alone in the large foyer, de Montmagny had already turned and bounded back up the stairs.

Hearing d'Aulnay's name had instantly reminded him of the pistole, Louie and Saint John. His next thought was how Jeanne Motin was faring. She was such a gentle and caring soul who had suffered silently in an unhappy marriage with d'Aulnay. His initial purpose for arriving in Mount Royale was just a memory now. The pistole could only be seen as blood money to him now, making it all a bad memory.

Several days later as the small ship charged with delivering LaTour made the turn north towards Bay of Fundy from the Atlantic, he could see his old Fort Lomeron ruins at Cap Sable had never been rebuilt. It was painful as he watched the shore slip by and remember his time there, along with the siege by his father guiding the English.

As the ship dropped anchor in front of the fortress at Port Royale he neither expected nor received a welcome. As he stepped onto the dock, a young officer with his escorting four soldiers demanded his paperwork. LaTour looked him up and down before he said "and who are you?"

The man stiffened and gave a curt "I am Gilles; the late Governor d'Aulnay's appointed lieutenant and acting adjunct to his authority here in his absence."

LaTour said dryly "of course you are." Jeanne Motin, d'Aulnay's widow, had slowly sidled into view and knowing LaTour since arriving in Port Royale decades before, stood looking at him apprehensively with dark circles under her eyes. She glanced furtively between Gilles and LaTour while wringing her hands, belying her fear and stress of Gilles and the unknown.

"Who is your sergeant" asked LaTour. Once identified, LaTour beckoned with his index finger, and when the man walked up to LaTour he was shown the Royal Commission to his Governance.

Looking at Gilles, he said "you are relieved of all duties here. Surrender all weapons" and turning to the sergeant said with disdain, "you will ensure he is placed on the next ship for France." After a pause he said viciously "if he gives you or anyone trouble before his departure... hang *him*... *slowly*."

Walking up to Jeanne with smile he bowed graciously, kissing her hand and said portentously, "you are even more lovely than I had remembered... It has been a been a very long time Madame Motin. Let us retire to the lodge, we have much to discuss."

After all the decades of trials and tribulations, Charles LaTour had taken a long path back to whence it all began for him in Acadia. The pair walked through the main gate with Jeanne clutching his elbow, smiling warmly as LaTour talked of his plans for Port Royale.

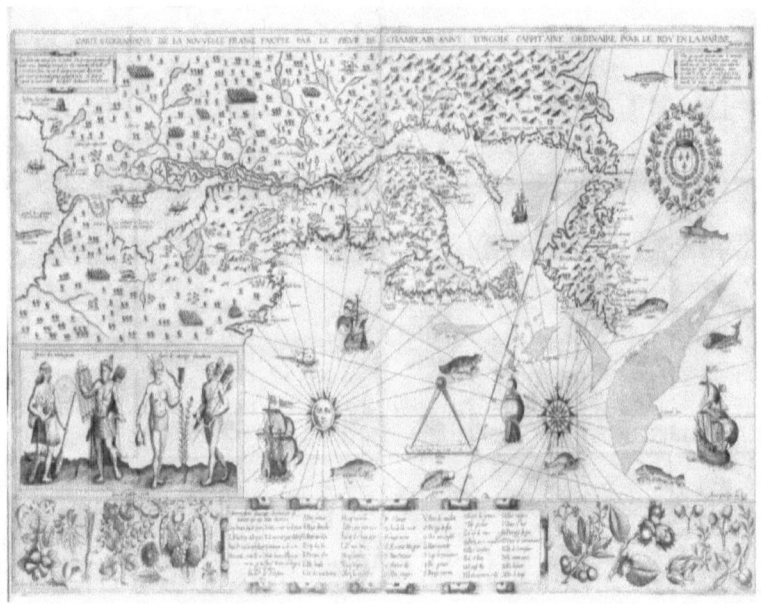

All that glisters is not gold;

Often have you heard that told:

Many a man his life hath sold

But my outside to behold:

Gilded tombs do worms enfold.

Had you been as wise as bold,

Young in limbs, in judgement old

Your answer had not been inscroll'd

Fare you well, your suit is cold.

William Shakespeare's play *The Merchant of Venice,*

(Act II - Scene VII - Prince of Morocco):

Places

Port Royale—Modern day Annapolis Royal

Isle Royale—Modern day Cape Breton

Mount Royale—Modern day Montreal

Kenepekachiachk—modern day Kennebecasis River

Wolastoq River – Modern day Saint John River

Kichisìpi River – Modern day Ottawa River

Kitcisìpiriniwak – Algonquin tribe on island in Ottawa River

l'Isle des Allumettes – modern day Morrison Island QC.

Characters

Charles de Menou d'Aulnay de Charnisay

Charles de Saint-Étienne de la Tour

Françoise-Marie Jacqueline—Officially known as 'Lady of LaTour'

Charles-François de Saint-Etienne (LaTour's son)

Claude de Saint-Étienne de la Tour

Jeanne Motin-- Charles d'Aulnay's wife

Giovanni Cellini-- San Sebastian gold merchant

Hernando Galeana-- Lighthouse keeper San Sebastian Spain

John Paris-- LaTour's main creditor Boston

Remy Martin-- d'Aulnay's lieutenant

John Reverie-- Boston Gold Merchant

Guilliame Desjardin-- LaTour assistant in France

M. Tourneau-- New France Trading Company Dock
Agent

M. Nicholas Gargot-- LaTour Lieutenant.

Gabrielle & Nadine-- Charles-Françoise LaTour
nurses.

Emmanuel Le Borgne-- d'Aulnay's primary financer in
Rochelle France.

John Paris-- La Tour's main financier in Boston

Richard Bellingham-- Governor of Boston 1641

John Winthrop -- Governor of Boston 1642

Tia'm – Mi'kmaq for Moose (LaTour's name.)

Mooin-- Mi'kmaq for Bear (Louie's name.)

Compton-- Bellingham's liaison for LaTour

Henri Membertou-- Chief of Mi'kmaq in Port Royale NS.

Manito-- Great creator

Níkmuesu –Osprey

Charles Jacques Huault de Montmagny – Governor of New France

Wolastoqiyik—Wolastoq Algonquin people (Maliseet)

Kitcisìpiriniwak-- Kichisìpi Algonquin people on modern day Ottawa River.

Ships

L'Amitye de la Rochelle -- LaTour's first ship

Grand Cardinal -- d'Aulnay's warship on lease from Le Borgne

Vierge -- d'Aulnay's ship

Saint-Clément-- LaTour's ship lease from Boston

Gilly Flower – English ship lease for Françoise return from France.

St. Francis – Ship sent from France for LaTour.

Providence-- Gargot shallop

1 Pistole, Redemption

Kenepekachiachk, Acadia (Modern Day Kennebecasis River N.B. Canada)

Early Spring, 1655

The winter had been the harshest in memory. Snow had fallen regularly until waist deep, and some areas were ten foot deep where it drifted. The incredible snowfall made passage impossible without snow shoes.

Níkmuesu had learned the art of making her snowshoes from Mooin, her partner. The time taken to split the wood and form shapes was a pastime while keeping warm by the fire while using the flames to shape her wood into ovals.

Mooin was in constant motion to keep wood supplied and hunt for their survival. The deep snow made it easier to harvest deer and moose that floundered in the impenetrable snow, providing food and hides. Their campsite was cleared back with the same large snowshoes leaving towering snow banks around the perimeter serving as windbreak to the frigid winds. They had an added benefit at the back of their wigwam of a small cave burrowed into the rock as part of their living space where the ice and wind could not penetrate.

As was the Mi'kmaq way of life, the two had adapted to every hardship while thanking the Great Spirit for their successes. Despite a hardy resolve, some local Wolastoqiyik, known as the Malecite people in

French, had not survived the harsh winter. Many were found frozen in their wigwams having surrendered peacefully in their sleep, exhausted and unable to rise to the demands of survival.

Having made a conscious decision to live with a basic sustenance had been a matter of her survival when rescued by Mooin from the clutches of an evil Frenchman a decade before. She was still awakened from sleep with horrific visions of her fellow settlers being killed and would lay with tears flowing at the memories.

She was driven by desire to succeed in her new life as Mooin's partner in the wilderness of Acadia as a means of emancipation from her previous values. She had adapted to native life under Mooin's quiet and patient tutelage. She was conversant in both

Mi'kmaq and Malecite languages, allowed her to blend in alongside Mooin with local meeting areas.

She had one prized possession that was her reminder of a different life left in France decades before. A small clear mirror, imported from Milan, had been a gift from her mother when she was a teen.
Overbearing guilt left her unable to look at the image in her mirror for a long time after her rescue. She realized her quest for wealth had cost the lives of forty settlers and with that knowledge came her responsibility of guilt.

Mooin had let her grieve for her mistakes only a short time before teaching new responsibilities for survival. The work load for survival gave little time for introspects and she functioned by doing as she was taught, emotionless and numb. She learned in time that God had many faces, and so with prayers to the

Great Spirit, she began to slowly heal her shattered ego and spirit.

What she now saw in her mirror made her stare. The stranger within looked vaguely familiar, but at midlife she had small lines that had not been visible before, and her long black hair had strands of grey showing. Her skin had weathered to a darker tanned hue that left most people wondering of her lineage. She actually looked Mi'kmaq when dressed in her buckskins.

She had never bonded with her son. It had been an unwelcome distraction from the excitement of building trade when she discovered she was pregnant. She had given birth while her husband had led a battle to regain their holdings and it had stung verily being relegated to domestic duties when she had been a business partner commanding a frontier outpost.

It had fractured their relationship as husband and wife with all the negativity of blame ultimately misdirected to her son. The plan to send him back to France to be raised by her sister had already been set when fate intervened. The battle for Fort Saint John had been brutal and lasted three days under her sole command. When she capitulated, she lost everything, and although she had negotiated for clemency, everyone at the fort was killed. Guilt would always be resident in her heart.

Her son would now be a teen she realized. It was regret beyond the guilt that made her heart ache. Níkmuesu knew that she would have to see him again, to know that he was being raised in a loving home, and know that she had done one thing correctly with a good outcome. Nogent-le-Rotrou was in the north of France and Níkmuesu missed it dearly as well.

Mooin had found a large split in the ice along the river bank allowing a fishing line to be cast with several hooks. After continuing on into the surrounding woods to hunt he returned with two rabbits and a partridge to find his line had two large eels on. It would be a good meal that night as Níkmuesu would know how to cook in her large metal pot using her herbs and spices. *The French know how to cook food* he thought with a chuckle.

Their wigwam was tied to the mountain side cave and gave a stunning view of the valley and river below. A flowing spring gave them all the fresh clear water they could use and game was plentiful, making an ideal encampment.

It took longer to get there as he had to remove his snowshoes occasionally when the snow was melted clear of the ground and wear them again when he encountered deeper wet snow. Later, as he walked into the orderly campsite, Níkmuesu was scraping a moose hide on a frame she had made and paused long enough to give him a small smile while holding his gaze. They could communicate effectively without spoken words and a glance could say volumes.

He looked at the hide and noticed the hide was scraped clean as well as could be done. Not a nick or mark in the hide meant top dollar, and no extra fat or meat meant the hide would tan well without rotting. She had learned well. He dropped the game and picked up another scraping tool to help her, working quietly with slow strokes as she did with a steady purpose.

He had learned to allow her space to start conversations. She had been fragile after her rescue and it took a great deal of his patience to coerce her back to productivity. He saw a beautiful woman where she could not. He felt her pain when she seemingly felt nothing. He had shown compassion she felt unworthy of, and it had taken time. She had told him once that he *knew* her better than anyone ever had. The only condition he had ever made was to never allow the wealth of coins be her life's priority ever again. When survival meant buying provisions from the traders in Saint John he had traded for their needs and spent with coin only as needed... which was seldom and he had only used three coins since hiding the wealth of coins from everyone.

They worked silently with each lost in their thoughts until the hide was ready for the next step. As had been passed down for thousands of years, Mooin had shown her that only the animal's brain, when boiled down, made an effective solution to soften the hide as it dried. Once it was smoke cured with heat or 'tanned' was as flexible as any blanket. Níkmuesu brought the small brass pot from the fire where she had prepared it, and they quickly brushed it on the hide. Their efforts were once again measured and seemingly without effort as they worked the clear liquid into the hide.

When done with the hide she turned to Mooin who froze immediately when he glanced into her eyes. He knew her well enough to know that she was troubled and was about to explain her thoughts. It was how she managed to rebuild herself, through inner reflection and then verbalize the findings... he knew this was going to be a major event by her trace movements. "We need to talk" she said quietly.

From the beginning, they had agreed to speak only in one language and alternate every week to build each other's first language. It was convenient for her because it was France that held her thoughts, and French was this week's language. As they began to process the game he waited for her to begin, but not until the pot was finally simmering on the fire did she utter thoughtfully "Mooin, I have thought of my son lately and it would ease my mind to know that he is safe and living a good life. I cannot change my past, but I can make a difference now. We more than have means to travel and live well in Spain. We could then travel to Nogent-le-Rotrou and see him from afar, to see and know that he is happy. I could perhaps give something to help him." Mooin remained silent and after a moment she added "a winter in Spain without snow is much easier than surviving here as well" she added dryly.

Mooin was uneasy as his world was being upset at the thought of leaving all that was tangible to his existence. He had known it would be a question of time before she would want more than the rugged wilderness could offer. She came from wealth in France and now wanted the comforts she had once known.

His greatest unease was being foretold a vision before leaving Port Royale decades before and he was cautioned then against the Frenchman's misplaced values. The vision had shown him as a travelling nobleman of wealth and this was the first clue that he was facing his destiny.

She knew that he would be uncomfortable leaving the forest that he deemed essential for life. The naked truth remained that the forest had indeed provided them everything needed for survival, but there was so much more than mere survival to a life well lived if she could help him see it. He had not responded for short time and seemed lost in a deep thought...meaning he was now unreachable. She had also learned how her partner thought, and knew him better than anyone else. All points had been made in the debate, so they sat quietly as the beautiful view began to darken and ate their hearty meal enjoying their companionship.

In the growing darkness he had thought long enough. "Are you no longer interested in our life here" he asked morosely. She sat forward with the firelight reflected in her eyes and said emotionally "This home is more than enough for us, and we are so comfortable here... no Mooin, I do not want to leave this forever, but I want to return where I came from and show you my life... to be comfortable and safe during the winter. We can return here for the summer and fall and provide aid for our people here. We can do this because we have the means to do it."

Mooin sat with a dejected look on his face and said sorrowfully "how can this 'Spain' be without snow in the winter? How can we hunt if I do not know where to hunt... I..." Níkmuesu was so excited that she cut him off in mid sentence and with the fire light dancing in her eyes she began telling him of life in a Spanish city, living in modern times. As the night wore on Mooin grew fascinated by her tales of travels between France and Spain as a child, and learning that the modern native people there also had ancient history with customs was hard for him to conceive. When she retold him the story of where his large Damascus steel knife came from, he was able to grasp the concept that Spain, Italy, India and the Middle-East were steeped in ancient traditions, yet they had advanced technology that enhanced life.

The clincher for him came as she eventually grew tired and cuddled into his chest as they always did in the evening, and said "I owe you my life and I will respect your final decision... but please take your time and consider it carefully." The big Mi'kmaq tossed another stick on the fire and pulled her in close with a grunt.

2 Pistole, Redemption

Port Royale

Early Spring, 1655

Charles LaTour, Governor of Port Royale in Acadia, sat beside his new wife in front of the fireplace. Her husband had drowned in Port Saint John and Cardinal Mazarin had seen LaTour as the best man to replace him. The two large wingback chairs were separated with a small table containing two delicate cups filled with hot cocoa. Jeanne had never had the new drink sweeping through upper aristocracy in Europe before Charles had arrived in Port Royale as the New Governor. Charles made close friends in Boston with the first known cocoa exporter while on an aid mission a decade before. Robert Compton had enjoyed the drink from the tropics and introduced it to a willing market in Europe. For LaTour, the drink always brought a flood of memories and it was the recent past that held his mind captive presently. He only just recovered from losing everything including… his wife in Port Saint John, by making the voyage to Mount Royale in New France to start life anew. The shock and surprise when summoned for his current role was replaced by excitement for a new adventure and chance for building Acadia as he saw beneficial for all… With fresh wood on the fire, he settled back with his cup and as he stared into the flames his mind replayed his arrival in Mount Royale.

On the dock he asked where to find the Governor and was directed to the largest building in sight. He first found a suitable inn and attempted to clean up in preparation of a good first impression. By late afternoon he mustered as much cultured air as his deflated ego would allow on the walk to the Governors house. He was out of options and he was "all in" on this play for his future, and his role today was of a nobleman with trade knowledge. He was ushered into a parlor to await the Governor after politely tapping on the large door knocker. He sat straight in his chair with his broad shoulders square waiting for the unknown. The butler had summoned Charles Jacques Huault de Montmagny, the duly appointed Governor of New France, who now was approaching so fast the butler was almost trotting as they entered the room. He was a large man with strong features and commanded with a fair sense of morality. He had been well received by the Algonquin people of the area... receiving the name Great Mountain. The irascible Governor met few men who stood as tall and looked him unwaveringly in the *eye. As he shook hands with LaTour he was impressed with his rough calloused large hands, the hands of a man familiar with work. He smiled as he exclaimed loudly "The great Charles de Saint-Étienne de la Tour! What brings you from Acadia? I am so pleased to have finally met you." LaTour's shock was complete when the Governor, who he had just met, recanted many of LaTour's triumphs stating he was legend in Mount Royale circles. When the Governor and LaTour discussed the fall of Saint John and LaTour's subsequent losses, de Montmagny immediately offered a liaison position with local Algonquin to build relations and trade.*

The two were instant friends, resulting in LaTour receiving a lavish suite in the Governor's Mansion. As LaTour expected, while they enjoyed sherry and their pipes after dinner, de Montmagny wanted to know all the details about d'Aulnay... he had heard the wild rumors about the Governor of Port Royale in Acadia requiring further explanation for confirmation.

LaTour was anxious for native interaction with the Algonquin people and begin learning the area. It was his intention to immerse himself in the culture as he and his father had with the Mi'kmaq in Port Royale decades before. He was shocked when de Montmagny told him that the area would be lethal without knowing local customs and he would not be allowed free travel unless accompanied. De Montmagny quickly explained the problems facing LaTour were not just trade, but warring Iroquois allied by Dutch then English seeking colonization on the lands claimed for France by Champlain. He offered LaTour as chair, sighed and began "Acadia may not have had any animosity between rival bands, or armed with muskets, but that is why I need your expertise to restore balance here. Four years *ago the Iroquois attacked the Algonquin fortress island Kitcisìpirinik and caused severe casualties. The tension here is building again, and I fear an all out war very soon. Your job as liaison is to interact, discover deficiency, and advise the Algonquin of the remedy... we need to aid our friends and repel our enemies while increasing trade exports."*

The magnitude of the job settled ominously as he and de Montmagny sat in the Governor's office. In the growing silence, only the ticking of the mantel clock could be heard. It was LaTour that broke the silence after weighing what he had gotten himself into. He could not determine if the Governor was placing the dangerous job on him because he had few if any options left. His reality was clear... he had no other option. "I assume you have a guide at my disposal and I need to assess what I have gotten myself into. I will begin by travelling to the sachem and make contact as soon as I can" replied LaTour with bravado. "That is the spirit!" exclaimed de Montmagny exuberantly.

Within a few days, France's new 'Native Liaison to the Governor of New France' was heading for l'Isle des Allumettes, the island Algonquin fortress, on the Kichisìpi River to the North West. LaTour had insisted upon stopping at the first available settlement for a change in attire. He needed the feel of moccasins and buck skins and he was soon fitted in traditional leggings mixed with his own fitted shirt. He had listened and adapted his learned Mi'kmaq language quickly and was conversational with his guides in no time.

As LaTour's entourage neared l'Isle des Allumettes they camped on the banks of the river one more night, his guides insisted on cold camping, concealed in the thick alder bushes. Iroquois were known to be in the area, and would attack in the night when drawn to camp fires. As LaTour lay on the cool ground, his muscles began cramping; prompting him to crunch numbers and realize that at fifty three he was getting too old for the lifestyle. He had been well trained in hand to hand combat and could handle his own in confrontation, but he now began to wonder if his destiny would end in this hostile land so vastly different from anything he had ever known.

Having listened carefully to his guides and preparing well, he met the sachem to present many gifts. The sachem was as impressed with how LaTour looked as he sounded, resulting in instant respect for the man preferring the name Tia'm. LaTour asked many questions and offered nothing until asked, earning more respect. He was genuinely impressed with the river toll system they had established for all river traffic. The palisade walls were a unique design and LaTour offered his insight to improve on them. They would never stop cannons, but that would come later. He had been surprised at the muskets at the fort and now realized how dire the situation was, with the Iroquois nation equally armed looking to destroy them. On a clear night, he could hear drums and chants from the distant shores and when he asked of the significance, learned it was Iroquois warriors building numbers. The sachem said they would attack eventually, and after a pause said matter-of-factly many would die.

As the leaves began changing, LaTour knew it was time for his return to Mount Royale before freeze up. The Kitcisìpiriniwak people of the island were as prepared as possible for both winter and war. LaTour promised to return after winter and bring needed arms and supplies as he departed, never knowing *that the Iroquois would attack and kill many of his*

new friends before his return.

Jeanne had been quietly watching him with concern as he had let his cup tip further until it started to spill without realizing in his distracted state. She set the cup and saucer down on the table firmly enough to make a rattle and stir him back to the present. The resulting recovery made him slop the now cold cup along with a sheepish apology. He reached his hand out after setting the cup down and took her hand saying "you are a gentle soul and a great comfort, I am sorry that I get lost in the past so often." She smiled serenely back at him and soothingly said "I am so thankful to have a strong man, yet so respectful. I have lived with ahhh, more colorful displays, over a spilled cup in the past." They smiled in quiet understanding at d'Aulnay's well known outbursts.

Where d'Aulnay had been LaTour's primary antagonist until his death in the past, the new threat for his contentment in Acadia came from d'Aulnay's principle financier, Ernest Le Borgne. Le Borgne had foreclosed on d'Aulnay in France, and was preparing to seize all holdings in Port Royale at the time d'Aulnay drowned in his canoe accident. Jeanne had no recourse against official paperwork allowing seizure of all personal holdings in Port Royale a year later. By the time LaTour arrived in Port Royale, Le Borgne had installed d'Aulnay's man Gilles as commander of the settlement. The insipient Governor LaTour arrived in Port Royale oblivious to Le Borgne's involvement, and immediately discharged Gilles on the dockside. It only took a glance at Gilles to see his cocky attitude displayed, along with Jeanne's apparent uneasiness to know that he would only be a problem to LaTour.

Le Borgne had attempted to seize everything in Port Royale. In his greed he failed to realize the fort was not d'Aulnay's for the taking, nor was the militia his to use for enforcement. LaTour came to realize that his appointment as Governor set precedence for France. Where trading companies had settled and began exporting resources to France's benefit, the Crown was now preparing to take full control... along with all the profits.

Pistole

A Novel of Historical Fiction

By Stephen Beyea

Greed, murder, deception, racism,

counterfeiting, religious persecution,

misplaced values and redemption are not

limited to the modern era. In the brave new

French lands of 17th century Acadia, two

warring Governors battle for their existence.

Based around an actual timeline of historical

events, fact and fiction retell the birth of a

Nation in Atlantic Canada.

www.ingramcontent.com/pod-product-compliance
Lightning Source LLC
Chambersburg PA
CBHW060240030726
47493CB00024B/1399